NEXT TIME I SEE YOU

By M.J. Bell

Chronicles of the Secret Prince:

Book I
Before the Full Moon Rises

Book II
Once Upon a Darker Time

Book III
How Dark the Light Shines

NEXT TIME I SEE YOU
A time travel novel

For Daniel, C.J., Brendan, Ben,
Sam, Sofia, Ethan, and Joe

AFTER

"I count him braver who overcomes his desires than him who conquers his enemies, for the hardest victory is over the self."
Aristotle (circa 384—322 BCE)

ONE

September 2017

Bad things happen to good people. I can't tell you how many times I heard my great-grandmother say that. If I had to guess, I would say it was more than a thousand. She moved in with us when I was a sophomore in high school, and whenever I went out with my friends, she would call out, "Remember, Kat, bad things can happen to good people too, you know."

I rolled my eyes the first dozen times or so. After that I just blocked her out. Old people are so out of touch with today's world, and I, being a punk-ass teenager, knew everything. Plus, those "bad things" she continually referred to, the kind that had her make the sign of the cross when she heard them on the news, only happened to strangers.

I continued to believe I was invulnerable even when I was old enough to know better. I had never been given a reason to think otherwise. The higher force in the universe, whatever or whoever it was, had blessed me. I had the perfect boyfriend, who would one day become my husband; I was in my second year at the University of Colorado Boulder on a full ride scholarship; and I had tons of friends and a loving family who all lived inside an invisible bubble with me, which protected us from those "bad things." Then on April 29, 2016, that bubble popped.

It's hard for me to imagine I could have ever been that

naïve and optimistic. I was, though. At least according to the thousands of pictures on my phone and in my social media posts. When I flip through the photos of that smiling girl now, it's like looking at someone else. And she's for sure not the girl I see in the mirror every morning.

In my defense, my naïveté and delusional thinking were not totally my fault. Like most young girls in this country, I grew up on the Disney princess movies and was ingrained with the ridiculous notion that if I was nice to others and worked hard, I too would find my Prince Charming and live happily ever after.

Even back then, I think I was aware it was just a fairytale. But unbeknownst to me, the seed Disney planted in my head took root deep inside my subconscious and sat there waiting for the right moment to sprout. That moment came on the day Michael, my very own Prince Charming, asked me out. I knew right then and there we were going to live an enchanted life that would put all other fairytales to shame.

It was the silly, romantic vision of an eight-year-old, but still, it blinded me. And being out of my mind with happiness didn't help. That's the only excuse I can come up with as to why I forgot about the element of evil that played a key role in every fairytale—a witch, a wicked stepmother, an evil fairy, or in my case, a maniac wielding a Smith & Wesson M&P15 assault rifle, who leisurely walked into the bar where Michael had met up with some friends. In less than five minutes, seventeen people were dead, including Michael, and my fairytale, the one I had unknowingly longed for my entire life, turned into a nightmare. And with my true love gone, there was no one to kiss me awake.

A chilly gust of air rattled the blinds on the bedroom window and blew over my bed sending a shiver down the full length of my body. A sane person would have snuggled deeper into the blankets, but I kicked all the covers to the floor and watched the goose bumps pimple my skin. A second blast of air lifted the blinds several inches away from the window. I shivered uncontrollably, wondering if this was what it felt like when the cold fingers of death crept over someone.

The thought of death—mine in particular—had been flitting in and out of my mind ever since the shooting. I was diagnosed as having "complicated grief" some time ago—a more chronic and emotionally intense grief. According to the shrinks, it's a rare condition associated with the horrific way Michael died. But I think they just like to put labels on people's afflictions. And whatever they want to call it makes no difference to me. It's not going to bring Michael back, and without him in it, my world has become a void of darkness and silence, no different than what I imagine death to be like.

I haven't found the strength to end my miserable existent yet, but that day has gotten a lot closer since I received the letter from the D.A.'s office informing me of the date of the Piece Of Shit's trial—I refuse to use the shooter's name. To me he will always be a POS.

I stared at the shadows and light dancing across the ceiling, listening to the demons whispering in my head as I envisioned someone sneaking a gun into the trial and shooting the POS. That's something I'd gladly stick around for.

A loud pounding on my door broke suddenly intruded on my fantasy. I jerked up and nearly fell out of bed. I then went stiff and held my breath.

"Kat, open up!" my best friend and current financial benefactor, Cathie, hollered.

The hammering echoed in my ears like the bass on a stereo turned to maximum and my head began to throb. I groaned, hugged my stomach, and rolled into a fetal position.

"Come on … you've been in there long enough. It's time to come out. Hiding isn't gonna help. You can't stay in there for the rest of your life."

"I'm not hiding. Go away. I'll come out when I feel like it," I yelled back and winced as my voice felt like gravel in my throat.

For a few precious seconds, the silence settled back over me like a warm, familiar blanket and I almost believed Cathie had given up. But bad luck, especially mine, doesn't just evaporate. It hangs around like a stalled low-pressure system holding the dark swirling cloud in place over my head, and sending small lightning bolts down every so often to remind me I will never be free of it. To prove me right, the pounding resumed in earnest, rattling the picture frames hanging on the wall next to the door.

"I'm not leaving this time, Kat," she called out, pausing her assault just long enough for her voice to carry through the wood. "If you don't come out right now, I'm going to call your mom!"

I rolled onto my back and muttered a few choice words. Having known Cathie since the seventh grade, I had no doubt she would follow through on her threat if I blew her off again. And if my mom was brought in, the unpleasant discussion of going into a rehab center for depression, would start up again. That would be disastrous. Thinking of the screaming—mainly mine—that would accompany that conversation made the throbbing in my head swell.

I snorted as the battering continued and sat up so fast the room spun. Fortunately, there was nothing in my stomach or it would have most certainly come up all over the pile of clothes scattered on the floor beside the bed.

"All right, all right!" I screamed to stop the pounding, which was making me feel sick.

"Are you coming out?" Cathie called back.

I knew in my heart Cathie was only trying to help, but I had buried my heart with Michael. All that remained was my brain, which at the moment was urging me to push her out the front door and lock her out.

With my lips pressed into a thin line, I crossed the room and jerked the door open. Cathie, who had her ear pressed to the wood, stumbled into me, then reared back, waving her hand in front of her nose.

"Whew! Have you taken a shower in like the last month?"

I rolled my eyes and pushed past her, putting forth my best effort not to weave too much, though my legs felt like gummy worms. I bounced off the wall only once as I made my way down the short hall and launched myself onto the sofa in the living room.

"Oh, no you don't!" Cathie barked, stomping up and

planting her hands on her hips as she stared down at me. "You are *not* trading in your bed for that sofa. You are going to get dressed and go out with me for some fresh air and real food."

I glowered at her and opened my mouth to protest. Before I could push the words out, she held up her phone and added, "Or I swear, I'm going to call your mom and tell her you haven't been out of your room for a week."

"It has not been a week! It's only been a couple days. And I'm not hungry," I fired back, but the loud gurgling in my stomach betrayed me.

"Uh-uh," Cathie replied with a shake of her head. "All the food I made up and left for you in the fridge before I went to my conference on Friday night is still there. And I know you didn't go out to get anything to eat. It's no wonder you're always tired. Your body has nothing to sustain itself."

"That's not true. I have eaten. I had a couple granola bars," I said defensively and laid my forearm over my face to block out both Cathie and the blinding sun shining in through the wall of windows.

"Oh, wow, really? A *couple* granola bars? Geez, I'm surprised you even managed to roll out of your room with all that extra weight on you."

She paused and I felt the cushion dip as she sat on the edge beside me and put her hand on my leg.

"Seriously, hon, you're really starting to scare me. I know I've never been in your shoes and don't know what you're going through, but it's going on seventeen months. Michael would hate that you've shut yourself off from everyone like this."

You're right, you don't know what I'm going through. The love of your life wasn't brutally murdered for no reason at all. My chest tightened and I pressed my fingernails into the palms of my hands.

"I don't see you making any effort to get better. In fact, it kind of seems like I'm the only one working to get you back on your feet," she continued. "I want to be here for you and I think I've been extremely patient. But I can't keep doing this if you don't start putting forth some effort too." She paused, waiting for me to say something. When I remained silent, she sighed.

"Your mom has been calling me since you haven't answered her calls. She's asking a lot of questions and I don't know how much longer I can put her off. And you know I won't lie to her. So please … come out with me for a little bit. Then I won't have to betray you the next time she calls. I don't have to go into the office until this afternoon, so we can walk down to Starbucks and get a latte and one of those chocolate croissants you like. It'll be my treat."

She was starting to sound like my mom. I moved my arm away from one eye enough to peek out, intending to tell her so, but the worry on her face stopped me.

When I lost my scholarship in April and had to move out of my apartment, Cathie talked her Aunt Stephanie into letting me take over the second bedroom of the apartment they shared while Stephanie was on a nine-month overseas work assignment. That saved me from having to move back home. Ever since, Cathie has had to put up with my nonsense on a daily basis and hasn't asked for a single thing in return. I owe her a lot more than a surly attitude, but at the moment that's all I had in me to give.

"Come on," Cathie repeated, her pleading eyes locking with mine. "Just come out with me for a bit. I promise if you do, I won't nag you for the rest of the week."

I looked up at her skeptically. "If I go out with you, you can't say anything to Mom either."

Cathie held up her right hand. "I won't. I promise."

I tried to focus on her face to see if she was telling the truth, but everything blurred together, which told me my blood sugar was too low.

"Fiiine!" I grumbled, trying to make it sound like I was giving in just for her and not because I knew I needed food. "But just so you know, I'm going to hold you to that promise."

I staggered to my feet and clomped back into my room. Sitting on the edge of the mattress, I stared at the piles of wrinkled clothes at my feet and fumed at Cathie for resorting to blackmail to get her way. Though in reality, I was more mad at myself than at her. She would never have been able to coerce me in the old days. But just as my desire to live had fled, so had my desire to fight. And the thought of the hell that would rain down if my mom found out how much time I'd been spending in my room sent a shudder all the way to the tips of my toes. Going out for a coffee was a small price to pay to avoid that scene.

I grumbled to myself as I dug through the clothes for something to wear and pulled out the first hoodie I came across. I would never have dreamed of wearing anything so wrinkled when Michael was still alive, but I had no one to impress anymore. After giving it a good sniff to make sure it didn't stink too bad, I pulled it on over Michael's old T-shirt, the one I still slept in every night even though it had lost his scent months ago.

I walked back to the living room in the hoodie and pajama pants I had worn for the past week. They had bright red lips and the words "Kisses" and "Sexy" printed in pink and red all over them. On my feet were a pair of plush unicorn slippers I had picked up in Las Vegas on a girls' weekend out.

Cathie gave me a disapproving look, but I just stared back, challenging her to say something. But we've been best friends for too long and she knows me too well, and all I got in return was a victorious smile. She then linked her arm through mine and practically dragged me through the door and across the balcony to the metal stairs that led down to street level.

Fall has always been my favorite time of year. I used to love everything about it: the cooler temperatures, the earthy smells, and how Mother Nature turned the mountains to gold—a gold that was free to all and required no mining to enjoy. Though fall didn't officially begin for another week and a half, the smell of it was in the air and some of the trees had already begun to change colors, showing off bits of the glittering gold amidst the green. But I barely gave it a glance as I was concentrating on putting one foot in front of the other and making it to the coffee shop without collapsing.

If anyone had been watching my struggle, they would have never guessed I was an avid hiker. Or at least I used to be, and have, in fact, hiked eleven of the fifty-three Colorado peaks over fourteen thousand feet. But it's been almost two years since I last hiked, and if Cathie hadn't had a firm grasp on my arm, which I suspect had more to do with keeping me from fleeing back to the apartment than supporting me, I'm not sure I would have made it the short trek to Starbucks.

Only when we got close enough to see there was an empty table on the outside patio, did I pull my arm free and staggered on my own to the empty metal chair. I sank down with a disgusted grunt, hoping to mask my weakness under the guise of antipathy. I could see right away Cathie wasn't fooled, but she kept her mouth shut and bounced off to get our order.

This particular Starbucks, because of its proximity to the campus of the University of Colorado, was a popular hangout for students no matter the time of day or night. Today was no different, and the line of customers extended out the door.

I pulled my hood up over my head and gazed blankly at the people coming and going, mentally debating with myself whether or not I could make it back to the apartment before Cathie returned. But even on my best day I wouldn't have made it much more than a block, as she had obviously pre-ordered online and was back in less than a minute with a caramel latte for both of us, two chocolate croissants and two blueberry scones.

I fixed her with my best scathing scowl, hating that she knew me so well. She ignored my look and pushed two of the treats across the table, then tried to hide her smile behind her cup as she lifted it to her mouth. But I saw the twinkle in her eyes and my spine went stiff. Before I could say anything, however, the sweet scent of the croissant and the caramel in the latte reached my nose and my stomach clenched painfully. I caught my gasp before it escaped, but the biting words I had intended to spew melted in my mouth.

Cathie, oblivious to my discomfort, filled in the silence with a rant about her boss. She had always been the ambitious one of the two of us, taking college accredited classes in high school and going to summer school so she could graduate in three years. When she got the job in May, fresh from graduation, she envisioned it as being the first rung on the ladder to success. But between her micro-managing supervisor and a wannabe dictator

CEO, she had become disillusioned with corporate America in a short four months.

Sixteen months ago, I would have been sympathetic to her plight. But that person died with Michael, and the person that was left didn't have the strength or desire to even pretend to care. Her words swirled into a fog inside my head as I nibbled on my croissant and indifferently watched some familiar faces come and go, wondering how all those people could look so happy in a world filled with such darkness.

That's when he looked around, and my world turned upside down.

TWO

I didn't pay much attention to him at first. He was just another guy standing in line, waiting to place his order like a dozen others. There was nothing special or unusual about his sandy-colored hair or his stubble beard that I call the "Hollywood" beard, since just about every actor in Hollywood who I think is damn sexy has one. But when he turned around and our eyes locked for a brief moment, my heart seized.

His eyes, a color somewhere between aqua and teal blue, were the most striking and peculiar shade I have ever seen. But it wasn't just his eyes that stalled my breath. A wave of dèjá vu hit me all at once and was so intense I felt like I was in the blast range of a nuclear bomb.

I know the word dèjá vu gets thrown around a lot in a joking manner, but this was no joke. One second I was fine, the next I was hot and queasy, my hands were clammy, and even with the chill in the air, beads of sweat dotted my forehead. But what freaked me out the most was the sense that I was no longer there in the moment. I had been pulled out of the scene and was watching it from afar—his every movement documented in a script I had already read.

I closed my eyes, took a deep breath, and tried to calm myself. But his allure was too strong and I couldn't resist darting glances at him every few seconds. As the line moved forward and he stepped through the door and out of sight, I stretched tall and leaned halfway over the table to see through the displays and the people coming and going.

"Watch out! Kat, what the hell are you doing?" Cathie hurriedly scooted her chair back to avoid the flow of milky coffee running across the table from the cup I had unknowingly tipped over.

I looked down at the cup lying on its side and then up at Cathie, who was frantically sopping up the liquid with handfuls of napkins.

"I'm sorry," I mumbled and dabbed at the mess with my own napkin so I could get back to the blue-eyed man in the shop.

When the coffee had been cleaned up the best it could with the few napkins we had, Cathie went inside to wash her hands. I eagerly flipped around to the window, but there were two teenage girls blocking my view. I shifed in my seat to see around them. However, no matter which way I leaned, they managed to be in the way.

I cursed under my breath and stood to get a better view. At that moment, the blue-eye man walked out the door with a venti cup in hand and crossed the street, completely unaware of the turmoil he had thrown me in.

I watched him bound down the stairs to the pedestrian underpass that went under Broadway and onto campus. When he disappeared from my sight, a small voice in the back of my mind urged me to follow. Before logic had a chance to bring me back to my senses, I obeyed.

"Hey! Where're you going?" Cathie called from the doorway.

Without turning around, I waved my hand and yelled back, "I'm going to get some air. I'll see you back at the apartment."

I stumbled down the stairs as fast as I could go and followed Blue-eyes onto campus. He showed no sign of knowing I was tailing him, but strode purposely through the maze of red-tile roofed buildings. At the Duane Physics Building, he walked through the doors of Gamow Tower, and thanks to the adrenalin surging through my veins, I wasn't too far behind him.

My chest heaved as I stood in the middle of the small entrance lobby that was quickly filling with a barrage of students rushing towards the exit from the hallways on my left and the elevators on my right. Classes had obviously just gotten out and the timing couldn't have been worse.

Acting like a crazy woman, I barreled through the crowd, darting glances at the faces as I pushed my way through. However, 95% of the students were men and I felt like an ant amongst giants.

I've never been one who enjoyed calling attention to myself, especially in a crowd of strangers, but the thought of losing Blue-eyes was more distressing than a little embarrassment. I steeled myself and yelled out at the top of my lungs, "HEY!"

The din around me immediately quieted and heads turned in my direction. I felt my cheeks heat up, but I ignored the strange looks and scanned the faces until I caught sight of him—Blue-eyes—talking to a man in the hallway to my left. His gaze was like a magnet to me, but I clearly didn't have the same effect on him. A few seconds later, he said goodbye to his friend, turned away, and continued through another set of doors and disappeared again around a corner.

"Sorry," I mumbled over and over as I shouldered my way through the mass of students to catch up before he got away again. Fortunately, around the corner was not another hall, but an alcove that led into a classroom.

I let out a sigh of relief and paused a second at the door to catch my breath and pull my hood farther down over my head. Then with a trembling hand, I pushed down on the handle and slipped into what I discovered was a balcony overlooking one of the many lecture halls.

I immediately dropped my gaze to the floor, as if that would make me invisible and no one would know I didn't belong there. But at the sight of two little gold unicorn horns sticking out of the bottom of my gaudy pajama pants, my stomach clenched with the recollection of the small rebellion I had staged before leaving the apartment.

I wanted to melt into the carpet, but instead, I turned to run out before anyone saw me. At the same moment my hand touched the door handle, I remembered Blue-eyes and I halted. He was somewhere in the room below and I could feel his draw, which was stronger than my urge to flee. I hesitated another second, then turned away from the door and scurried to a seat in the darkest corner. I cowered in the chair with my knees drawn into my chest and my head buried between them, praying no one would notice me.

Every muscle in my body remained tense and ready to bolt, but the minutes ticked off and no one came. I heard the door open and close several more times, and after what seemed like an eternity, I lifted my head and braved a look over the railing at the floor below.

The lecture hall looked like so many others I had sat in during the two years I attended classes at CU. Rows of stadium-style seating rose up from the floor, and dual movie screens were pulled down in front of a wall of blackboards. In front of the screens was a long display table. Occupying the center of the floor was a square kiosk equipped with audio equipment.

Three-quarters of the seats were filled with occupants lost in laptops propped open on the trays of their chairs. Not a single person seemed to know or care I was in the balcony. Or it might have been they were so used to freaks coming into their classes, they were oblivious to them. Whatever the case, it was to my advantage. I slowly released the breath I'd been holding and unfolded my legs to sit up so I could get a better look around.

Blue-eyes was easy to pick out, even though all I could see was the back of his shaggy head. He was sitting in an aisle seat in the second row with a laptop on his tray like everyone else. *Turn around*, I said inside my head, hoping he would be able to pick up on my telepathic message.

All at once, something inside my brain clicked on and I realized where I was and what I was doing. "Holy shit … I've become a frickin' stalker!" I whispered to the shadows.

I groaned out loud, feeling like I had been punched in the stomach and slumped deeper into the seat. But before I could process what madness had come over me, the sting of a thousand needles began pricking the tips of my fingers. I sucked in my breath and held it, hoping the tingling would go away. Instead, it quickly moved into my hands and started up my arms, signaling a full blown anxiety attack was just minutes away.

No, no, no, this can't be happening now. I squeezed my eyes together, willing my heart to remain calm and not start thumping erratically against my chest until my ribs ached. If that happened, the next thing would be the walls of the room would close in on me and I would feel like I was suffocating. Then a stabbing pain would slice through my heart like the bullet that ripped through Michael's, and I would be reduced to a despondent blob of tears and snot within seconds.

"Oh shit, oh shit, oh shit," I mumbled, realizing it was already too late to leave. I should never have let Cathie drag me out of the apartment. Ever since the shooting, these kind of attacks would randomly hit me when I was out in public, adding my name to the long list of lives the POS destroyed that April night.

I bit down hard on my lower lip and pressed my fingernails into the skin of my palms, but that did little good. My breath came in short bursts and I trembled all over, and not because of Blue-eyes this time.

One of the many shrinks I had gone to over the past year gave me a technique of mentally reciting the multiplication tables to abate an attack. It was supposed to occupy my brain and take it off whatever had triggered my anxiety, but my bad luck was holding out and I couldn't make it past three times three.

With a moan, I bent in half and pulled the neck of my hoodie up over my nose and mouth to breathe in the carbon dioxide. Then, rocking back and forth, I prayed to whatever entity might be listening to have pity on me.

I was vaguely conscious of the door opening and closing on the other side of the room and the sound of shuffling feet going down the steps, but no one bothered me. The attack was still in the beginning stages when a booming voice came through the speakers. I jumped clean off the seat and lifted my head.

The balcony lights, as well as a majority of the lights on the main level were out, leaving a single spotlight shining down on a short, squatty man standing at a podium. The beating of my heart echoed so loud in my head, I could barely make out what the man was saying, but I wasn't interested in him anyway. I noticed Blue-eyes had moved to a chair next to the audio-visual equipment and all of my attention was focused there.

"... Einstein's theory of general relativity says gravity can bend time. Some believe this implies time travel is possible."

Those words broke through my trance and my gaze shifted to the man at the podium.

"While the scientific community has had no problem accepting the majority of Einstein's theories, most are still hesitant to accept the possibility of time travel," the man went on.

"Today's distinguished guest, Dr. Marcus Mallory, a respected theoretical physicist, academic, author, and former professor here at CU, has what you might call a difference of opinion on the matter, coming about as a result of a life-long study on the hypothesis of time travel. After more years than he is willing to divulge, he now believes he is on the verge of a monumental breakthrough.

"Dr. Mallory's classroom days are over for the most part, but he still roams about campus like an old ghost." He chuckled as he looked over his shoulder at a tall shadow of a man standing at the end of the long table. "That is where I found him and begged him to come and update us on his research. I was exceptionally pleased when he agreed to carve out two hours of his time and share some exciting news with us. I have no doubt he'll use his charm and knowledge to turn many of you over to his way of thinking. But enough of my babble, for I am, as I'm sure you are, anxious to hear what the good doctor has to say. So please join me in a warm welcome for Dr. Mallory."

A splattering of applause circulated the room as a tall African-American man with graying hair at his temples stepped up to the podium. His rich baritone voice flowed over me like molasses, and as I listened to him talk about time travel, my breathing slowly returned to normal and the tingling dulled to a buzz.

For way too many months, my bed had been the only thing I was interested in, and I can't say quantum physics or the idea of time travel *ever* piqued my interest. But within the first half-hour, I was completely enthralled with what Dr. Mallory was saying, and a spark of life reignited within me. By the end of his talk, every cell in my body was on fire and my brain was working overtime trying to process what I heard.

Much of what he said was beyond my understanding, especially the equations and the logistics involved, but I had no trouble comprehending that he had found the means and method to make time travel possible and was in the process of building a time machine. And he was hoping to test his theory before the year ended.

I remained in the back corner of the balcony long after the room cleared, contemplating Dr. Mallory's words and the "what ifs." What if I went back in time and stopped Michael from going to the bar that night? What if I was able to stop the POS from killing all those people?

Countless possibilities and questions pummeled my mind and I lost track of time. A loud yell startled me out of my thoughts. I went rigid and stared down at the floor below where a security guard stood, pointing his finger up at me.

"You aren't supposed to be in here. You need to leave. I'm locking up now," the guard said.

My cheeks burned as I rose and hurried to the door before he could question me further. The weather had turned, as it so often did in Colorado, and a brisk wind nearly blew me over as I rushed out of the building, my unicorn slippers shuffling along the concrete.

The smell of rain was thick in the air, but the threat of getting drenched didn't dampen my spirits as I was lost in the thought that the Universe was telling me to go back in time and save Michael. That's why it sent me Blue-eyes. To lead me to Dr. Mallory's talk. It was a crazy thought, bordering on the edge of insanity, but really no crazier than the thought of killing myself. And the more I thought about it, the more sense it made to my troubled brain.

THREE

As I slowly walked back through the campus, two questions in particular took the forefront of the hundred different thoughts colliding with each other inside my head: Was Dr. Mallory for real? Is time travel even possible?

I'm a huge fan of Dr. Who and the Back to the Future movies, but I never believed time travel was real. I knew those shows were merely created for entertainment value and had very little scientific merit. And from the slides Dr. Mallory showed in his talk, his time machine was clearly not as glamorous as a DeLorean, or as quirky as a police box. In fact, with its glowing green lights, it looked more like a weird Halloween decoration than a time machine.

The slides only showed a small scale model of the machine sitting on a table, not the real thing. A machine that would accommodate a human would have to be a hundred times larger than the model, if not more, or so I imagined. Something that big would require a building the size of a hangar or large warehouse to fit in.

"Shit!" I uttered, realizing Mallory hadn't mentioned where his lab was located. I dropped down on a stone bench and buried my head in my hands. I hadn't gotten started yet and I was already facing a major roadblock—how to find the machine.

My chin began to quiver with the thought of having to go on without Michael, but I forced those thoughts away and focused back on the time machine. The man who had introduced

Mallory said he spent a lot of time on campus, but I couldn't picture that large of a machine being in any of the university's buildings. If it were, there would have been plenty of buzz going around, and there had been none. That I heard of anyway. So why would Mallory hang around CU?

All at once, a few more of my brain cells fired up and it dawned on me that one man could not have possibly built the machine on his own. And what better place for Mallory to find cheap and willing labor for a science project than on a college campus filled with physics students? That meant someone else out there knew the location. Possibly even one of the attendees at the lecture.

I thought back, trying to picture the classroom, but the only image I could muster up was the blue-eyed man. My pulse escalated and heat rushed through me as I pictured his blue-eyes. But something else nagged at the back of my mind. He had run the visual part of the presentation. Did that mean he knew Mallory?

"Ohmigawd! He might be able to tell me where to find the machine," I said out loud.

The thought had barely registered in my head when another sent me reeling. Hunting down Blue-eyes could be just as time consuming as hunting down the machine. And why waste the time when any other mathematic/physics major could probably tell me who worked with Mallory. Or at least direct me to where to go to find out.

I jumped to my feet and began pacing, racking my brain to come up with who I knew in the physics department. In my three years at CU I had met a ton of people, but the only name I could think of was Jeff, an old buddy of Michael's.

My stomach dropped. *Oh, crap! Not Jeff!*

Jeff and Michael had been close friends since high school, but he and I never meshed. I actually didn't like him and hadn't tried to hide the fact. He made me feel uncomfortable and gave me the impression he didn't think I was good enough for Michael. That didn't sit well with me. In return, I did my best to pretend he didn't exist. I haven't seen him since the funeral, so it's possible he won't remember that I was kind of a bitch to him. But if he does remember, I'm going to be screwed.

My stomach locked tight with anticipation and stayed that way all the way back to the apartment. When I burst through the door, I was out of breath and cold.

Cathie stood in the kitchen on the phone and spun around at the sound. I took one look at her puffy red eyes and the little air left in my lungs came out in a whoosh. She was not the weepy type. In fact, I had only seen her in such a state two previous times: when her dad got into a serious automobile accident, and when Michael was killed.

I took a hesitant step toward her, but her next words into the phone stopped me cold.

"She just came in." Cathie paused a moment and listened before adding, "Yes, everything seems to be fine. Sorry to have taken up your time, Sir." She punched the screen with her finger and turned on me. "Where the *hell* have you been?"

I squared my shoulders and lifted my chin at the accusatory tone of her voice.

"You've been gone for hours! No call, no text … nothing. You just took off, and all I could think of was you were out there—"

She didn't finish the sentence, but she didn't need to. I was well aware of what she was going to say. She thought I had finally gotten up the nerve to end my life.

A wave of guilt crushed my annoyance and nearly buckled my legs. Cathie was the best friend a person could ask for and I had been nothing but a total jerk in return. In a heartbeat, I crossed the room and wrapped my arms around her in a tight hug.

"I'm so sorry, sweetie," I whispered in her ear. "I didn't mean to worry you."

Cathie sagged against me for a split second, then pulled back. "You've been gone for three and a half hours! Why didn't you call or answer my texts?"

I flinched at hearing how much time had passed. "I didn't have my phone with me, so I couldn't call." I didn't add that it probably wouldn't have entered my mind to call anyway. "And I had no idea you'd be so upset. You've been on me to get out and get some fresh air and that's what I was doing. I took a walk around campus and ended up in a lecture. I didn't plan to stay for the whole talk, but it turned out to be quite interesting." I gave her my best smile, hoping it would hide the fact I wasn't telling her the whole story. I could only imagine her reaction if I told her I wanted to go back in time to save Michael.

Cathie stared at me, then took hold of both of my arms and gave me a little shake. "Don't you *ever* do that to me again! Do you know who I was talking to when you walked in?" She didn't pause for even a heartbeat to let me answer. "The police!"

My stomach dropped and I took a step back. "Are you serious? What the hell?! Why did you call the police?"

"Why? You're seriously asking me why? You don't step a foot out of your room for days, and then you disappear without saying a word. What am I supposed to think? I know you're having a tough time, but you won't let me in. You won't let anyone in."

Her words trailed off, but they had hit the mark and another wave of guilt swept through me.

"I'm so *so* sorry," I said, meaning not just for the worry I'd put her through, but also for not confiding about what was going on in my head. "I really didn't intend to be gone so long. It was kind of nice, though, being out among people who didn't give me that pitying look you know I hate." Cathie's eyebrows raised and I quickly added, "I'm not saying you do that. You don't. You've been my rock."

A tear slipped out of the corner of Cathie's eye. I swallowed the lump in my throat and went on. "You're my best friend. I truly don't know what I'd do without you. I know I've become a burden, but that's all going to change soon. I'm going to make more of an effort … I promise. And I swear I'll tell you or text the next time I go somewhere. Okay?" I clamped down on my tongue knowing that was a promise I couldn't keep.

Cathie cocked her head to the side and gave me a puzzling look. "You seem different. What happened?"

"Nothing," I replied too quickly. Then, realizing my error,

I hurriedly added, "I mean, I don't know. I guess getting out of the apartment cleared my head. And you know that lecture I mentioned? It was a physics talk. I know it's totally out of my realm, but I found it incredibly interesting. And it got me to thinking that maybe I could jump start my life if I took some classes outside of neuroscience. Like maybe some physics classes."

Cathie's eyebrows shot up and her eyes grew wide, but I cut her off before she could say anything and back me into a corner. "Do you remember Jeff, that friend of Michael's? The one with the longish hair, glasses, and bushy goatee thing?" I tried to keep my voice even and not show too much excitement. I didn't want her to get any more suspicious than she already was.

"Are you talking about Jeff Newton?" Cathie replied, her voice carrying a hint of disbelief.

"Yes, that's it! Jeff Newton," I confirmed with a nod of my head. "I'm so bad at remembering last names." I turned and headed toward my room.

"Isn't he the guy you didn't like?" she called after me.

"Yeah, but that was a long time ago. I'm going to go take a quick shower." I slammed the door to put an end to the conversation.

Inside my room, I pulled the boxes of Michael's belongings I had packed up shortly after his death out of the closet. Most of it was useless junk, like his toothbrush, old binders of school notes, beat up hockey pucks, old earbuds, concert T-shirts, and so on. I knew it was all worthless, but I couldn't bear to part with any of it and lose one more piece of him.

It took me several minutes of digging to find his phone. It was dead, of course, and in my combined state of nerves and exaltation, I fumbled multiple times trying to get the power cord plugged in. I then sat and stared at it while it charged enough to be turned on.

The next five minutes were pure torture. When I couldn't wait another second, I hit the power button and held my breath until the screen light blinked on. I hurriedly scrolled through the list of contacts to Jeff's name and plugged the number into my phone before I could chicken out. It rang once, then twice. On the third ring, I realized I had no idea what to say. And my mouth had gone so dry I didn't know if I would be able to speak anyway. I lifted my finger to hit the end button just as a hesitant voice answered, "Hello?"

A lump of panic tightened my throat. I definitely should have thought it through a little more before I called.

"Hello?" the voice repeated.

"Um, hi … is this Jeff?" I stammered into the phone.

"Yeah. Who's this?"

"It's Kat … Katelyn Chambers … Michael Bellwood's girlfriend. Do you remember me?"

"Yeah, of course. Um … how're you doing?" Jeff replied, his voice revealing his shock at hearing from me.

"Good. I'm good. I hope I'm not bothering you."

"No, not at all."

"Oh, good." I swallowed hard knowing it was too late to turn back. "Are you still at CU?"

"Yeah, I am. Just started back up a couple weeks ago. I'm in the graduate program now."

"Yes!" I muttered.

"I beg your pardon?"

"Oh … I'm just happy to hear you're continuing your education." I almost added, "Unlike me," but didn't. "Actually, that's the reason I'm calling. I've been thinking of switching into the physics program and was hoping we could meet up for coffee so you could tell me a little about it," I gushed in one long breath.

"I thought you were in nursing?"

I bristled. He knew I wasn't in nursing. However, instead of firing back, I kept my voice sweet. "No, I was in neuroscience, but I've recently developed an interest in physics."

"Oh, that's cool," Jeff replied.

I waited for him to say more, but he remained silent.

"So would you be willing to meet and talk to me about it?" I coaxed.

"Yeah, sure. I could do that," Jeff replied. "I have a Tuesday, Thursday class that starts at 9—"

"That's perfect!" I cut in. "We can meet tomorrow before your class. How about 7:45 at the Starbucks on College?"

"Um … yeah. I guess that could work," Jeff said hesitantly.

"Great! I'll see you in the morning then. And thanks so much." I punched end before he had time to think it through and back out.

I took a quick shower, then spent the rest of the afternoon, right up until Cathie called me for dinner, surfing the internet and reading up on everything I could find on time travel.

It was gratifying to discover Einstein, Hawking, and Thorne, the top-noted authorities in physics, all agreed time travel could be possible. But they also agreed that it would take an advanced society to pull it off, and we're not even close to being that society yet.

If I had been in my right mind, reading that might have discouraged me from going on. But I just shrugged it off, thinking new, ground-breaking discoveries took place every day in the world of science. And who was I to say this wasn't one of them?

I continued my research after dinner, hoping to find evidence that a circulating cylinder of light could in fact bend the space time continuum like Mallory believed it would. But all I found were complex theories involving wormholes, black holes, cosmic strings, the speed of light, and paradoxes. When my head started to spin and I could barely put two thoughts together, I called it a night.

At 6:30 the next morning, I was up and dressed in the only pair of semi-clean jeans I could find in the pile of clothes on the floor. I was standing in the kitchen, pouring myself a cup of coffee, when Cathie stumbled out of her room still in her pajamas. Out of the corner of my eye I saw her jerk to a stop.

"You're up early," she said.

I could tell she was trying to sound casual, but she did a lousy job of hiding her shock.

"I have some things to do today," I replied, pretending to be just as indifferent as she was trying to be and failing just as miserably.

"Oh?" Cathie grabbed a cup from the cupboard, filled it with coffee, and leaned her butt against the counter.

We had been friends long enough that I could tell she was dying for me to tell her what I had planned, but I didn't want her to start hammering me with questions I couldn't answer. I took my coffee and nonchalantly walked to the sofa to get away from her scrutiny.

"Sooo, what kind of things do you have going?" she brazenly asked.

As much as I wanted to tell her the truth, I knew it would freak her out, and I already had too many obstacles in my way.

"I'm checking out the physics program. Remember? I told you about it last night." I flicked on the TV to the morning news and pretended to be interested.

Over the banter of the TV personalities, I heard a clank as Cathie set her coffee mug on the granite countertop. A second later, she was beside me on the sofa.

"You were serious about that? I mean, physics? Are you kidding? You hate math!" Her voice raised several decibels.

"That's not totally true. I'm not a fan of math, but I don't hate it. And like I said yesterday, the lecture I went to was fascinating. The more I think about it, the more it seems like going in a completely different direction will help me move on."

I added the last part in hopes it would break her skepticism. It worked. Her face went from suspicion to sympathy in a nanosecond. But as her eyes turned glassy and her chin started to quiver, my small victory evaporated.

She sniffed back a strangled sob and leaned in to give me a hug. "It makes me so happy to hear you say that." She squeezed me harder. "It's about time you started fresh and got back on track."

I hugged her back and tried to push away, but she wouldn't let go. When she finally released me, my cheeks were burning hot and I was pretty sure my face was the same color red as the little hearts dotting her pajama shorts. I hurriedly turned away and gathered up my phone, purse, and keys before she could see the guilt I had no doubt was written all over my face.

"I'm meeting up with Jeff this morning to get some info on the program. So I'll see ya tonight." I then hurried out the door before she had me spilling my guts.

I hated to have to lie to her, but if she knew what I was really up to, she would take me straight to the psych ward and sign me in.

FOUR

I wasn't expecting it to be so cold when I walked out of the apartment. It was still too early for snow, even in Colorado. But as everyone here likes to say, "If you don't like the weather, wait five minutes." The heavy gray clouds blocking the sun and my crystalized breaths proved how accurate that saying was.

Grumbling to myself about the fickle weather, I wrapped my light jacket tighter around me, hunched my shoulders against the biting wind, and headed to Starbucks. As I walked, I mentally practiced what I would say to lead Jeff around to telling me who might know more about the machine.

Thanks to the nasty wind, Starbucks was bulging with customers who would otherwise be congregating around the tables outside. I collected my caramel macchiato latte and scone and looked around for a spot. Finding none, I turned to the window and looked mournfully out at the closed table umbrellas rocking in the wind. It looked as uninviting as I knew it was, but there was not even a corner inside to stand in.

I lifted the collar of my jacket and headed out, sitting at the table closest to the door to savor the small wafts of heated air that floated my way every time someone entered or exited. The random gusts of wind played havoc with my hair, but that was the least of my worries. In all the time I had known Jeff, I never took the time to *really* get to know him. He went to my high school and I saw him around, usually tagging along after Michael, but he never had a girlfriend, so we seldom went out together. Then at CU, my circle of friends were always around, and though Jeff came to most of our gatherings, he stayed on the fringe and I never attempted to pull him in.

So pretty much, all I had left to work with was my charm. At one time, I was quite good at turning it on. Hopefully, it will be enough to make Jeff forget all about those other times.

I spotted Jeff over the rim of my coffee cup when he was about a block away. His head was down and his shoulders were hunched, but the signature Star Laboratories cap and camouflage jacket I've never seen him without was a dead giveaway. He walked straight to the door without looking up, probably because he didn't expect me to be sitting outside in the cold. I called his name and his head jerked around. He stared at me blankly as if he didn't know who I was. That didn't surprise me. I don't look anything like I used to. I've lost a lot of weight, my cheeks are hollow, and my eyes are sunken with deep, dark circles under them that I can't cover up even with a whole tube of concealer. I blushed at his shocked look and ran my fingers through my tangled hair, wishing I had worn a hat.

He seemed unsure, and for a moment, I thought he might turn and run the other way. But after a long pause, he shuffled over to the table.

"Kat?"

"Yes, it's me. I guess it's been awhile." I could feel a rush of heat moving up my neck.

"I'm sorry. I didn't recognize you," he said, then visibly flinched. "I mean … you know, I haven't seen you since Michael's fun—" He lowered his eyes and shifted from foot to foot, clearly not knowing what to say.

"It's okay. I know it's been awhile. Why don't you sit down. Or did you want to get a coffee first," I said, wanting to ease his discomfort.

"No, I'm good," he said, which I took as meaning he wanted to get this over with as quickly as possible.

He dropped onto the chair, pushed his glasses up on his nose, and stared down at his lap.

I folded my hands on the table, smiled, and plunged right in. "I want to thank you for agreeing to meet with me. You're the only person I know who's been in the physics program." I paused. "I did tell you I was thinking about switching majors, didn't I?" I didn't give him a chance to answer. "I was hoping you'd give me the scoop of what to expect and fill me in on the professors."

Jeff's shoulders noticeably relaxed and he finally looked at me. "I don't know how much help I can be. Your best bet would be to talk to your advisor. They're better qualified to tell you what it takes to get in."

"Yes, I realize that. I plan to talk to him later today," I lied. "But I was hoping you could give me an insider's point of view on the program. I attended a lecture yesterday given by a Dr. Mallory."

A light clicked on in his eyes.

"Were you at the lecture too? I didn't see you there."

"No, I wasn't, but I know Dr. Mallory and his work," he replied.

"You do? Then you know about his time machine?"

Jeff nodded, but didn't elaborate. He never was a man of many words. At least, not around me. I clasped my hands together to keep them from shaking and stretched my smile a little more.

"Dr. Mallory's talk inspired me to do some research on time travel. From what I found, it sounds like most physicists agree it's possible, but we don't currently have the capability to warp space-time. To make that to happen, we would need to travel the speed of light or get close to a black hole. Nothing I read mentioned using circulating beams of light like what Dr. Mallory talked about. So what do you think? Is Dr. Mallory's theory viable? Will it work?"

That was all it took to break through Jeff's reluctance. His entire demeanor instantly changed and he began rattling off terminology, theories, and equations so far over my head he might as well have been speaking Chinese. I twisted the blue topaz promise ring Michael had given me around on my finger as I listened and nodded my head from time to time when he said something I actually understood.

I let him go on for a while before breaking in to bring the conversation around to the point of the meeting.

"It's mind-blowing to discover how far science has come," I said, trying to sound as if I had followed along with him the whole time. "But all you've just talked about is traveling into the future. What about going backward in time? Does Mallory's theory work just as well for that?"

"Of course, as of right now, since no one has done it, it's all conjecture. Personally, I don't get the point of traveling to the past. The universe has a set of laws that don't—" Jeff started, but I cut him off.

"Yes, I've read over some of the objections and I know the problem of paradoxes. But like you just said, no one has ever done it, so there's really no way to know for sure. And couldn't that same logic apply to the laws of the universe? Couldn't it be that the laws aren't as cut and dried as you think, and it *would* be okay for someone to go back to, let's say, right a wrong? You know, like … prevent Kennedy from being assassinated kind of thing."

Jeff scoffed softly. "Why does everyone think stopping Kennedy's assassination is a good idea? Who's to say the world would be a better place had Kennedy lived?" He placed his elbows on the table and leaned in. "The world as we know it today depends on Kennedy dying on November 22nd. If he hadn't, the lives that we have right now would not exist. *Nothing* in this world would be the same."

A lump formed in my throat and my voice wavered. "I realize changing an event in the past would create some differences in the future, but those differences don't have to be bad. Don't you think if someone actually had the ability to stop something horrific from happening, something that impacted hundreds or thousands of lives, it would be a good thing and would be their duty to do so?"

He shook his head again. "You don't understand the innumerable consequences that could occur if even one minor incident is changed in the past. I'm not saying all effects would be bad, but some of them could be. And even if it's just one, it could significantly change the world.

"For example, if Kennedy had lived, U.S. and Russia could have gone to war, resulting in massive portions of the world becoming nuclear waste sites. That is not a farfetched conclusion. A majority of historians agree we were heading towards that end. My point is … no one knows what we'll get if the past is somehow changed.

He held up his index finger. "Another point you probably don't understand is, you can't travel back decades or hundreds of years in time. That misnomer was adopted when H.G. Wells' *The Time Machine* came out. But the reality is, you can't travel back to a time before the machine was built. If you think about it, you'll see how that makes sense. So it's pointless for us to sit here and debate whether or not someone should go back and save Kennedy. The simple fact is, there's no possible way to do so. And I can't see how there ever will be."

It felt like an anvil had been dropped on my chest and my arms and legs went numb. I had placed every last bit of hope on the time machine giving me back my life. But if I couldn't go back … I stopped those thoughts from taking root. Jeff had to be wrong.

"Are you okay?" he asked.

I opened my mouth, but no words came out. My vision blurred with tears, but it didn't prevent me from seeing the apprehension wash across Jeff's face. All at once, he pushed his glasses up on his nose, stood, and looked around helplessly. No other brave soul was sitting out in the bitter wind, though, and there was no one to come to his rescue. He cleared his throat and pushed his chair back from the table as if he was going to leave.

"It's okay, I'm fine," I croaked, grabbing his arm before he could run away. A small seed of hope lingered inside me and I couldn't let him go as long as it was still alive. "I've been having, um, … stomach issues that throw me a little off balance sometimes, but it goes away quickly."

Jeff looked wary and continued to stand. "Do you need me to get you something?"

I forced a smile and gestured to the chair. "No, please sit. I'm okay. I promise I won't faint on you or anything like that." That was the second promise I've made in the past twenty-four hours I wasn't one hundred percent sure I could keep.

He hesitated, then reluctantly sat, although he remained stiff and looked ready to bolt should anything else happen.

I took a deep breath and steeled myself for the answer to my next question. "So you're saying it's impossible to travel back to a time before Mallory's time machine is finished since his is the first one?"

"That's correct. Or to be more precise, to a time before the machine was first turned on. But as I previously stated, everything to do with time travel is based on theory. There are no definitive answers to any question as yet. Once we get the testing phase of the machine under way and have results to analyze, we'll have a better understanding and should be able to answer a few of the questions."

The second I realized my idea was doomed, the rest of his words were a hum in my head. But one word—"we"—broke through.

"You just said "we." What do you mean by that? Are you working with Dr. Mallory?"

"Yes. Well, technically I work for Dr. Bukowski. He's the experimental physicist on the project. Mallory developed the theory and Bukowski applied the science to build the machine. I've been on the project for over a year, working nights and weekends. I thought you knew that."

"*No*, I most certainly did *not* know that!" I crossed my forearms on the table and leaned forward. "So you've actually had a hand in building the first time machine?" I couldn't hold back the awe in my voice.

"Sadly, no. I would have liked to have been on the project from the start, but the machine was already assembled when I started."

"Wait ... what?" I nearly came out of my seat. "It's already been built? But I thought ..." I tried to recall what Dr. Mallory had said in his talk. "Mallory insinuated yesterday it was still in the process of being built."

"You must have misunderstood. The machine itself was finished at the end of 2015, and was originally turned on in March 2016. But a major malfunction took it down after only two weeks. All the circuitry had to be completely rebuilt. We also had to install three industrial generators to provide supplemental power. The work's just recently been completed and we're almost ready to go back online. Then we can start the first testing stage."

His words hit me like a sledgehammer. I sprang to my feet, as if I had been mechanically ejected from the chair, and bent halfway over the table, putting my face right in front of his. "You're saying the machine was turned on a year and a half ago?" My words came out much louder than I intended, but the rustle of the wind helped muffle them.

Jeff's smile vanished and he sat back, too shocked to do anything other than nod his head.

"What exact date?"

"M … March 7th."

"March 7th," I repeated and swallowed hard. "So technically someone could go back to March of 2016. Is that right?"

The crease in Jeff's brow deepened. "Hypothetically, yes. But we would know if someone had come through the portal during those two weeks. There's nothing to substantiate that anyone did."

I stared into his eyes for a long moment before my knees gave out and I slowly sank back onto the chair. I swayed slightly as the rollercoaster wave of emotion twisted and turned within me. I love rollercoasters, but this had been one hell of a ride and I was ready to get off.

"Are you sure you're okay?" Jeff asked hesitantly.

I licked my lips and swallowed hard. "I'm fine. The wind just took my breath away. But I'm curious how you can be so sure no one came through the portal while the machine was on?"

"The security cameras and sensory devices set up around the machine would have captured any movement. So not even a cockroach would have been able to get in without being detected."

"There was no way around the cameras?"

"No. Multiple cameras were documenting every angle and every minute the machine was on."

"Every minute?" I repeated more to myself than to Jeff.

"Well, almost every minute. There was one small glitch in the camera system, which they think might have been from a power surge, and four minutes of the feed was lost."

My chest swelled with excitement, but I did my best to keep my voice even. "A power surge could do that?"

"That's what they're saying. In my opinion, I don't believe it was so much a power surge as it was the fact they initially put in an inadequate system. I'd appreciate you not sharing that with anyone."

I shook my head and gave him my best, "of course I wouldn't" look. "Couldn't it have been someone from the future who erased those four minutes so no one would know they were there?"

"That isn't likely. First of all, that person would have needed the password to access the computer in order to delete the footage. The password is changed weekly. Second, they would have also had to know how to modify the data in the system to delete the shift in the gravity chamber during that time. In other words, the traveler would have needed inside knowledge of the project and the processes, which means they would have had to be connected to the project. With that being the case, I can't see any reason why they would want to hide the evidence. In fact, it would be the opposite and I think they would have gone out of their way to *ensure* their presence was recorded and leave as much proof as possible that the machine worked."

"Yeah, maybe," I said, still struggling to conceal my excitement. "When did you say that happened? The small power surge?"

"Two days after the machine was turned on."

Could that have been me? Did I actually go back in time and make the changes to the system so no one would know I was there?

It sounded outlandish even to my feverish mind, but there were too many coincidences to ignore. The Universe led me to Mallory's talk, and then led me to Jeff, who could let me into the lab and show me how to run the equipment and change the data in the system. The pieces were all fitting together very neatly.

I suppressed a smile and sat up straighter. "You know, I can't imagine what it would be like to witness the first test. Are they going to allow outsiders in to watch? I would seriously give anything to see it."

"No, Mallory wants to keep it on the down low. At least through the first couple go arounds … in case something goes wrong."

"Oh." I didn't have to fake being crestfallen. "That's too bad. What about just getting a glimpse of the machine?" I leaned forward. "Do you think that would be possible? Would you let me come by one day while you're working? Before the testing starts?"

From the glazed look that darkened Jeff's eyes, I could tell he was searching for a way to say no, so I hurriedly added before he could come up with an objection, "Michael always said you would do something great one day. It looks like he was right. He'd be so proud of you if he were here."

Jeff's face paled a little and I knew I was on the right track.

"I'm not going to lie to you … I've been struggling since Michael's death. But I'm trying to work my way out of it. That's why I'm thinking about joining the physics program. I need a challenge that will give me focus and something new to look forward to. I realize, of course, it'll take years before I get up to speed and am able to work on a project such as this one. But I think seeing what I have to look forward would inspire me to keep going. What do you think? Would it hurt if I just took a quick look?"

Jeff's shoulders slumped and he remained silent for such a long time I thought I had lost. When he did finally look up, his eyes were glassy.

"I never knew Michael to love anyone as much as he loved you. I hope you know that."

His statement took me by surprise. My hand flew to my mouth to hold in the sob that sprang into my throat.

"He would hate to see you this way." He paused, looked down at his hands, and then back at me. "I can't see how getting a look at a machine will make a difference. But I do owe Michael a lot, and I know he would want me to help you in any way I can. And letting you have a glimpse of the machine won't have a negative impact on the project, so I guess it would be okay. I would appreciate you not telling anyone about it, though."

I bit down on my bottom lip to keep from shouting out, "Yes!" as a surge of anticipation swept away the longing ache in my chest that had been there for over sixteen months.

"This week is already full, and I have a grant proposal to finalize next week, so I can't do it then either. But maybe sometime that following weekend or ..."

"The following weekend is great!" I cut in before he could push it back any farther. Grabbing my phone, I pulled up the calendar. "Saturday the 23rd then?"

"No ... let's do the 24th. Sundays are a quieter day at the lab, and I'm there alone from three to nine. I'll text you that weekend and let you know if it'll still work."

"That'll be awesome. What's the address of the lab?"

"It's off 36 on the way up to Lyons. I'll text you the directions."

I had the feeling he was telling me what I wanted to hear to pacify me, and would come up with an excuse on the 24th to put me off. But I wasn't going to give up.

Jeff suddenly stood and awkwardly slipped the strap of his computer bag over his shoulder, looking very much like a thirteen-year-old who was about to ask a girl out for the first time. "I should get going," he said in haste. "I don't want to be late for my class. It was good to see you again. I'll talk to ya later."

He walked away before I could say anything more than, "Bye."

I felt bad about bringing up Michael's name to get Jeff to consent, but only for a moment as other thoughts quickly moved in—like how do I stop the POS?

FIVE

I sat at the table long after Jeff left, even though the wind was turning colder by the minute and I was shivering inside my jacket. There was so much to think about, so much to do, and so little time. I chuckled out loud as that thought drifted through my head. If Mallory's machine worked as he claimed, time would never again be an issue.

A swarm of butterflies took flight in my stomach at the thought of being in Michael's arms once again. It was going to be hard to hold back and not run to him the second I got to 2016. But I'd read about the paradoxes associated with time travel and how they could tear the fabric of space time in half. I didn't know exactly what that meant, or what it would do to the universe, but the article made it clear it would be bad and I didn't want to be responsible for that. My goal was to improve the future, not destroy it.

All at once, the wind and traffic noises faded out as my brain latched onto the realization it would be next to impossible for me to go anywhere around campus in 2016 and not run into someone I knew. Would that also tear the fabric of space time? Would traveling back ruin the future for everyone I loved?

A knot of panic squeezed the butterflies out of my stomach, but then a thought came to me. If I could find a way to get into the time machine and go back in time, surely I could find a way to make sure no one saw me. I just had to keep a level head and let the Universe guide my way.

A strong gust of wind rattled the chair across from me, rousing me out of my thoughts. I shivered and looked around. The weather had deteriorated further in the short time I had been sitting there and I hadn't even realized it. My breath came out as a little white cloud, as I gathered my things together with frozen fingers and turned to the coffee shop to get warm.

Just as I reached for the door, a group of goths bounded out. They brushed past me and sauntered down the street, the musky scent of patchouli and cigarette smoke trailing behind them. I let the door swing shut without entering and stared at the group. No one else on the street gave them so much as a sideways glance, though.

I had to bite down on my lip to keep from squealing. This was the answer. I could dress as a goth and no one would know it was me. I looked up at the sky in awe at how quickly the answer had come, and the last doubt as to whether the higher force in the universe was orchestrating this blew away with the wind.

Instead of warming up inside Starbucks, I raced back to the apartment, plopped down in front of my computer and started a list of what I would need: a wig, black combat boots with buckles, spike bracelet, temporary tattoos, a fake ID, and a gun.

My hands shook as I typed out the letters G. U. N. I had never owned a gun before, never even touched one, but I had seen plenty of actors in movies and on TV use them and the process looked simple enough—load bullets in, aim, and pull the trigger. The hardest part would be aiming at a living, breathing human being.

A sharp pain suddenly pierced my heart. I closed my eyes and took in several long, slow breaths. The thought of killing another person was horrifying, but it was the only sure way I could think of to stop the POS. I had to become a murderer, just like him. I stopped myself from going down that path. I wasn't at all like him. He's pure evil and killed for his own pleasure. Whereas I didn't want to do it, but I had no other choice. It was either him or Michael.

A tear leaked out of the corner of my eye as I looked at

Michael's picture sitting on the desk. It was taken on closing day at Keystone Mountain two weeks before he was killed. His face was ruddy from the cold, except for a white outline around his eyes from his googles. He looked happy and his eyes sparkled with life, nothing like how he looked lying in his casket the last time I saw him. I gulped back a sob.

Taking the POS's life would no doubt haunt me for the rest of my days, but it was a sacrifice I had to make to save the lives of the seventeen people he killed and the thirty-eight others he had injured. I looked back at the photo.

"I'll do whatever it takes to stop that POS and bring you back," I whispered, swiping the wet off my cheek.

I squared my shoulders, pulled up Google, and started a search for what I needed. Thirty minutes later I had found the perfect wig— black, chin-length bob with bangs and heavy red highlights—the complete opposite of my hair. I also ordered two temporary tattoos, one, the Chinese symbol for courage, and the other, the Chinese symbol for love. Anyone who knows me knows I'm too big of a chicken to get a tattoo, so I planned to place them in plain sight, one on my neck, the other on my front collar bone.

I owned several pairs of black leggings and had black shirts as well, so I didn't have to buy anything in the way of clothes. And I knew of a little consignment shop in Denver that would be able to supply a pair of used boots, the accessories, and hopefully a long black coat.

Once I had my disguise put together, I sat back, closed my eyes and pictured the girl I would become. The image that floated into my head was a clone of Quorra from *Tron: Legacy*, minus the fabulous body and skin-tight, leather unitard. It hadn't been my intention to copy that look, but I hit it pretty much square on and it worked. To make the transition complete, I decided to order a pair of brown contacts to cover my blue eyes.

From there I set my mind to thinking of a fake name to go with my new look. I threw out a lot of names before coming up with Olivia Flynn. It too was a play on the characters from the Tron movie, Olivia being the name of the actress playing Quorra, Flynn being the last name of the male lead character. I doubted anyone, other than me, would ever put that together, but it was fun to know my alias had a story behind her.

"Okay, Olivia Flynn, as soon as your wig and contacts come in, we'll take a photo and get a fake ID to make you official."

It was a relief to have all that figured out, but that relief lasted only until I turned back to the computer for my next task. I typed the words "where to buy a gun," in the search box on my laptop and stared at it a long time before clicking the little magnifying glass to start the search.

I had not been brought up in a family of gun advocates. There was only gun that had ever made it into our house and that was my dad's deer rifle, which was handed down to him from his father. And technically, it didn't make it *into* the house either, as it was kept up in the rafters in the garage, out of sight and out of mind. So I knew nothing about where to go or anything about buying a gun. And I knew of no one to ask.

Fortunately, the internet provided all the information I needed as to where to purchase the gun and the requirements for a background check, which was the part I was the most anxious about. There were even sites telling how to avoid a background check. That surprised me. I had assumed all that was strictly regulated. I clicked through several of those links just to see what they had to say, and then it occurred to me that these were the kind of sites a criminal would go to and the police would be monitoring.

I grabbed the mouse, closed the site, and hurriedly scooted back from the desk. What was I thinking? I stood and started to pace, imagining if the police checked into the rest of my search history, how much more incriminating it would look.

The sound of the front door opening, then clicking shut halted me in mid stride. My brain, already in full panic mode over my internet searches, rushed to the assumption the police had come to arrest me. I looked around for a place to hide. Before I could force my feet to move, a soft knock sounded on my door. I took a step back and bumped into my desk, knocking a cup of pens over.

"Kat, are you in there? Are you okay?" Cathie called through the door.

My pulse raced as if I had just finished the 400-meter dash. I bent over, put my hands on my knees, and dropped my head to catch my breath.

"Is everything alright? I'm coming in," Cathie added when I didn't answer.

The knob turned and I lifted my head. The dual computer monitors glowed with the search page on how to buy a gun.

"Crap!" I mumbled and rushed to the door to block Cathie's view.

"Hi!" I said, cringing on the inside at the squeakiness of my voice. Cathie's brow furrowed and I hurried on before she could ask questions. "What are you doing home?" I looked at my wrist for the time, but it was bare.

I slipped out of the room, pulling the door closed behind me with a resounding click and headed into the living room. According to the clock on the stove it was 1:15. Whatever happened to the morning? I fixed a fake smile on my face and turned to her.

"Why aren't you at work?" I asked, rephrasing the question.

Cathie gave me a funny look, then shook her head and walked into the kitchen. "I forgot my lunch this morning and didn't feel like going out for fast food." She stuck her head inside the fridge. "How did it go today?"

I thought I detected a hint of suspicion in her voice, even though it was muffled, and immediately jumped to another conclusion that she knew what I'd been doing. My mouth went dry and I struggled to come up with an answer. But then she looked over her shoulder and raised her eyebrows in question and I realized she was asking me about my meeting with Jeff.

"It was good. Jeff was actually a big help." The words had barely passed my lips when another thought popped into my head and I blurted it out without thinking it through. "He was a little bit distracted. He had searched online looking to buy a gun and was worried he was now on a watch list."

Cathie guffawed. "Are you freakin' kiddin' me? I thought he was supposed to be a smart guy?"

I bristled at her insinuation. "He is. I think that's a legitimate concern. I've heard the media reports on how the government spies on people and such. So … you know, it's possible."

Cathie pulled out a leftover box, lifted the lid, and sniffed the contents. "Come on, you can't be serious. You actually think the government has the time to spy on everyone who buys a gun? We're talking like probably tens of thousands of people who do that on a weekly basis. If he'd been searching for chemicals or bomb making equipment, yeah maybe. But an ordinary guy like him buying a single gun?" She shook her head. "That's not going to put him on a watch list. The bigger question is why in heaven's name does he want to buy a gun?"

I suddenly felt like a fool. She was right, of course, and I should have known that from the start. My brain had obviously not fully recovered from its sixteen month hiatus. If my plan was to succeed, I was going to have to get back to the smart, level-headed person I used to be. Squaring my jaw, I lifted my chin and slid into a lie without even blinking.

"He's going deer hunting with some friends." I snatched a piece of celery from the box of chicken wings Cathie had set on the counter to avoid looking her in the eye.

"So then he's got nothing to worry about. What did he have to say about physics? Do you think it's something you might actually be interested in pursuing?" Cathie probed.

I couldn't believe she had so willingly accepted my flimsy answer, and I didn't realize how much tension I had been holding in until the flood gates opened and it drained away. Feeling so much lighter, I sat down on the barstool beside her. Within minutes, we were back into our comfortable banter like old times as we shared the leftovers and she caught me up on some of the stuff going on in our friends' lives.

For that hour I almost felt like my old self, except my old self would not have had to lie. Thankfully, Cathie didn't appear to pick up on my fabrications. When it was time for her to head back to work, she leaned over and gave me a hug, making me feel all the more guilty. I closed my eyes and hugged her back, using all of my strength to keep it together. When she pulled back her eyes were glassy. She opened her mouth, then closed it without saying anything, and turned away to gather up her keys and the satchel she used as a briefcase-slash-purse on her way out.

She paused before stepping out the door and looked over her shoulder. "I've missed you," she whispered in a strangled voice. Our eyes met for a moment, then a wide smile split her face in two. "How about ordering in Thai tonight?" she added in a louder voice.

My chin started to quiver and I knew if I tried to speak, my voice would crack. I nodded my head in response and prayed she would leave before I completely broke down.

Cathie let out a half squeak, half sob, and closed the door without saying anything more.

As soon as I heard the click, I folded my arms on the countertop and dropped my forehead onto them. I hated liars more than anything, and I never thought I would become one. But there was no other way. If something went wrong, the less Cathie knew, the better it would be for her. On the other hand, if my plan goes the way I hope, all the lies would be erased and there would be nothing to regret.

SIX

After Cathie left, I went back to my laptop and began the next chore I was dreading—gathering information on the POS. He had dominated all media outlets for months after the shooting, but I had purposely avoided as much as I could and refused to watch, listen, or read any of it. I already knew all I wanted to know about him: he was caught red-handed outside the bar loading his guns into his car after he killed Michael. I didn't care why he had done it and didn't want to know about his childhood or any of the other tidbits of his life the media always loved to shove down our throats. But from the hundreds of results that came up when I typed his name in the search bar, it looked like I was the only one who didn't care.

My heart ached and my breathing became labored as I opened and read the first article. The second one I read turned my stomach inside out. Then when I read he was a neuroscience graduate student, I hurried into the bathroom and threw up the lunch I had just eaten.

Neuroscience was *my* field and the POS even took it away from me. I shuttered at the thought of having passed him in the halls of the Muenzinger building as I sat on the cool tile floor in the bathroom, my back and head resting against the wall.

It wasn't just that he was in the same program at CU as I was. It was that I knew he had to have spent years studying the workings of the brain to get to the level of graduate student. How could someone be that smart and put in that much time and not know there was something wrong in his head? He had to have known. And he also had to know he could get help, but instead he chose murder. That was pure and simple evil.

At some point, I must have dozed off, for I suddenly jerked up, shivering from the cold. My legs had also fallen asleep and stayed that way as I stumbled back into the bedroom, grabbed a sweatshirt from the floor and a blanket from the bed, and sat down at the desk. I stared at the screen of my laptop, which still had the article open. I didn't want to read any more about him. He was a monster and my stomach was still roiling, but if I wanted to find him in 2016, I had to do the research. I reluctantly pulled up the next article.

For the next couple hours, I read the details and scope of the POS's plan and all the meticulous preparations he had gone through. The sick feeling stayed with me and my cheeks were streaked with tears until I read about the number of people who had known how disturbed and dangerous he was. People who were in a position to stop him, but did nothing. That's when a whole new level of rage took over my anguish. He had talked to others about his desire to kill, had amassed an arsenal of weapons and ammunition, and no one raised a single red flag.

And here I was worried I'd be put on a watch list for searching how to buy a gun. What a laugh!

With the plethora of articles and information on the POS and the attack, I quickly filled up an entire spiral notebook with notes and printed out articles. Pretty much everything I needed to know was in there, even where to find him.

But finding him was only the first step. I also had to get close and engage him in a conversation in order to lure him to a secluded spot where I could shoot him without getting caught. And I had no clue how to go about doing that. Beside the fact we had very little in common, the articles reported in the months leading up to the attack, he had disconnected from just about everything, including school. He was an introvert and loner, who spent most of his time locked inside his small apartment amusing himself with role-playing video games—games I had never been interested in and had no experience with. Other than that, his only other interest was murder.

I groaned and slammed both hands down on the keyboard. A fleeting image popped up on the dual monitors as I dropped my head into my hands, but I was more concerned with coming up with something that would interest a maniac killer than I was the image.

For a nanosecond I thought about trying to flirt with him, but I wasn't *that* good of an actress. I also threw out using neuroscience, as the other doctoral candidates in his program said he would have nothing to do with any of them. The only other idea I came up with that I imagined had even the slightest chance of working was to offer to sell him a gun. But how does one bring up a subject like that in a casual conversation without looking suspicious? It would really only work if we were at a gun range. However, I couldn't recall any article mentioning a specific range he had visited. There were a lot more articles to read, though.

I reluctantly raised my head to do more digging. On the dual screens, big as life, was an image of the POS standing next to his car, being handcuffed on the night of the shooting. The saying, "my blood ran cold," never held any meaning to me until that moment. All the air in the room seemed to vanish and I couldn't breathe, but I couldn't take my eyes away either.

I had caught an occasional glimpse of his mug shot in passing after the shooting. It was everywhere and was impossible to avoid. But I never looked long and hard at him. His eyes were big and round in the photo, like in his mug shot, but in this image there was a smug look of victory and pride in them as well. I stared at the maniacal sneer plastered on his pale face and had no doubt that if he was standing in front of me at this moment, and if I had a gun, I could easily pull the trigger without a single drop of remorse.

I reached for the mouse to close the window. Just as I was about to click on the X in the top corner of the page, the elongated white skull with long teeth on the front of his T-shirt triggered a memory. I hurriedly shuffled through the stack of articles I had printed out. It took me a few minutes to find the one I was looking for, as I had compiled quite a heap. I ran my finger down the page, skimming the paragraphs until I found it:

> *"In the months leading up to the massacre, Mr. James became more obsessed with the Marvel character, the Punisher. Dozens of Punisher posters adorned his apartment walls, he dyed his hair black, and embarked on a rigorous physical and weapons training routine."*

I sat back with a satisfied grin. "The Punisher is going to be my way in," I whispered. "I've got you, you sick son-of-a-bitch!"

After reading all the articles and the vivid details of the shooting I was physically and mentally drained and cold from the inside out. I crawled into bed and curled up in a ball with every blanket I had on top of me. I don't know how long I laid there, but when a knock on my door finally roused me, the sky outside my window was dark.

"Kat, you in there?" Cathie called.

I swiped the back of my hand over my eyes and croaked out, "Yeah."

"I was thinking of ordering some Pad Thai for dinner. Does that sound good? Or would you rather have pizza?"

At the thought of food, my stomach rumbled. "No, Thai sounds good," I replied. "I'll be out in a sec."

I swung my legs over the side of the bed and sat up too quickly. I held onto the desk for support until the room stopped spinning, gritted my teeth, and stood. Then I slowly hobbled into the bathroom, leaned against the sink, and looked into the mirror. If it weren't for my blue eyes and the dark circles under them, my face would have disappeared into the white wall behind me. I dropped my chin to my chest.

Oh God, am I doing the right thing? Or am I just fooling myself again?

I tried to bring up the memory of Michael's arms around me, but it was too far faded. Choking back a sob, I lifted my head and stared into the mirror.

"You *have* to do this. You have to get your life back. That means you have to shoot the POS no matter how disgusting the thought is," I whispered to the person staring back at me.

With a nod of my head to confirm the statement, I splashed cold water on my face, dried it, and dabbed some concealer under my eyes. I grimaced at my reflection, then walked into the living room to have dinner with Cathie, praying I'd be able to keep it down.

SEVEN

The next morning, I drove to East Colfax in Denver and parked across the street from a pawn shop I had found online. I knew my previous worry about someone watching my online searches was ridiculous, but I still couldn't bring myself to search for gun shops. So I searched for pawn shops instead. That's how I found Shorty's Pawn and Guns. With the word "guns" in the name, I figured it would be a good place to start.

I sat in my car, staring at the red painted building with metal bars on all the windows, trying to get up the nerve to walk in. Traffic on the street was constant, but not heavy. Other than two women—one in demin shorts cut so high her butt cheeks showed, the other in a tight mini skirt and tank top that I had no idea how she managed to fit into—all the other people walking up and down the street were male.

For a moment, I seriously contemplated going back to the apartment and waiting for the wig to arrive so no one inside Shorty's would know what I really looked like. Then I realized it didn't matter. My driver's license had my real photo and every other piece of information they needed about me, so they were going to know who I was no matter what I was wearing.

Several times I reached for the car door handle, then dropped my hand back into my lap before it occurred to me someone might think I was casing the joint.

You can do this! I told myself, then said out loud, "Yup, okay … here I go."

I pulled the handle and reluctantly got out of the car. I stood beside the car door until the stoplight at the corner turned red, then hurriedly jaywalked across the street. I walked stiff-legged past the row of bicycles and lawn equipment that occupied the sidewalk in front of the building and through the heavy metal door before coming to a jarring halt.

The inside of the shop was nothing like what I had imagined. A strong scent of burned gun powder and stringent glass cleaner stung my nose as I looked up at the wall in front of me that was lined with racks of rifles halfway down its length. The other half had a collection of animal heads: deer, elk, bear, moose, even a buffalo head. I had envisioned the store having items, or actually junk, piled up everywhere, but the shop wasn't overly crowded and every item was neatly and orderly displayed.

To my left, a long glass case held a variety of rings, watches and jewelry. Next to it was another glass case of collectibles. The cash register was next, facing me, and to the right of it was a glass case of wicked looking knives. There were more cases beyond that, but from where I was standing, I couldn't see what was in them.

I slowly walked along the jewelry display, pretending to browse the selection. From there I moved to the front of the room and the musical instrument section. I then browsed through the tools before moving on to the small, stuffed animals.

The gentleman standing behind the counter, who had been eyeing me from the moment I walked in, moved past the knife case and stopped behind the first of three cases of hand guns.

"Are these what you're looking for, miss?" he asked.

I started at the sound of his raspy voice and twirled around, knocking a stuffed pheasant off its stand. My cheeks flamed as I hurriedly set the bird upright and met the man's amused gaze.

"Are you looking to purchase a gun today?" he repeated.

I opened my mouth, but no words came out. I cleared my throat. "Yes, I am," I replied.

With the pretense over, I lifted my chin, marched over to the gun counter, and bent over the display, my nose coming within inches of touching the glass.

The array of weapons gleaming in the light looked tremendously dangerous and I had to suppress the shiver that ran through me. I set my jaw and tried to look as if I knew what I was doing, but I'm sure the man saw right through me. He was kind, though, and didn't say anything until he saw me linger for a moment on a gun that was similar to ones I'd seen in movies. He unlocked the sliding panel and pulled out the weapon, laying it on a small black square of velvet on the top of the counter so I could get a closer look.

"You've got a good eye, Miss. The Glock 17 is one of the most popular handguns on the market."

I stared at it, resisting the urge to turn and walk out the door. *Don't be a wuss. This is to save Michael,* I chastised myself. I reached out, picked up the gun, and almost dropped it. It was so much heavier than it looked and what I expected it to be.

The man smiled. "Like I said, the Glock is a big seller, but it's not right for everyone. How's it feel in your hand?"

My bewildered look must have told him what he needed to know, for he walked to the next case and pulled out another gun. He placed it on a second velvet square next to the first.

"Try this one. It's got a little better grip for a lady's hand, and is the right size to carry in a purse."

I recognized the name Walther on the barrel of the gun. A Walther PPK was the gun James Bond used. If the brand was good enough for 007, it was definitely good enough for me.

"Walther makes a good piece." He took the gun from my hand and slid the barrel back to show me how it cocked. "The slide on this CCP is among the easiest to rack of any you'll find. And I think you'll like this grip better."

He went on to show me the safety, the 8-round magazine and thumb button release, the three white dot sights, and a whole bunch more stuff about the disassembling and cleaning that I didn't pay attention to because I only planned to use it once. I just nodded to everything that he said and wanted to get the gun and get out of there as quickly as possible before I lost my nerve.

Fifteen minutes later, $300 poorer, and with one more item on my list checked off and tucked deep inside my purse, I rushed to my car and sped away, giddy with relief, but also with a sense of foreboding.

EIGHT

Every waking minute of the next ten days was spent researching, making preparations, and trying to think of any variant that might possibly arise and derail me. My disguise, along with toiletry items were stacked in the corner of the room. I also had several changes of clothes laid out—all black—as I figured I would be in 2016 for multiple days.

My desk was a clutter of sticky notes that had addresses, names, and numerous other bits of information I didn't want to forget: the name of the closest motel to the lab—or at least what I assumed was the lab going off what Jeff had said about it being behind a warehouse off Highway 36—the phone numbers to a couple different car rental offices; a list of classes in the graduate neuroscience program; the POS's make of car; his favorite restaurant; and the most important piece of information of all, the address to where I would lure him.

It was no problem finding the motel and car rental places as they were businesses and easy to look up. But I didn't know where to even begin to look for a secluded place within the city, as it needed to be a residence with easy get-away options for after the deed was done.

I'd lived in Boulder for three years, but in that time I never had any reason to explore the residential side of the city. I knew the campus, the Hill, and Pearl Street like the back of my hand, but beyond those was mostly foreign territory.

For the better part of the week, I drove around searching for a place that would work, and it was just by happenstance that I came across it. Or maybe it was the Universe intervening again to make sure I would succeed. Whatever the case may be, the spot couldn't have been more tailor-made for my purpose if I had plotted it myself.

When I first drove by the jungle of foliage, I thought it was nothing more than an oversized wooded lot. I had no idea a small house was tucked behind the mass of bushes and trees until I got out of the car and walked the ground. The empty wooded lot beside the house added to its appeal, for it also eliminated the worry of snoopy neighbors witnessing the act. But the pièce de résistance was the cemetery across the street. Dead men don't have eyes or cell phones, and I could disappear into the emptiness afterward and make my escape with no one being the wiser.

The scheme I had concocted to sneak into the building and into the time machine to go back to 2016 was complicated, but I had every step ingrained in my head. Still, I mentally ran through them again and again to keep them fresh: *Once Jeff lets me into the building, I'm going to pick an appropriate time and excuse myself to go the ladies' room. There, I'll prop open the bathroom window so I can sneak back in once I hear they've turned the machine on. If there isn't a window in the ladies' room, I'll locate a side door exit and tape down the latch so it won't catch and lock. But if the building has a high-tech security system, the door option will be out and I'll just have to play it by ear and count on the Universe to provide and show me a way in.*

The bigger issues that I was most anxious about was getting the password out of Jeff and getting him to show me how to run the machine and delete the camera video. He was so enthusiastic when he talked about physics and I hoped that enthusiasm would extend to the machine and he would want to show it off. When he did, I'd video the controls and processes on my phone, which would be sticking out of the side pocket of my purse, to ensure I didn't forget a step.

On Sunday, I got up before dawn and repacked my backpack for the tenth time. I was ready to go, even though I had no idea when I would be leaving. The spiral notebook I had filled with the POS articles was going with me, along with a document I compiled with the information from all the sticky notes. In total I had put in over seventy hours of research on him and on quantum physics, but I was still a bundle of nerves.

Jeff had yet to text me and I was starting to wonder if he would cancel. Each time my phone beeped with a new post from one of the social media sites, I jumped, even though I was staring at the phone. Thank God, Cathie had gone to the mountains with friends to check out the fall colors or I would be having to come up with a whole new set of lies to cover my nervous prowling.

When three o'clock rolled around, I couldn't take another second of waiting and not knowing. I picked up my phone and typed out a message.

Hey, we still on for tonight?

I held my breath for his reply. It took him exactly nineteen minutes to respond. I know, because I counted off every second.

Jeff: *Sorry, I forgot*

I stared at the message, trying to decipher if it meant he forgot, but we're still on, or was he saying he couldn't do it? My stomach twisted at the thought of going another day, or worse, another week without Michael. However, before I could type out a reply, another text came in.

Jeff: *Come by at 7 tonight? Take 36 toward Lyons. 3 mi. outside of town on the L is a white warehouse. Lab is behind that and up the hill, bldg on the L. Text if you get lost*

My eyes teared up after reading the first sentence and it took me several seconds to read through the whole thing.

Got it. See you @ 7

A bubble of anticipation swelled within me and I wilted against the cushion of the sofa. I was really going to do it—go back to 2016, save Michael, and put everything back the way it was before.

I didn't know when Cathie would be home and I for sure didn't want to be in the apartment when she came in. It would only take her one second and one look to know I was up to something, and I didn't want to have to lie to her face again. So I jotted a quick note, telling her I was going home to have dinner with my parents. I then grabbed my loaded backpack and my leather messenger bag that carried the gun and headed out the door two hours early.

As I pulled the door shut, I paused and looked over my shoulder. I had lived in the apartment for five months, yet, not one thing about it looked or felt like home. Everything in it was Cathie's aunt's, as it should be, for if my plan worked the way I hoped, I wouldn't have ever lived here. I would be living with Michael in our own apartment.

However, if something went wrong … I stopped myself. The Universe had gone out of its way to set me on this path and I had no reason to start questioning it. I shut the door holding onto the belief that the next time I walked through, it would be me and Michael stopping by for a visit.

NINE

Jeff was right. The lab was easy to find. I knew it was the right place when I spotted his very distinctive, beat-up green jeep parked in front.

A large sign posted at the bottom of a short hill leading up to the building warned it was a restricted area and no trespassing or unauthorized vehicles were allowed. I proceeded up anyway and drove slowly around a circular driveway.

The building looked like an airplane hangar built on the side of a house. The single-story house had a pitched roof and large picture-size windows on each side of the door. The hangar was at least two stories tall, about the length of a basketball court and had no windows at all.

I had been too nervous to eat all day and my stomach was growling, but there was plenty of time for me to drive back into town and grab something to eat. Even doing that, I still had over an hour before Jeff was expecting me and nothing else to do. I pulled in behind the warehouse at the bottom of the hill by the lab and sat in the car to wait.

At 6:30, I drove up the hill and parked next to Jeff's car. I closed my eyes. *You can do this.* I took in a deep breath and looked over at Michael's pocket watch that hung on a chain from the rearview mirror. It had been in his pocket on that April night and was hit by one of the bullets that ripped through him. The bottom half of the cracked crystal was gone, and the dial had a small, ragged hole from the bullet that had forever frozen the hands at 11:27.

I rubbed my thumb over the rusty-colored bloodstain that surrounded the hole. "I'm going to fix this and bring you back, my love. Everything's going to be all right," I whispered.

At 6:50, I got out of the car, walked to the door, and knocked. There was no response. Just as I lifted my fist to knock again, I noticed a small intercom speaker attached to the side of the door frame. I pushed the button below the speaker and waited.

Seconds later, I heard static, then a mechanical voice said, "Gimme a sec."

I was perspiring like a professional dancer when almost five minutes later I heard a click and a buzzer and the door opened.

"Hi!" My voice squeaked like a smitten teenager. I internally cringed, cleared my throat, and started again. "I'm sorry I'm a little early. I didn't want to take the chance I couldn't find the place."

"It's okay, you're fine. Come on in." Jeff stepped aside to let me pass as he continued. "Sorry for the wait. I was in the middle of something and couldn't stop."

"That's okay," I said and winced at the sound of a mechanical lock clicking back in place.

As Jeff turned back to me, I quickly plastered a big smile on my face in hopes it would hide the sinking feeling that had come over me.

"I can't tell you how much I appreciate you letting me in to see the machine. It's really sweet of you to do this for me," I continued.

"No problem," Jeff replied, walking around a large reception desk and heading down a narrow hall to the left.

I followed right behind him, making small talk to calm my nerves. "So you've been here working with Dr. Mallory for a year?"

"Getting close to a year and a half," Jeff replied. He stopped in front of a door halfway down the hall, used a keycard to open it, and gestured for me to go in.

"I imagine it's—" My words trailed off as I stepped into a cavernous room and came to an abrupt halt. For a moment I felt like Dorothy getting her first look at the Emerald City. The whole room was bathed in a green light coming from a mammoth clear, plexiglass tunnel that took up most of the room from end to end. Masses of wires, cables, and thick rubber tubes snaked across the floor and up and around the outside of the cylinder, and circles of green lights glowed from within. There was a faint shape inside the cylinder at the end closest to the door, but I couldn't tell what it was through the glare of the lights.

"Is that it?" I asked.

Instead of mocking my stupid question, Jeff nodded his head. "Yup, that's it. It's not a DeLorean, but it will still take you back to the future."

"How? How does it do that?"

"It's complicated, but the simple answer is in Einstein's special-relativity equation, $E=mc^2$, which tells us energy equals mass times the speed of light. And since we know light has energy, it must then have mass, and mass exerts a gravitational force. Einstein also posited in his general theory of relativity that time and space are connected and matter warps spacetime through gravity. Dr. Mallory expanded on that theory and generated a new hypothesis in which states the vortex created by the gravity of circulating beams of laser lights will twist space, and thus time, into a loop that can be used to travel through time."

As I tried to digest his explanation, a question popped into my mind and I blurted it out without thinking. "Why would it be so disastrous if someone went back in time and changed something?"

Jeff hesitated a moment. "That question has been debated in and outside of the physics world for decades. The truth is, there's no definitive answer. But I can tell you, you don't want to go too deep down that rabbit hole or it'll make you paranoid and you'll start wondering if our past has already been changed and we just don't realize it. And that is a possibility I suppose, because our current reality would have evolved from the modified version of the moment and we'd have no reason to suspect it had ever been any other way."

He folded his arms over his chest. "Einstein supported the theory of a block universe, which suggests the past, present, and future exist in a four-dimensional block of spacetime and all events across time and space are on an equal ontological footing, with no sense in that any present event is more real than past or future ones. So everything that has happened or will happen has already been set in stone.

"The other principal theory, the Alternate Timeline theory, states if someone were to travel to the past and change an event, it would create an entirely new universe. Two separate universes would then exist, the original, with the future reflecting the event as it took place, and a new one, with the timeline going forward from the change.

"There are arguments for and against each stance, but at this point it's all speculative. The only thing both sides do agree on is, if a person were to travel back in time, they could never return to the future they left."

I choked on my breath. "What do you mean, they can't return? The machine can't bring you back?"

"No … I mean, yes, you can return through the machine, but that's not what I'm talking about. What I mean is, it would be virtually impossible for a time traveler, who is a physical being, to go back in time without being seen, or heard, or touched. Unless, of course, the lab is empty when that traveler arrives and they return immediately without leaving the room. But any contact with another individual, however inconsequential, would have an impact on the future in some way since that meeting had not taken place in the original timeline. And as I said before, there is no way to know what that impact might be. You've heard of the Butterfly Effect, right?"

I sagged and nodded my head.

"It's an exaggerated version of what could happen, but it does work to paint a vivid example of how the smallest variation can create a tremendous ripple effect on the future. And imagine … if a tiny insect could have that much effect, what kind of impact would a human traveler from the future have? It could be catastrophic."

I tilted my head and frowned in confusion. "It almost sounds like you're against time travel. If so, why would you want to work on a project like this?"

Jeff held up his hands as if warding off an evil spell. "Oh no, I didn't say I was against time travel. I'm all for traveling into the future. But going backward in time is an altogether different matter. Personally, I don't see how revisiting the past is in mankind's best interest."

I understood his way of thinking, but it didn't sway me. Coming back to a different future was what I was counting on.

"Mallory showed slides of a scale model of the machine in the talk I sat in on. It had green lights like those." I pointed to the machine. "Do they have a purpose, or are they just for show?" I casually asked to change the subject.

"Those are the rotating lasers that create the time warp."

My brow creased. "And they glow like that all the time, even when the machine is turned off?"

"No, only when the machine is on."

My heart and breath stalled at the same time. "So are you saying the machine is on right now?" I asked softly to confirm I had understood correctly.

"Yeah. It was turned on last Friday to test the power levels. We don't want to risk running into the same issue as last time."

A long silence followed as I stared at the machine and tried to get my emotions under control. Then suddenly, as if someone had slapped me on the back of the head, I snapped out of my stupor. The timeline had been sped up, which suited me just fine, but I still had work to do to get back and save Michael.

I scanned the room, noting the placement of the blinking red lights of the cameras positioned high up on the back wall. There was only one other door that I could see. It was at the far end of the room. But according to the large yellow warning sign that read, "High Voltage, Restricted Area," it wasn't an exit.

To the left of the door, a small area had been partitioned off for what looked like a control room. The top half of the wall facing the machine was glass to give the occupants inside a clear view of the machine room. Through the open door I could see dozens of monitors in varying sizes and just as many keyboards set up on a long tabletop. Panels of switches, dials, levers, and blinking lights lined the wall behind the monitors.

I swallowed hard at the sight of the extensive equipment. While I considered myself tech savvy, realistically, I'd only ever dealt with normal everyday kind of tech stuff, like apps, smart phones, tablets, and basic computer software.

It's going to be okay. The Universe will help me figure it out, but first I've got to get back into the building.

I turned to Jeff with what I hoped was an apologetic smile. "I guess I shouldn't have had that second cup of coffee earlier. Is there a ladies' room here, by chance?"

"Yeah, sure. Let me show you."

He walked me back to the reception area and pointed down the hall behind the desk. "I'll leave the hall door propped open. Come back to the control center when you're finished."

I thanked him and hurried past several small offices to a door that had a gender symbol for women instead of the standard stick figure. *Geeks,* I thought as I pushed the door open.

I didn't expect it to be fancy and it held up to my expectation, which was okay, because the only one thing I cared about was the rectangular window high up on the wall. It wasn't large, but it looked like I could probably wiggle through if I put forth a little extra effort.

I wasted no time climbing onto the toilet seat and stretched up on my tiptoes to reach the latch at the top. From the buildup of grime around the latch, it looked like it had seldom, if ever, been opened. It took some straining and grunting, but I finally got it twisted around. The bigger problem was that it was a hopper style window that tilted out from the top about eight inches, which was not wide enough for a child to crawl through, let alone me. I yanked on the frame as hard as I could to see if the hinges that kept it from opening all the way would give, but they were strong and wouldn't budge past the designed inches.

Cursing under my breath, I looked over my shoulder for something to use to break the hinge. The dingy little room held a toilet, a sink, and a waste can. That was it. No closet or cabinet or anything else. I turned back to the window for a closer look. The hinge was attached to the metal frame with one small screw. If I was able to remove it, my problem would be solved.

I jumped off the seat and dug through my bag for something I could use as a screwdriver. When my fingers brushed my key chain that held a small, flat, metal disk with different size appendages around the outer edge, I smiled. My dad had given it to me when I first started to drive. I attached it to my keychain only to appease him and never expected to need it. I raised my eyes to the ceiling and whispered. "I love you, Dad!"

I was getting a little nervous about the amount of time it was taking, but the window was the surest way back in and I couldn't leave until I had the screws out. I climbed back onto the toilet with fob in hand and went to work on the screw.

It was awkward to stretch up, fit the disk into the groove of the screw, and turn it, especially as the toilet seat rocked back and forth. The far side was even trickier as I had to stand with one foot on the overturned trash can and one foot on the sink. The trash-can quivered beneath my weight and I had visions of the bottom caving in and me falling and cracking my head on the floor. Thankfully, the can held up long enough for me to get the screw out, but the size of the dent in the bottom said I had finished just in the nick of time. I turned it upright and stuck it back in the corner, hoping that if Jeff checked the room before he left, he wouldn't notice the dent.

I wound a rubber band around the slider and the latch on the frame to keep the window closed, knowing a little pressure from the outside could easily break it. I then scrubbed the black grease from the screws off my hands as rapidly as I could and swiped the dots of sweat from my forehead with a paper towel.

I glanced over my shoulder to make sure the loose hinges weren't noticeable, then opened the door and ran smack into Jeff, who was standing just outside. My stomach dropped and my cheeks instantly heated up.

"Excuse me," I squeaked, as I side-stepped him and walked stiffly back to the time machine room as if there was nothing out of the ordinary and I hadn't just spent an exorbitant amount of time in the restroom.

I didn't dare look back at Jeff in fear he'd be able to see the guilt on my face. I stopped in the doorway of the control room with my back to him.

"You have some serious technical equipment in here. Does it take all of this to run the machine?"

When Jeff didn't answer, I made the mistake of looking around. His mouth was pressed in a thin line and he was glaring at me through narrowed eyes.

Shit! I racked my brain for an explanation that would sound somewhat legitimate. "I … um—"

"Why are you really here? And before you lie to me again, I heard all the banging in the bathroom."

My stomach dropped to my feet at the same moment my mouth dropped open. But before I could formulate an excuse, he added, "You obviously came here with an agenda. I don't know what it is, but I'm positive it's not because you want to switch your major."

My brain went blank, leaving me with nothing to say. I swallowed hard and strained to pick something out of the air.

Jeff blew out a long breath and raked his fingers through his hair. "I think it's time for you to leave." He stepped aside and swung his arm around, gesturing toward the exit.

A sense of panic immediately replaced the shame of getting caught. "No, please, wait. You don't understand," I said frantically in an effort to stall until I could figure out what to do.

Jeff took a step forward, breaching my comfort zone of space. "Oh, I understand!" he yelled in my face, making me wince. "I understand you're not the trustworthy person I've always believed you to be. Do you realize I put my job on the line to let you come here? Or do you even care what could happen to me if someone found out?

"So just admit it. You have no interest in physics at all, do you?" He paused to let me answer, but I just stared past him. He snorted in disgust. "I thought as much. So I'm not going to ask you again. Please leave."

His face was flushed and his hands were balled into fists, but I didn't move. I still needed to know how to work the machine and how to delete the camera video.

"I'm sorry. You're right … I'm not switching my major. But I did go to Mallory's talk and I found it fascinating. I just wanted to get a glimpse of the machine and I didn't think you'd let me in without a good reason."

"You're right, I probably wouldn't have. What were you doing in the bathroom? Why the pounding?"

"Oh … that was just a spider on the wall. I was trying to knock it down with my shoe." It was the lamest possible explanation and I knew it as soon as the words came out. But it was the first thing that had popped into my head.

"That's it! I'm done with your lies." He took hold of my elbow and started guiding me toward the door.

"Okay, wait!" I said, pulling my arm free. I bit down on my quivering lip and lowered my eyes, debating how much of the truth I should tell him. But my panic had reached an all time high and thinking clearly was not possible at the moment.

"I want to go back to March of 2016 and save Michael," I said fervently, looking up through my eyelashes.

Jeff took a jerky step backward. I sucked in my breath and waited for him to say something, but he just stood there gawking at me as if I had grown horns.

I lifted my head. "I'm serious. I'm going to go back in time. I was just in the bathroom taking the hinge off the window so I could sneak in later tonight after you leave."

Jeff stared at me for several moments more, then exploded. "Are you fucking insane?" A large vein bulged on his forehead and his fists clenched and unclenched like he wanted to hit something, but instead, he turned and walked away. He took only a few steps, then spun around and stormed back.

"Do you have the slightest clue the dangers involved with time travel?" He held his hand up, palm side out to stop me from replying. "Save your breath, because I know you don't. And I doubt that you care we haven't performed a single test on that machine yet, either. That means we have no idea what will happen to live matter that enters the gravity field. If we miscalculate the amount of exotic matter needed to offset the field, you could be torn apart. And that's only one of an infinite number of malfunctions that could happen, not to mention, the whole damn thing could blow up again."

His eyes were wild and bulging, but I just shook my head. "Nothing is going to happen to me. I make it through just fine."

He let out a howl as he threw his hands in the air, his fingers spread wide. "And this comes from a girl who knows nothing about physics!"

"I don't need to know physics. You told me yourself that I make it through."

"What?" Again, he gaped at me. "You are completely out of your mind and have no idea what you're talking about."

"No, listen." I shook his arm to get him to look at me. "You told me four minutes were erased from the security camera two days after the machine was turned on. It was written off as a glitch, but it wasn't a glitch. It was me. I erase those minutes after I come out of the machine so no one will know I was there."

Jeff mumbled something I couldn't make out and moved to the table. He placed his palms down and bent halfway over, staring at keyboard in front of him.

I wanted to say more, but I had a feeling it would only make matters worse. I stood back and silently prayed I hadn't made a mistake in divulging my plan. By doing so, I had inadvertently put everything, including my future, in his hands. He could make or break me, and if I get broken a second time, there was no chance of recovery.

It seemed like an eternity passed before he straightened and turned his head in my direction. His face was etched with pain and his voice cracked with emotion.

"You know I loved Michael. He was like a brother to me. If I thought there was the slimmest chance of bringing him back, I would be the first one through that portal. But there's not. You can't go back in time and change the past. The universe won't allow it."

"How do you know?" I croaked out. "There's never been a time machine or an opportunity like this before." I moved closer and looked up into his bloodshot eyes. "You have to know that a power surge would not erase those minutes from the video. It would take a person to manually delete them. That person was me. I know it without a doubt, which means you either run the controls and send me back, or you show me how to run it and I go back on my own. Either way, everything works like Mallory says it will and I make it back just fine."

Jeff's nostrils flared. "You don't—"

"Don't you see? There's some other force at play here. It led me to Mallory's talk. It also led me to you, because it knew I couldn't do this without you." Jeff hadn't been included in my original plan, but it suddenly made sense that he was supposed to be part of it.

Jeff blew a frustrated breath out through his teeth. "Even if you do make it into the past, the odds the future turns out the way you want are against you.

"Say you do save Michael," he continued. "Then somewhere in the future he becomes a total douche who cheats on you and dumps you. That puts you right back where you started, depressed and brokenhearted. Or what if in the future he drives drunk and kills a whole family? Could you live with yourself knowing you were partly responsible for that?"

"Oh, come on, he's not going to do either of those things, and you know it!" I exclaimed.

"No, I don't know!" he yelled, throwing his hands up in the air again. "That's the point I've been trying to get through your head. I only know the Michael that was. You're smart … you know people can, and do, change. And I don't know about you, but I don't happen to know anyone from the future who can let us in on what the future holds for any of us."

A rush of heat moved up my neck as my temper flared. "I'm talking about bringing back the man we both love. I thought you would be as excited as I am with the possibility of saving him," I fired back.

Jeff's jaw hardened as he bent toward me, looking very much like he was going to strangle me. "Jesus, Kat! Did you not hear a single thing I just said?" He shouted in my face. "This has nothing to do with what I want or what *you* want for that matter. But it does have everything to do with violating the laws of physics and affecting the very foundation of what our existence is based on.

"You think this is Hollywood and all you have to do is waltz into a time machine and everything bad that has ever happened to you will turn into sunshine and roses. Well, let me tell you, it doesn't work that way. This is the real world and every move you make in the past will impact the future in some way. That's assuming you make it out of the machine alive in the first place. More than likely, you'll be maimed or killed. How is that going to make anything better?"

"I don't care if it kills me! I'm as good as dead now and I don't want to live without Michael." My voice was croaky with guilt and tears. "You don't know what's it's been like. It's my fault Michael's dead."

I watched Jeff's face go from shock to pity. He opened his mouth and I knew he was going to challenge my statement, so I rushed on before he could.

"Michael and I fought that night about moving in together. He said there was no reason to be in such a rush, which I interpreted as he didn't love me enough to want to live with me." My throat closed up and it was hard to spit out the next words. "I over-reacted and said some awful things. I … I told him to get out. That's why he went to the bar. He wouldn't have been there if it weren't for me. He wasn't supposed to die that night. So I *have* to go back and make it right."

Jeff stared at me for several long seconds, then closed his eyes and shook his head. "God, how could I have been so stupid? How could I not have seen this coming?"

Confessing my shame out loud drained my last drop of energy. I stood rigid trying not to cry as each second that ticked off tightened the vice around my heart.

"This is messed up. You're messed up." His voice sliced the quiet like the crack of a whip and I jumped.

"I …" My voice broke. I swallowed hard, squeezed my fists

tight, and started again. "I didn't come here to ask for your help. It's fine if you don't want to be part of it, but that doesn't change a thing. It's not going to stop me either. I'm going to go back in time through that machine and save Michael with or without you."

Jeff turned his back on me and faced the glass wall. The eerie glow of the machine turned his face green and I could see his tortured look reflected in the glass. The weight I was already carrying on my shoulders increased. I hadn't wanted to involve anyone else, but he backed me into a corner and now I had no choice.

I couldn't say which was louder, the grinding of my teeth or the pounding of my heart, but together they reverberated inside my head until I thought it would burst.

"This is too much for me to digest. I need some time to think," Jeff said without turning to look at me. "I'm asking you as a friend to not do anything or go any farther with your plan until I get back to you. Can you promise me that?"

I didn't trust my voice, but I knew he could see me in the glass so I nodded my head in response.

"I need to hear you say it out loud … that you won't come back here later tonight."

"I won't. I swear," I said without hesitation, knowing it would be pointless to sneak back in without knowing how to operate the controls.

Jeff's eyes locked with mine in the glass. "Go ahead then and show yourself out."

I nodded again and turned. I was just about to step through the hallway door when Jeff called after me.

"Just so you know, I'll be setting the emergency lockdown when I leave tonight. If any motion is detected inside the building, a gate will fall at the entrance to each hall and the police will be notified immediately. You won't be able to get near the machine before you're arrested."

A gasp slipped through my lips as if someone had punched me in the gut and I almost doubled in half. It was only my determination to not let him see the effect his words had on me that kept me upright. Steeling myself, I walked out of the building. However, the second I was safely inside my car, I crumpled over the steering wheel and sobbed loud, hiccupping sobs.

How could I have been so stupid? If I had just stuck to my plan, everything would have been fine. Now, Jeff was in control. If he decided not to help, he could make it so I would never be able to step foot inside the building again.

An intense pain pierced the center of my chest and my breath whooshed out, just like the first time I lost Michael.

TEN

The drive home was a blur, and how I managed to get to the apartment unscathed, I'll never know. Muffled music drifted out from under Cathie's closed door, which was a blessing. I stumbled into my room and collapsed on the bed, burying my face in the pillow to stifle the next torrent of tears.

For the rest of the night, I fluctuated between trying to stay optimistic and feeling as if my life was over. When the dawn's pink glow filtered in through the blinds, I was exhausted and sick to my stomach.

I heard Cathie getting ready for work and rambling about the apartment. The next thing I heard was my phone ringing. I sat straight up and automatically swiped across the answer tab, though I was still half asleep.

"Can you meet tonight at 7:00?" said a voice on the other end.

"Huh?" I replied, my mind still shrouded in a fog.

"Can you come to the lab tonight at 7:00," the voice repeated.

Jeff's impatient, brusque tone finally registered in my brain. In the next heartbeat, I was fully awake. "Yes! I can be there," I croaked into the phone.

"Okay, see you then."

"Yeah … all right," I murmured, though he had already hung up. I stared down at the phone wondering why he wanted to see me. Had he decided to help me after all? After the torturous night I had gone through, I was afraid to hope, but it was better than thinking about the alternative—him turning me in.

The clock on my phone showed 3:09. I blinked at the numbers and lifted the phone closer to my face to make sure I was seeing it correctly.

Realizing I had slept through most of the day, I let out a squeal and scrambled out of bed to rush to the shower. I took extra time on my hair and makeup to ensure both were perfect, even though I knew looking nice wouldn't influence Jeff one way or the other. That still left me with almost three hours to wait, which might as well have been an eternity.

The seconds ticked off slower than if the clock was winding down as I paced the apartment and rehearsed what I would say to Jeff if he told me he wouldn't help. My friends had frequently teased me about my knack of being able to talk someone into doing things they didn't want to do. I never saw it that way, but I prayed with all my might they were right and that the ability would work on Jeff. At the very least, I hoped to talk him out of turning me into Mallory and not activate the lockdown security, so I could hold onto some hope for a better future.

The lab was no more than fifteen minutes away, but when the clock showed 6:15, I couldn't stand to stay in the apartment another second. The sun had settled behind the mountains and the air was still, as if it was holding its breath to see what would happen next. My hands were clammy as I got behind the wheel of my car, but my mind was focused. The Universe had brought me this far and I was determined to hold onto the belief that it wouldn't waste its time for nothing.

I turned off the highway into the drive of the warehouse and looked up the hill to the lab. There were two cars parked in front of the door, Jeff's and one I didn't recognize. My confidence slipped a notch and instead of driving up the hill, I turned in behind the warehouse and backed into a parking space to watch.

I tried not to let the negative thoughts in, but I couldn't help but wonder if the meeting was a setup after all, and Jeff was intending to turn me over to the police. As those thoughts and others raged through my mind, a sudden fury filled my belly. I could understand him being mad at me for using him, but how could he turn his back on Michael, his best friend?

My chest rose and fell as I smoldered and stared at the door. Then, just as I decided to leave, a tall, gangly, young man came out of the lab and got into the second car. My fingers were on the key, ready to start the car, but I paused and watched him drive away without glancing my way.

What the hell? My mind bounced back and forth between wanting to leave and wanting to see what Jeff had to say. At 7:12, my phone buzzed with a new text.

Jeff: *Are you coming?*

I was still conflicted, but as Jeff was the only one who could help me get Michael back, I knew I couldn't leave without at least hearing what he had to say.

Just turning in now, I texted back, then started the car and drove up the hill, parking in the spot vacated by the car that had just left.

I hadn't even removed my finger from the intercom button when the door jerked opened and Jeff stepped aside to let me to enter. He didn't look at me and didn't say a word. As soon as the mechanical lock clicked in place, he started down the hall toward the lab. I followed in his wake, my apprehension building with each step.

When he reached the control room, he finally turned and look me in the eyes. His face was pale and he looked as uncomfortable as I felt. My stomach was a ball of knots, but I waited for him to speak first.

"The Kat I knew before was intelligent and had common sense and would never have considered sneaking into a time machine to solve her problems. She also wouldn't have needed someone else to tell her it didn't work that way and she's not going to accomplish what she thinks she's going to." He paused.

An intense pressure in my chest made it hard to breathe and my eyes burned with building tears, but I was determined not to cry. I opened my mouth to plead my case again, but he went on before I had a chance to speak.

"I know you. You're stubborn as hell, but what if I showed

you documentation on the effects of high intensity gravity on live matter? Would that change your mind or make you see how insane your idea is?"

I gave a slight shake of my head.

He closed his eyes and pursed his lips. "I figured that would be your answer. So now I'm in a conundrum, because I know you'll go ahead and try to execute your crazy plan on your own. That'll not only jeopardize the project, but you'll be torn apart. I couldn't live with that guilt on my shoulders for the rest of my life. So what am I supposed to do?"

He searched my face for an answer, but I don't think he found what he was looking for. He tilted his head back and looked at the ceiling. "I can't believe I'm going to do this," he muttered more to himself than to me. Then louder, "You probably don't know this, but I've had a crush on you since the day we met."

That was the last thing I expected him to say, but suddenly so many pieces fell into place. All those years the signs were right in front of me and I had missed them.

"I was going to ask you out, but Michael beat me to it. So I bowed out."

"Jeff—"

"No, please … you don't have to say anything. It's okay. You two were meant to be together. That was obvious right from the start and I harbored no hard feelings.

"You talk about your loss, but you don't seem to realize I lost Michael that night too. The thought of losing you too is … I don't think I could handle that."

I wanted to say something, but for the first time in my life, I was at a loss for words.

"I spent last night thinking about what you said," Jeff went on. "How it would take a person to manually erase the video. That thought has always been in the back of my mind, but since I couldn't imagine why a physicist would want to hide their arrival, I never explored the idea. I can see your logic, though. So I called in a colleague and we spent the day going over the equations and rechecking every process. We both came to the same conclusion that the machine is operable and could send someone into the past. But only if a knowledgeable person familiar with the system and the processes is at the controls."

I didn't understand what he was saying as my brain was still trying to catch up to his earlier declaration.

"I don't want you to kill yourself, so I will be that person for you. But I do have a stipulation and it's non-negotiable," Jeff added after a long pause.

I think I nodded my head, but in my state of shock, I wasn't one hundred percent sure.

"I have no idea how you plan to save Michael …"

I opened my mouth to tell him my plan, but he stopped me with his next words.

"And I don't want to know. That will just give me one more thing to worry about. My stipulation is, you must stay completely away from Michael. What I mean by that is no personal contact with him, no going by his apartment, no calling, no giving him a glimpse of you in the distance … nothing. You have to give me your word on this and swear you won't try to contact him."

"Why? Would that create a paradox? What if I accidentally bump into him?"

"It has nothing to do with paradoxes. And nothing much would happen if you bumped into him, unless you interact with him. I'm asking this for Michael's sake. Seeing you looking like this would—" His cheeks turned pink as he seemed to realize what he had said, but it didn't bother me. I knew I had completely let myself go.

"Don't worry. The last thing I want is for Michael to see me like this. Or anyone else I know, for that matter. I've already put together a disguise that I plan to wear. I guarantee you no one will know who I am."

Jeff stared me for a long moment, and I couldn't be sure, but I think there was a hint of admiration in his eyes.

"Also, keep in mind your every move will have an impact on the future. So try to keep your interactions with others to a minimum. You'll arrive there on March 9th and will have eleven days to accomplish whatever you're going to do. That's not saying you *have* to stay there the full eleven days. The sooner you come back, the better actually. And remember the absolute latest you can return is 10:20 p.m. on March 20th. The machine blows up at 10:21. If you haven't completed the return process, you'll be stuck in 2016."

I nodded my understanding.

He looked down at a manila file folder on the corner of the table. "Here are the instructions on how to erase the camera footage. This is the password." He tapped the top corner of the folder. "They keep a file of all previous passwords since they're changed so often and it's easier if we know what has already been used. The top one is for the week of the sixth, the next one is for the week of the thirteenth, and the last is for the twentieth. So you're covered even if you stay the entire time.

"You arrive at 9:13, which gives you seven minutes to get into the control room and erase the camera footage. At 9:20, the system automatically backs up to the Cloud and cannot be altered from that time forward. The cameras record only what goes on in the lab, so once you're in here you won't have to worry about the video feed. Just don't go back into the lab."

He opened the folder and pointed to the top sheet. "This page has the instructions to change the data. It's not overly complicated. If you follow the steps exactly and enter everything as I've noted, you'll have no trouble. The rest of this," his thumb fanned through several more papers, "tells you how to reset the machine when you're ready to come back. I'll walk you through the entire process now so you can ask questions. It's paramount you are comfortable performing each task. Your return in one piece will depend on it."

I had a feeling he added that last part in an effort to scare me out of going through with it. But he didn't know I was serious when I said I didn't want to live without Michael.

The next hour, he went over every step in detail with me. By the time he was finished, my head was spinning with information I only half understood. The whole time I kept thinking of how movie stars only had to set a dial, flip a switch, and voilà, they would be back in another time. I didn't think it would be that simplistic, of course, but I didn't expect it to be as complicated as it was either.

The laser lights needed to be rotating at a certain velocity and in a certain direction to create the intense gravity field that twisted time back on itself. Something Jeff called a BEC then had to be pumped into the pod to offset that same gravity field and keep me from being spaghettified when I entered the portal. There were also dozens of dials and meters to set, and even more computer commands that had to be entered. It was mindboggling and additional proof a higher hand had directed me to Jeff. I would never have been able to figure it out on my own and remember everything that had to be done.

I was feeling completely overwhelmed, but I didn't want Jeff to know. I must not have done a good job of hiding my dazed look, though, for he added, "It's a lot to take in, I know, which is why I wanted to walk you through it. I've written the instructions out as precise as possible, but if you're like me, seeing the process makes the words easier to follow. You'll be fine as long as you don't rush through it and you follow the instructions to the letter."

I gave him what I hoped was a reassuring smile, but in my head I was wondering what would happen if I missed some miniscule detail.

Thankfully, he wasn't looking at me. He had turned to the corner behind the door and was pointing to a MacBook sitting next to a black box that looked much like my TV cable box.

"The camera box you'll find there should look similar to this, though not as sophisticated. That's to your advantage. The original one worked with iMovie, so you'll just bring up the file and delete the appropriate frames using the program. Pretty simple."

He looked back at me for confirmation. I nodded. I used to be a nut about filming videos whenever my friends and I went out. I'd then edit them on iMovie and post them all over social media.

"The majority of grant money and every other penny Mallory raised for the project went into the machine and the hardware and software equipment. Security was an afterthought. The initial system in 2015 and the first part of '16 was a basic model.

One password accessed all of the computers. We've upgraded the system since, but back then the cameras were activated by motion and took pictures at several frames a second. The video files will be in a folder labeled "Security."'"

He paused and raked his fingers through his hair. I could practically see the wheels spinning in his head and I knew the feeling. My thoughts were churning just as fast.

He suddenly reached in his pocket and pulled out a plastic card the size of a credit card. "You'll need this as well. It's my key-card to get back into the building and into the lab. It originally belonged to a guy who worked here at that time, so I know it will work. According to the log books, the teams were gone by six at night. But I suggest you wait until maybe eight or so before going in to be sure."

I started to nod my understanding and remembered the emergency lockdown system. "You haven't mentioned how to turn off the emergency lockdown. I should probably know how just in case it's set."

Jeff's cheeks turned pink. "There isn't an emergency lock-down, and there never has been. I told you that just to make sure you wouldn't sneak back into the building."

I looked at him through wide eyes, but I couldn't get mad, and I couldn't blame him. I would have done the same if I had been in his shoes.

Jeff turned back to the table of monitors and keyboards. "Now that you've seen all that's involved, do you still want to go through with it?"

My chest swelled with emotion. "I have to," I said. Without thinking of what I was doing, I threw my arms around him. "Thank you so much. I know I couldn't do this without you," I whispered into his shoulder.

He turned in my arms and hugged me back. The embrace lasted far longer than necessary, but I needed it as much as I think he did. Plus, I didn't want to pull away until I had my emotions in check.

I quickly swiped my fingers under my eyes as I stepped back and looked up at him. "Don't worry. I'm going to be fine. But …"

My voice cracked. I went on anyway. "… if something happens, or if I don't come back, please don't blame yourself." I forced the corners of my mouth up into what I hoped was a confident smile. "I may just find I prefer 2016 and decide to stay there."

Once again, my acting fell flat and Jeff's mouth didn't so much as twitch at my poor attempt of a joke.

"I know you don't want to hear this, but I hope you can be realistic for a moment," Jeff said. "No axiom has been observed to prove the past can't be changed, but greater minds than either of us believe that to be true. Even if you succeed in keeping Michael from going to the bar, that doesn't automatically equate to the two of you living happily ever after in the new future."

I didn't correct him about what I was planning to do. It was far better for him to think my plan was to keep Michael from going to the bar than what I was actually going to do. I smiled the first genuine smile of the night.

"You know, I can't wait to tell you, "I told you so," one of these days. And you're not going to have a clue as to what I'm talking about."

Jeff pressed his lips into a thin line and shook his head. "We'll see."

Our eyes locked for a moment and I sensed he wanted to say something more, but instead he just added, "Are you ready to do this then?"

I jerked back. "Right now?" I had come hoping he'd agree to help me, but it never entered my mind he would be ready to send me tonight.

"Do you need more time? I'd prefer to wait until after a few actual tests have been run if you're good with that."

"No, I don't want to wait! I'm ready. My backpack and disguise are still in the car from yesterday. I'll … I'll go get them." The words came out in a rush and I nearly tripped over my own feet in my haste to get to my car.

Jeff held the door open for me as I retrieved my backpack and helped me apply the tattoos so they would be on straight. It took me a bit to get in my disguise with makeup and all. When I walked out of the bathroom, Jeff did a double take. Then his chin jutted out and his brow furrowed as he leaned closer and stared into my eyes.

"Holy shit, are those brown contacts?" he exclaimed.

I laughed for the first time in a long time. It felt good. "Yup. I told you I wasn't taking any chances of accidentally running into someone I know. No one would ever expect me to turn goth, so it's almost as good as being invisible."

Jeff gave a nod of approval, then walked me through the web of cables and tubes to the machine. He had mentioned earlier I'd be inside a pod that would protect me from the gravity field, but as I couldn't see it from the control room through the glow of lights, I imagined it to be something like the escape pods in the *Star War* movies. But in actuality, it was nothing like them, and in fact, looked more like a casket. I stopped short and gulped back a sense of dread as Jeff kept on walking and rambling on about the process.

I've never considered myself claustrophobic, but I had never been in a tight space such as the pod either, and the thought of it freaked me out more than a little bit.

"Are you okay?" Jeff had stopped next to the pod and was looking back at me with concern.

"Huh?" I said, tearing my gaze away from the metal casket.

"You don't have to do this right now if you don't want to. There's no reason to rush."

"No!" I shouted louder than I intended to. "I'm ready," I hurriedly added in a softer tone. "It's just that I wasn't expecting the pod to be so long … and narrow."

"It has to be the same shape as the cylinder to create the anti-gravity field around you that will protect you. You won't be in there for long. Just close your eyes and think of Michael. When the hatch opens, you'll be safely through the field and in 2016."

I gave him an insincere smile and hoped he couldn't tell how nervous I was.

"Sooo … are you ready?" Jeff asked.

I licked my lips and clutched my backpack tighter as I nodded my head. As he lifted the lid, I checked my Fitbit. It was 9:07.

The pod was longer than I was tall, so there was plenty of room at my feet for my backpack and messenger bag. But the side walls were extremely thick making the inside even narrower than it appeared. There was enough room for me to lie with my arms at my side, but a football player or anyone much wider than me would never have fit.

Jeff helped me settle in, then handed me a gas mask. He must have noticed the blood drain from my face for he quickly reassured me. "It's just a precaution since we're using a gas."

"Gas?" I squeaked.

"Yes, the BEC." He looked at me quizzically, then added, "You know, the exotic matter that creates the anti-gravity field? It's a critical step. Don't you remember?"

As soon as he mentioned exotic matter, I vaguely remembered him saying something about it.

"Fuck! You don't remember?" He pulled the gas mask back. "Come on, get out. I'll take you through the steps again." The tone of his voice displayed his exasperation.

"No … I remember. I'm sorry. I just didn't realize the exotic matter was a gas. I'll be fine, don't worry. I've got your notes and they're very detailed. I'm good. Let's just get on with it so I can get there and back."

Jeff studied me a moment, then shook his head as he wiggled a tube attached to the side of the pod to check the seal. "The gas will be cooled to absolute zero, so you might feel a chill once it's been added. You won't have any lasting effects from it since you won't be in there for an extended period of time. The lid will automatically open when the pod clears the field at the other end. If all goes as it should, I won't be here when you climb out."

"Thank you again for helping me. No one else will ever know what a hero you are, but I'll be eternally grateful. You're doing a good thing here."

"I hope so," Jeff replied.

His face was grim as he helped me put on the gas mask and reached up for the lid. "I'll be here for you when you get back," I heard him say softly as the lid clicked closed.

I took in a shuddering breath and closed my eyes. *I'm coming Michael. I'm coming to save you.*

BEFORE

"Anger is an acid that can do more harm to the vessel in which it is stored than to anything on which it is poured."
Seneca (circa 4 BC—65 AD)

ELEVEN

March 2016

Kat sat up the second the lid of the pod sprung open, jerked off the gas mask and vigorously rubbed her arms to get the blood circulating again. Jeff had mentioned it might get cold inside the pod, but that was an understatement. It had been freezing. She flexed and curled her fingers and toes to work out the stiffness and grimaced with pain. But the time on her Fitbit glowed 9:13, and achy joints or not, she knew she had to get going.

With the grace of a newborn foal, she climbed out of the pod, retrieved her backpack and bag and stashed the gas mask in their place inside the pod. Her knees didn't want to bend, but using the side of the machine as a crutch, she made her way around the end of the machine. She was groggy and lightheaded, but cognizant enough to set the stop watch on her Fitbit and peek out to see if there was anyone around before stepping out into the open.

A light was on in the empty control room, but the rest of the lab was dark. The same as it was when she got into the pod. A fleeting thought that the machine hadn't worked flashed through her mind. Then she remembered Jeff saying if he wasn't there, she would know she had made it.

She held her breath and slowly scanned the room a second time. Then squinted through the glare of the green lights on the control room window. The entire place looked deserted. She pressed her back against the plexiglass as a bubble of laughter made its way up her throat.

Holy shit, it worked! If her joints weren't stiff from the cold, and if time had been more plentiful, she would have done a happy dance, but instead, she limped as fast as she could across the floor.

The room looked much like it did when she left Jeff. A long table with multiple monitors and keyboards, the back wall panel of dials and switches, but the corner where the security camera equipment sat had nothing but two empty boxes waiting to be taken out to the trash.

Kat hung onto the door for support and surveyed the room. *Calm down. I know the tape gets erased, so the box has to be here somewhere*, she told herself to abate the panic that had started to take hold.

She stumbled to the long table, pushed aside papers and stacks of files and looked in every drawer and every cabinet. After scouring the entire room, she went back to a small, square, white box she had noticed sitting behind one of the monitors. It didn't looked like a video box, but it was the closest thing to one that she could find.

Her fingers felt as fat as sausages as she turned on the MacBook that the box was plugged in to. Out of the corner of her eye, she could see the seconds ticking off on the stop watch as she typed in the password. She opened iMovie, then the day's video file from the security folder, and fast forwarded until she came to the frames that showed a dark-haired girl dressed in black climb out of the pod at the far end of the plexiglass tunnel.

It was the first time she had seen a full view of herself in disguise, and for a few seconds she forgot all about her need to hurry. If she hadn't known for a fact the stranger who was skulking around the machine was her, she would never have guessed. A satisfied smile spread across her face and with renewed vigor she went back to work.

The edited video finished uploading with nine seconds to spare. She sat back, blew out the breath she'd been holding, and stared at the date and time in the top right corner of the screen. It read, 3/9/16 9:20 PM.

2016 … I'm really here. This is really happening.

Kat shuddered at the thought of what she had come to do and her fingers fumbled on the keyboard as she went through the process of changing the data per Jeff instructions. She was still a bit lightheaded, but even with that, it took less than ten minutes to make the changes.

Once she finished all the necessary tasks, she stuck her arms through the straps of her backpack and hefted the messenger bag strap over her shoulder. So far, it had all gone as planned and she had no doubt she was going to stop the POS and get her former life back. But first things first, which was a three-mile hike to the motel she had chosen. She didn't cherish the thought of walking along a dark, two-lane highway at this time of night, but since it was a weekday, she hoped there wouldn't be much traffic to worry about.

Kat could almost feel the world spinning on its axis, or maybe it was just the residual effects of the machine, but it all came crashing to a halt when a buzzer sounded as the hall door opened and a man entered.

The man was studying a sheet of paper in his hand and didn't see Kat standing inside the control room at first. But at the small squeak she made when she sucked in her breath, he stopped short and looked up.

His sandy-colored, shaggy hair kissed the collar of his shirt and his "Hollywood" beard darkened his jawline, but she wasn't looking at that. She was staring into his eyes, which were a peculiar, but familiar, color that she had only seen once before and would never forget—a color somewhere between an aqua and teal blue.

"You!" she said more to herself than to him.

For a split-second he was embarrassed for staring. Then the realization she didn't belong there made its way to his brain and his embarrassment dissolved.

"Who are you? How did you get in here?" Blue-eyes asked bluntly.

His rich, baritone voice sent a trickle of shivers down Kat's spine, but her mind was spinning with the question of what was *he* doing here?

When she didn't answer, he moved toward the control room. "You aren't supposed to be in here. How did you get in?" he asked again, a little more forcefully.

Her stomach twisted and she took a step backward, bumping into a chair. "I … um, I'm here to pick up some notes from Dr. Mallory's office," she stammered out.

His eyebrows drew together. "This isn't Mallory's office."

"Yes, I just realized that." Kat's cheeks were already pink, so she didn't have to pretend to look embarrassed.

"His office is down the hall behind the front desk."

"Oh, right … thanks. I'm sorry to have bothered you." She sheepishly walked to the door, sidled around him, and started toward the exit. But suddenly, he was right in front of her, blocking her way.

"How did you get in here. The front door and this lab both have keycard locks. I would have heard the buzzer go off if either had opened and there was no buzzer."

"Oh?" The word slipped out in a hush.

Before she could think of a lie, he added, "What do you have in your bags?"

Kat put her arm protectively around the messenger bag and her cheeks grew hotter. "Just personal stuff."

His breath-taking eyes turned darker and a tic appeared in his jaw. He stepped around her and went back to the control room, where he picked up the receiver of the landline phone on the table and started punching numbers.

"What are you doing? Who are you calling?" Kat said, her voice trembling with panic.

"I'm calling my boss to check out your story."

Kat moved faster than she thought possible and closed the distance between them, slamming her finger down on the lever of the cradle to end the call. "No, wait, please." Her heart was pounding and her mind was whirling so fast she couldn't think of what to say. But she knew for certain she couldn't let him make the call.

"Please don't," she pleaded. "I'm not here to steal anything. I swear."

"Then what are you doing here?"

Between the shock of finding him in the lab and getting caught, she could barely think. But a small voice in the back of her mind told her to trust him. She licked her lips and swallowed hard.

"I'm from the future." She held her breath and waited for his reaction.

His brow came together and his eyes drilled into her flushed face. Then, he let out a loud guffaw. "That's a good one. But I highly doubt they would choose a goth to be the first time traveler." He laughed again.

Kat squared her shoulders and lifted her chin a little higher, but held her tongue until his laughter died to a snicker. "Like it or not, it's the truth," she responded indignantly. "How else would I know that …" she pointed to the machine, "is Dr. Mallory's time machine, which was built by Dr. Bukowski?"

Blue-eye's brow raised and he choked on his laughter. He bent over and coughed. When he looked back at her through a lock of hair that had fallen over his forehead, his eyes were wet and wide in disbelief.

"Where did you get those names?" he asked as he slowly straightened.

"I told you already. I'm from the future. I came through the machine." She lifted her shoulders toward her ears, cocked her head, and nodded. "Yeah, it works … yay!"

She hoped he would be so thrilled to hear of the machine's success, it would take the focus off of her. But instead, his face turned dark and without warning, he pulled out a chair, took hold of both her upper arms and pushed her down onto it. Just as fast, he grabbed the back of another chair, whipped it around, and straddled it so they were face-to-face, the back of his chair between them.

"Okay, so tell me everything. Every step you took. All the

processes you went through to get here. And don't think you can bluff your way through, 'cause I'll know if you're lying. If you leave out one detail, I'm calling the cops."

Kat fidgeted under his intense glare and looked down at her hands. "I didn't do anything but get into the pod. Jeff was the one who set the controls on the machine—"

"Jeff who?" he interrupted.

"Jeff Newton."

"You're lying. No one by that name works here or has ever worked here, so there's no way he would have knowledge of the system. And you wouldn't have made it through in one piece without someone on the project helping you."

Kat's eyes widened with fear that he would hold true to his promise and call the police. "I'm not lying!" She reached out and put her hand on his knee. "I swear I'm not. Jeff started working here …" She had to stop a second and think back to what Jeff had told her. "I think it was sometime early summer of 2016. I'm not sure of the exact timeframe, but I do know it was shortly after the machine blew up."

"Blew up?" Blue-eyes perked up. "When did it blow up?"

"Eleven days from now. On March 20th. It was some kind of major power surge. That's all I know."

"Son of a bitch! I've been telling Bukowski the substation couldn't handle the draw the machine would need." He leaned back and his brow creased in thought, but surprisingly, he didn't look upset.

Kat folded and unfolded the strap of her backpack as she watched him and worried this unexpected run-in would mess up the future.

Several long, agonizing seconds passed before he looked up. "What's your name?"

The question caught Kat off guard and she almost blurted out her real name. Fortunately, she caught herself just as she opened her mouth. "Oo … livia Flynn. My friends call me O."

As his gaze slowly moved over her from head to toe, he made no attempt to hide the skepticism on his face. "What year did you come from?"

"2017."

"Humph." He crossed his arms over his chest. "Let me take a wild guess and say you're not a physicist. In fact … I'll go one step farther and say you're not a scientist of any kind." When Kat didn't contradict him, he went on. "So why are you here? Why did Mallory send you back in time?"

A dozen or so thoughts flew into Kat's mind all at once and she hesitated to sort through them. She knew there was little chance she would succeed in convincing him she was a physicist, however, none of the other ideas were any more realistic than that one, which left her with only one option—to tell the truth. But what if he tried to stop her?

"You seem to be having trouble coming up with your next lie, so let me make this simple for you. Save your breath and tell me the truth. I'll pick up on a lie anyway. And if you think I wasn't serious about calling the cops, you might want to think again," he added.

She flinched and looked up. His eyes were so damn beautiful, like a Caribbean Sea, and before she realized what she was doing, she plunged in. "I've come to stop a disaster."

His eyebrows rose sharply. "A world-wide disaster, or an American disaster?"

"A … personal disaster."

He gaped at her in disbelief. "A *personal* disaster? That's the best you can do? You think I'm going to believe Mallory and Bukowski would use their multimillion-dollar investment to send a girl …" his eyes raked her up and down, "who by the looks of it walked in off the street, back in time to what …" He groped for the right words. "… keep her boyfriend from breaking up with her? Come on, do I look like a moron?

"Mallory didn't spend his life working on this hypothesis and pound the pavement, sacrificing everything to get the funds to build the machine just to have it be used for personal vendettas."

Kat's chin lifted. He was making it sound as if her mission was petty, but it wasn't. It wasn't entirely personal either. "It's not like that. I'm not here to get revenge. I'm here to save hundreds of people from a massive amount of pain and suffering."

One corner of his mouth turned up in a cynical sneer as he exhaled a snort through his nose. "Mallory—"

"Doesn't know I'm here," Kat cut in. "No one does … other than Jeff, the guy who helped me on the other end. The machine was just recently turned on for the first time since it blew up. They haven't even begun the testing phase yet, but I didn't want to wait. I saw an opportunity to give a whole bunch of people another chance at life and I took it."

"Wait." He held his hands up in front of him. "You're telling me you went through the gravity portal before it was even tested?" He didn't give her time to nod her head in confirmation before he went on. "That's … I can't …" He shook his head. "What the *hell* were you thinking?"

He gaped at her for several long seconds at a loss for words, then added, "Do you realize what could have happened to you if something had gone wrong?"

"Yes, I do. Jeff had a similar reaction as yours and he explained it all to me. Actually, that's why he decided to help and run the controls. He knew the risks would be too high if I tried to do it without him."

Blue-eyes frowned. "It doesn't sound like this Jeff guy knows any more about physics than you do."

Kat squared her shoulders. "He knows a lot about physics, as well as everything there is to know about the machine. He's one of the smartest men I know. Look." She dug into her bag for the pages Jeff had printed out for her.

"He gave me this step-by-step procedure on how to set the machine for when I'm ready to go back. And the fact that I made it here just fine should tell you he knows what he's doing."

She held out the sheets for him to see, but he didn't even glance at the pages. His gaze was locked on Jeff's keycard that she had pulled out and laid on the table along with her phone as she dug through the pack.

"That can't be," he said more to himself than to Kat. A deep crease cut a line between his eyebrows. "Where did you get that?" he asked, not taking his eyes off the card.

Kat looked down at the table to see what he was referring to. "The card? Jeff gave it to me so I can get back into the lab when I'm ready to leave."

"Jeff gave it to you?" he repeated. "Where did he get it?"

"I'm assuming they gave it to him when he started here."

Her stomach twitched with the sense that something was wrong. She picked up the card and held it tightly in her hand. "Why?"

"It's mine."

She pressed the card against her chest protectively, even though she knew he could easily take it from her if he wanted it. "No, it's not. It's Jeff's. He gave it to me."

He didn't take his eyes off the card in Kat's hand as he stood and reached into his pocket, pulling out a duplicate plastic card. "See this?" He held the keycard out and pointed at the bottom corner. "It's an infinity symbol. I'm sure you already knew that, but what you don't know is how it got there.

"My mom was an artist. Not famous or even well known, but to me she was the greatest artist of all time. Her thing was to hide an infinity symbol in every one of her paintings. She was ingenious in the way she went about it, and they were near impossible to find. It sometimes took me hours, but I always found it.

"When she died last year, I got an infinity tattoo on my bicep. But I didn't want the standard symbol, so I designed one myself that incorporated her initials. I sketched it here on my keycard."

He pointed at the two loops of the symbol where Kat could see, now that he was pointing it out, a forward and backward C. "There's only one card with a symbol like this on it … mine."

Kat's throat tightened. She didn't have to look at the card Jeff gave her to know it had an infinity symbol in the bottom corner. She had noticed it when he handed it to her, but thought nothing of it at the time, and never looked close enough to know if the two Cs were there.

She squirmed under Blue-eyes' intense scrutiny, dying to know the answer, but scared to find out. Scared that this accidental meeting was the reason he had left this job, or the reason he was fired, whichever the case may be.

She couldn't resist the temptation for long, though, and a minute later, she tentatively moved her hand away from her chest. They both leaned in closer as she opened her fist and exposed the card.

Kat inhaled sharply at the sight of the Cs on each end of the symbol, which were identical to the ones on Blue-eyes' card. He didn't say a word and moved to the window to stare out at the machine.

Kat swiveled around in the chair. "I'm sorry, I …" she started, but there was really nothing she could say.

"It's okay. It's every physicist's dream to have the hypothesis they're working on advance to theory. And hey," he shrugged, "I've just witnessed the arrival of the first time traveler—possibly the greatest science breakthrough in modern history. There are no words to describe what it means to me."

He looked over his shoulder. "So do you know why I left the project?"

Kat shook her head. "No, I'm sorry. I don't know anything about you," she replied, glad that it was true and that all she did know was that he drank coffee.

He turned back to the window. The buzz from the lights of the machine filled the silence that grew between them and Kat glanced toward the hall, debating whether she should chance sneaking out while he was distracted. However, the notion that the Universe had placed Blue-eyes on this side to help her held her in place.

All of a sudden, Blue-eyes walked back and sat down in the chair, and twirled Kat's chair around so she faced him.

"I'm Daniel Christoph," he said, holding his hand out for her to shake.

Kat blushed, but took his hand. "Hi." She could feel her cheeks getting hotter by the minute, but she couldn't look away.

"So is Olivia Flynn your real name?"

Her nose wrinkled as she grimaced. "No, but I don't think it's a good idea for you to know my real name."

He shrugged in acceptance. "I don't suppose much has changed in just a year, huh?"

"I'm sorry, but I can't tell you anything at all about the future."

"Can't or won't?"

Kat pressed her lips together and lifted her shoulders in place of an answer.

Daniel laughed. "So you're telling me I'm not going to get the winning lottery numbers out of you? That would be a damn good explanation of why I left my job here … you know, winning the lottery."

Kat laughed along with him. "You of all people should know the odds of winning the lottery are pretty lousy. But miracles do happen, and people do win. If you're one of them, it's not going to be because I gave you the numbers. I couldn't tell you a single number that's been drawn in the last five years."

The laughter eased some of Kat's tension and she genuinely smiled into his eyes that were holding her prisoner the same as if she was strapped to the chair. She had originally thought his eyes were aqua, but now that she was close and staring directly into them, she could see a distinct circle of blue and a circle of green in each, which gave them the unique hue from afar.

All at once, a fire that had laid dormant in her stomach for over sixteen months sparked back to life and a slow heat began to spread. When it reached her chest, she started and blinked rapidly. Her gaze dropped to the keycard she still held in her hand and she hoped he wouldn't notice the blush moving up her neck.

They both started to speak at the exact same moment and both abruptly stopped. He motioned with his hand for her to go ahead.

She cleared her throat. "I was just going to say that I think I should probably get going." She stood and stuffed the keycard and her phone back into the bag.

Daniel visibly jerked. "Where are you going to go?"

Kat pointed in the direction of Boulder. "Into town."

"Why? What do you plan to do? "

"I already told you I can't say."

Daniel jumped to his feet. "You said you came to prevent

something from happening. But didn't Jeff tell you that you can't undo an event that has already become history in your timeline?"

Though Kat was physically exhausted, she was even more tired of hearing that.

"Well then, I guess you have nothing to worry about, do you? And since my plans have nothing to do with you, you don't have to worry about me either," she huffed and strode purposely to the door.

"Wait!" Daniel called after her. "I could give you a lift to wherever you're going."

"No, thank you. I'd rather walk," she replied without turning around.

Daniel stared at the empty doorway long after the buzz of the front door opening ceased. He had signed onto Mallory's project not because he was a proponent of time travel, but because he was interested in delving deeper into the effects light and gravity had on spacetime. The time travel aspect of the machine was Mallory's folly. Daniel had gone along with the dream only because he didn't believe it would ever be possible to send a person into the past or future. Discovering he was wrong was not only unsettling, it went against everything he believed.

He placed his hand on the back of the chair to steady himself as his mind raced. He was a proponent of Hawking's Chronology Protection Conjecture that proposed the laws of physics would prevent time travel on all but submicroscopic scales to protect the universe. But if this girl really was who she claimed to be, and the evidence was clear she was, then Hawking's conjecture was false.

Daniel collapsed onto the chair. *Jesus, what have we done?* He couldn't begin to comprehend what would happen to the universe if people had the means to change the past whenever things didn't go their way. It would violate the law of causality and everything that mankind's physical existence was based on would be null and void. That could then bring on total chaos and possibly even the collapse of the entire universe.

Daniel let his head fall back and looked at the ceiling. If that happened, he would be partially responsible.

He twisted around to see the time on the monitor behind him. He hadn't paid attention to the exact time Kat left, but he was sure it hadn't been more than fifteen minutes. He pushed himself up from the chair, rushed out of the room, and bolted down the hall.

It was almost 10:30 on a Thursday night, which meant traffic going into town would be light, and few Boulderites would stop and pick up a goth hitchhiker this late. That gave him the advantage. As long as he caught up to her before she entered town, he could follow her to wherever she was staying. He would then have the rest of the night to figure out how to stop her from inciting utter mayhem.

TWELVE

The sliver of moon floated in and out of the clouds, glittering in the intermittent puddles from an earlier rain shower and turning them into black mirrors that were only visible when Kat's foot landed in one. But she didn't care, because her combat boots had thick soles and kept her feet dry. Plus, there were far too many other issues on her mind to worry about puddles, or cars less than three-feet away zipping past her at way too high of speed, or the rustling brush on the other side that might or might not be a wild animal or possibly a snake.

Jeff and Daniel both insinuated traveling through the machine was the most dangerous part of her journey, but neither of them knew what she was about to do, or the evil she was about to encounter. The hazards of the machine were nothing in comparison.

She had started out walking at a brisk pace, but as the lights of the city drew nearer, the reality of her journey began to weigh on her and her feet dragged as if a 50-pound barbell had been strapped to each ankle.

Daniel sped up when Kat appeared in his headlights and moved into the left-hand lane to keep her from seeing him as he drove past in his eight-year-old silver Jetta. He turned off the highway at the junction of Broadway, one of the main thoroughfares of Boulder, drove down the street a short distance to be away from the intersection, and pulled over to the side of the road. He turned the car and the lights off and slouched in the seat to avoid drawing attention as he waited for her to catch up.

It was well after 11:00 by the time Kat appeared in the rearview mirror. When Daniel saw her turn onto Broadway and head toward him, he pulled the hood of his sweatshirt over his head, tucked his chin to his chest, and listened to the crunch of her boots on the gravel. Her footsteps approached the car, then passed without the slightest pause.

Kat hugged her coat around her and looked up as she neared the strip club she had discovered while scoping out the area for a motel. On the other side of the club was a homeless shelter. A block farther down was the motel she planned to stay at. It was not the best part of town, but it was the closest to the lab and it was cheap.

As the sound of voices drifted to her, her steps slowed and her muscles tensed. She warily glanced from car to car in the club's parking lot. They all appeared to be empty, but she picked up some movement in the shadows at the side of the homeless shelter. At the same moment, two men exited the club, stumbling into each other and talking boisterously.

Her pulse accelerated and a chill ran up her spine. She never used to be so skittish, but thanks to the POS, every stranger spooked her nowadays. Clenching her teeth and folding her arms over her chest, she crossed the four-lane road and walked as fast as her feet would go without breaking into a full run the rest of the way to the motel.

She burst into the dimly lit, sparsely furnished lobby and went straight to the plexiglass square in the wall that cordoned off the registration desk from the public. She pressed her nose against the barrier, but the small room behind was as empty as the lobby.

"Hello?" Kat called out, shifting from foot to foot as she waited for someone to appear. When no one did, she took a step back and looked down the length of the narrow ledge used as a counter for a bell or some way to summon a clerk. Instead, she found a small tabletop stand stating the front desk was closed and would reopen at 5:30 a.m.

"Ah, shit!" she muttered, knowing from her reconnaissance this was the only motel within walking distance. She folded her arms on the ledge and dropped her forehead onto them. Her legs and feet ached from the three-mile trek and she didn't know how much farther she would be able to go. She grimaced at the thought of calling a taxi, knowing her funds were tight and a trip around town to find another cheap place to stay could end up being quite expensive.

But that wasn't even the biggest issue at the moment. She had taken the SIM card out of her phone and left it in 2017 to avoid creating an issue with two identical SIMs working on the same network at the same time, so she had no way to call. And the only phone in the lobby was on the registration desk behind the plexiglass barrier.

Kat turned and slid down the wall of the counter to the floor. The thought that the past was fighting to stay the same slipped into her mind, but she clenched her jaw and pushed it away. She didn't want a thought like that to sit in her head for even a second. This was just an unforeseeable turn of events and nothing more.

Bone tired and chilled from the night air, she was half tempted to curl up on the floor and spend the night right there. If there had been a lock on the door, she might have actually bedded down. But knowing a group of men were lurking around the shelter a few yards away made her skin crawl. That left her with only one option—continue down the road until she came to a gas station and use their phone to call a taxi.

She gave each calf a brisk rub to work out the cramps and moaned as she pushed herself to her feet. Then with a heavy sigh, she walked out into the night.

Daniel watched Kat over the edge of the car's dashboard as she crossed the street and hurried on, lit by the security lamps of a large storage facility. When she darted back across Broadway and disappeared into a small cluster of trees in front of a motel, he started the car.

His eyes were fixed on Kat standing inside the lobby when he drove past the driveway. A second later, he felt the bump of his car going up and over the curb. With a jerk, he twisted the steering wheel hard and veered the car back onto the street just in time to miss a metal post of a street sign. It was a stupid near miss and not like him at all. But having a vision of the universe imploding inside his head wasn't typical either.

At the gas station two corners down, he pulled in, parked on the dark side of the building, and turned off the engine. The situation was bad enough without putting his life, and possibly someone else's, at risk. He stared out the side window as he tried to get his head straight and figure out what to do next.

The lights of the canopy over the pumps at the gas station flicked off when Kat was still a half block away. "No, no, no!" she muttered. Picking up her pace, she jogged, or more like stumbled, the rest of the way. She choked back a sob of relief as she drew near and saw an inside light shining through the windows and an attendant moving about inside.

Kat hurried to the door and pounded her fist on the glass. The elderly attendant stopped his sweeping and looked over his shoulder.

"We're closed," he called out, pointing to the rectangular sign hanging on a chain before going back to his cleaning.

"Please, I need to use your phone," Kat yelled, her mouth as near to the glass as possible without touching it to make sure he could hear her.

The attendant moved a few feet closer to the door and squinted at Kat. "We're closed, lady. Sorry."

"Please, I just need to use your phone. It'll only take a minute."

The attendant hesitated a moment before he hobbled to the glass, scanned the empty lot, and looked suspiciously back at Kat. "Where's your car?"

Kat's stomach tightened, but she didn't falter. "I don't have a car. I got in a fight with my boyfriend and he dropped me off back there along the highway." She pointed back the way she had come. "My phone must have fallen out of my pocket when I got out, so I have no way to call a taxi to come get me. Please, I just need to use your phone. Can you let me in for just a moment?"

The attendant's gaze scanned the lot again. "Look, lady, I ain't no fool. I open this door and your little pack of thug friends hiding out there somewhere jump me and rob the place."

"No! I swear there's no one else here with me. I'm all by myself."

The attendant turned his back and started to walk away.

"No, wait! Please. Can you at least call a cab company for me? You don't have to let me in, just call for a taxi and ask them to pick me up out front here. Please … I have no other way of getting home."

The attendant paused and looked back over his shoulder. "You got money for a cab?"

"Yes, I do!"

The attendant scowled at her, but reached into his pocket and pulled out his phone. Kat had the number for the cab company memorized and called it out before he asked.

"They said it'll be about ten minutes. You can wait out there by the pumps," he said, then turned and shuffled to the back of the store.

Kat sagged with relief, walked to the cement island, and plopped down between the gas pumps. Her leg muscles ached from the long walk and her eyes drooped, but the strong smell of gasoline stung her nose and she had no fear of falling asleep.

The temperature had fallen from the time she left the lab, and she was still cold from the machine, so even with her long coat on, she shivered uncontrollably. To take her mind off her misery, she tried to mentally tick off the steps of her plan, but an image of

Daniel's face kept popping up and she couldn't stay focused.

It had been a long time since she was attracted to anyone other than Michael, and the strong connection she felt to Daniel confused her. He was handsome, yes, but so were a hundred other guys she knew. It wasn't that kind of connection anyway. It was deeper than that. She had felt it the very first time she saw him at Starbucks, and it was even stronger at the lab. Initially, she thought the attraction was the Universe's way of getting her to follow him to the time machine. But that didn't explain why he was here now.

The crease in her brow deepened. Did the Universe want him to work with her to make it right? Kat sat up straighter as another thought came to her. Was her success dependent on his help?

Ah, shit! Kat closed her eyes and slumped against the cold gas pump. She had hated having to involve Jeff in her plan, but at least he was a friend and had a stake in the results. And it wasn't totally her decision. Jeff hadn't given her much of a choice.

Daniel was a different story, though. He was a stranger and had no tie to her. And he could just as easily turn her in as help her if he found out what she was about to do.

A Yellow Cab pulled into the drive and the passenger side window rolled down. "You my ride?" the driver called out.

Kat's knees popped painfully as she got to her feet, and she inwardly groaned as she lifted her backpack and climbed into the backseat. The sound of a car engine turning over drifted in as she pulled the door closed, but her brain was too tired to give it a second thought. She leaned forward and told the driver where she wanted to go to, then settled back in the seat.

Daniel waited a few seconds after the cab pulled out before he followed, making sure there was always at least two car lengths between them as the taxi drove to the east end of town and pulled into a hotel. He parked across the street and watched Kat get out and go into the lobby. Seconds later, she returned and got back into the cab.

The same scenario repeated at the next two hotels. Finally, at the third, she paid the driver and trudged around the building to a door on the side. Daniel pulled into a parking spot that gave him a view of the side door as well as the lobby entrance.

A few minutes after Kat entered the building, a light went on in a room on the third floor. Daniel sat in his car and watched, even after the light went out.

An hour later, he was satisfied she was in for the night and reluctantly drove home to get a few hours of sleep. Tomorrow was going to be a long day and he needed to be fresh and on top of his game.

THIRTEEN

Kat opened her eyes and squinted into a bright patch of sunlight shining through a crack in the curtains. She turned her head away and rubbed her fists in her eyes, then frowned as an orange loveseat came into focus. She had no loveseat in her bedroom. And certainly Cathie and her Aunt Stephanie had too good of taste to have such an ugly orange thing in their apartment anyway.

At that moment, the fan on the air conditioner unit clicked on. Kat started at the sound and her memory came flooding back. She wasn't at home in her room. She was in a hotel in 2016.

She closed her eyes and filled her lungs as a torrent of thoughts tumbled through her mind. There was so much to do and so little time now that she was paying twice what she had anticipated for the hotel. She had only brought $673 in cash with her, which was the sum of what was available on her credit card, plus, $200 she borrowed from the emergency fund Cathie kept in the apartment. With the extra cost of the room, and the rental car on top of that, her cash would not last long.

Kat rolled to her back and looked around the room. It was furnished in typical hotel motif: several mass-produced prints on the walls, an oval cherrywood coffee table in front of the loveseat, and a long dresser/desk/TV stand combo along the opposite wall. As her gaze landed on the glowing green 8:03 on the alarm clock sitting on the shelf attached to the headboard of the bed, she sat up with a small squeal.

She had intended to get up before dawn and secure a spot near Michael's apartment before he came out of the building. She had promised Jeff she would stay away from Michael, but she was no better than a junkie who had gone too long without a fix, and her aching need to get a glimpse of him was stronger than the disgrace of breaking a promise or any kind of rational thinking. But now that she had overslept, she would have to go another day without her fix, for Michael was already on his way to his internship job in Denver.

Tears pooled behind her eyes as the doubts from the night before infiltrated her thoughts. She didn't want to believe the Universe had reversed its course and abandoned her, but it was hard to dispel the notion with everything that had gone wrong since she got to 2016.

Falling back on the bed, she stared up at the ceiling feeling more exhausted than ever.

"You've done so much to help, please don't stop now. I don't have much time here to set things right. I can't afford to have anything else go wrong," she whispered, hoping and praying that whoever had brought her this far was listening.

Kat's body ached, but she rolled to her side, sat up on the edge of the bed, and cursed again for oversleeping. The information she had collected on the POS said he arrived early for class, and the first class of the day started at 9:30, according to the graduate school schedule she found online last night in the hotel's business center. He may not be in that particular class—his school records and schedule were one thing she couldn't access on the internet—but she was prepared to sit outside the classroom buildings for every scheduled class until he showed up if need be, because she figured locating him on campus was by far the faster and easiest route.

She hurriedly dialed the car rental office on the hotel phone to reserve a car, the cheapest one they had. Fortunately, the pick-up location was less than a mile away and she could walk there to save money. But that meant she didn't have time to shower, which wasn't that big of deal since she had no plans to get close to anyone except the POS. And she may not even be able to get close to him if he didn't have a class today.

Bile suddenly rose into her throat at the thought of having to interact with the POS face-to-face. She rushed into the bathroom, emptied her stomach, and rinsed her mouth out in the sink.

She had tried to think of another way to get the POS to the house, but there really wasn't any other. And the whole plan depended on him going to that address. Shooting him on campus or at his apartment complex was too risky and the chances of getting caught were too high. If she was caught, the chaos that would ensue when they ran her fingerprints and discovered there were actually two of her would ruin everything, especially her future that she was trying so hard to save.

You brought me here, and I'm counting on you to help me finish, she silently said to the Universe.

She blew out a big breath, straightened her back, and looked into the eyes of the stranger in the mirror. "Okay, Olivia Flynn, let's do this!"

FOURTEEN

Daniel pulled into the parking lot of the office building next to the hotel and checked his watch. He had wanted to be back no later than 6:00 a.m. to ensure he wouldn't miss Kat. But the myriad of questions rolling around in his head had kept him awake until almost 4:00 a.m., and he slept right through the radio alarm when it went off. Twenty minutes later, he awoke with a jerk to the sound of Blake Shelton's *"Came Here to Forget."* He jumped out of bed, pulled on some jeans and a hoodie, and drove like a madman back to the hotel, praying the whole way that she hadn't left yet.

He arrived a half hour later than he wanted, tense and pissed off. He pounded his fists on the steering wheel and gnashed his teeth, but there was nothing he could do but sit, wait, and see if she came out.

Kat's hand shook as she grabbed the messenger bag with the gun and the Punisher comic book she hoped would be her golden ticket to get the POS to talking. The weapon weighed less than two pounds, but she could feel the pull of it on her shoulder. She set her jaw, rolled her shoulders back, and walked out the door wearing the white skull T-shirt.

The temperature on her phone showed 45 degrees and

the sky was a deep blue with only a narrow band of wispy clouds painted across the mountaintops. But with the adrenalin pumping through her, and her long black coat soaking up the heat of the sun, drops of perspiration quickly formed on her nose and temples and under her arms. As she walked, she mumbled out loud the Punisher facts she had memorized to keep them fresh in her mind.

A chubby man with a few long hairs carefully combed across the bald spot on the top of his head looked up with a smile at the tinkling of the bell as Kat entered the rental office. His smile rapidly vanished as he looked her up and down, however, and he didn't rise from his chair behind the counter.

"Excuse me, can you help me?" Kat asked, looking directly at the man.

With a grunt and a frown, he pushed himself up and waddled to the counter.

"I don't know that I can. I'm afraid we don't have anything readily available at the moment," he huffed, his jowls jiggling like the flab under an old woman's arm.

Kat gestured with her head to the line of cars parked out front. "Are those your cars?"

"Yes, they are, but I'm afraid they have all been reserved." The man patted a stack of rental agreements on the countertop to prove his point.

Kat glanced down and back up. "Is one of them reserved for Olivia Flynn?"

Recognition lit up the man's eyes. He held her gaze as he surreptitiously slid his hand over the name on the top agreement. "I'm not at—" he started, but Kat cut him off.

"I'm Olivia Flynn, so I guess one of those is my car. And I'm in a hurry, so if you don't mind, I'd appreciate you giving me whatever it is you need me to sign so I can be on my way."

The man had the decency to blush, but his eyes remained cool. "I'm going to need to see a driver's license and a credit card."

"I'll be paying cash," Kat replied, handing the man the fake driver's license she had gotten from the same Frat boy who had made her first fake ID when she was a freshman at CU.

He studied the picture on the license several seconds, looked up at Kat with narrowed eyes, then back down at the license. It would have been obvious to a five-year-old he was trying to find fault with it, but he obviously didn't have the training or the eye to be able to pick out the minor discrepancies. After scribbling the license number on the agreement, he returned his gaze to Kat. "Your credit card?"

"I already mentioned I would be paying cash not using a card."

"Don't take cash. We take credit cards. It's company policy. There has to be a card on file to cover damages or additional charges that may be incurred."

Shit! The credit card she had brought with her was the one her parents had given her to cover emergencies when she started college. It was in her dad's name, and the only reason she brought it along was because she knew hotels required having a credit card on file and her own card was maxed out. She wasn't expecting to put actual real charges on it, though, and didn't feel right doing so.

"I can't let you take a car off the lot without a credit card," the man reiterated, his eyes gleaming with victory.

Shit, she thought again. She needed a car to get around and get back to the lab after shooting the POS. Reluctantly, she fumbled with her wallet, making a concentrated effort to keep her hand steady as she pulled out the credit card and handed it to the clerk backside up so he wouldn't see her dad's name on it.

At that moment, the doorbell tinkled and a couple entered. The clerk looked up with a smile. "I'll be with you folks in a moment," he said as he swiped her card through the reader.

His smile vanished as he turned to Kat and handed her back the card without looking at the name printed on it. Then, without further ado, he assembled the remaining paperwork, making it clear he was anxious to get rid of her. As soon as the printer rattled to life and spit out a long receipt, he slid the agreement around for her signature and moved on to the couple, missing the smug smile that tugged at the corners of Kat's mouth as she coolly signed her name.

Kat was aware she was running out of time, but she also knew she needed to get something to eat as it may be her only chance for the rest of the day. After a quick pass through a fast food drive-up, she drove to the lot where she and her neuroscience classmates always parked. There was only one empty spot left, which told her what she already knew—she had most likely missed the POS.

Her clunky boots were not fit to run in, but she did her best and speed-walked through the campus to the Muenzinger building, which housed the majority of psychology and neuroscience classes. She came to a stop in the middle of the porte-cochère that led into a central courtyard and watched as a few straggling students hurried through the doors and into the building.

For two years she had roamed the halls of Muenzinger. They were two of the best years of her life. She didn't realize until that moment how much she missed it.

With a new ache in her heart and a longing to be back in the classroom, Kat turned to leave and stepped right into the path of a student rushing up the passageway. "Oh, sorry," she automatically mumbled, then froze as she looked into the face of Madison Kelley, a long-time friend of hers.

The little bit of color on Kat's face, the only thing that kept her from looking like the walking dead, drained. But Madison didn't notice and hurried into the blackness behind the dark-tinted glass doors without giving Kat a second look or saying, "I'm sorry" or "Excuse me."

Kat's mouth dropped open and the sting of her friend's brush off was just reaching her heart when she realized Madison hadn't recognized her. The hurt instantly turned into elation and a satisfied grin replaced her shocked look. She had hoped the goth attire would fool her friends, but truthfully, she didn't believe it would.

Score one for the home team! Kat thought, savoring the small victory, which she needed more than she realized.

Her step was a little lighter, though still skulking in a goth-like fashion to stay in character, as she crossed the plaza and settled on a bench nestled between two trees on the side of football stadium. The strips of cold metal making up the bench weren't the most comfortable and she had to shift her butt this way and that to find a spot where they didn't grind against her bones. It was going to be a long wait before the class ended, and if the POS wasn't in attendance, it could be even longer.

Though the sun was shining brightly in the cloudless sky, the air was crisp and smelled of wet earth. Kat's eyes drooped with the hum of traffic and after almost nodding off, she shoved her ear-buds in her ears and turned the music up to near blaring. But her eyes still sagged. Just as she was about to lose the battle, a stream of students, some walking, some on bikes, spilled out of the passageway.

Kat sat up straighter and unconsciously held her breath as she searched the faces, paying extra attention to lone males. Many of the faces were familiar and her longing for her old life grew steadily stronger.

But all too soon, the rush of students dwindled to a trickle. Kat wilted a little on the inside and slumped back onto the bench. The next scheduled class was at 12:30 in a different building, which meant she would need to move soon to get there early enough to catch him.

She leaned forward and squinted at the passageway, focusing on the faces of the last few stragglers. "Come on, show yourself," she whispered, hanging onto the hope that he would appear. She really didn't want to have to sit there all day waiting around.

As three girls emerged from the shadows, Kat did a double take. It was Madison, Emma, another old friend, and herself. She had been so focused on the POS and where he would be that she didn't take into consideration she also had a Thursday morning lab in Muenzinger in 2016.

Seeing herself chatting and laughing with her friends was surreal and mesmerizing at the same time. She seemed so happy and carefree. Kat smiled. It really had been the best of times back then. She held a 3.8 GPA, had a great circle of friends, the perfect boyfriend—everything she ever wanted. But in a little over a month's time, it would all be lost unless she was able to find the POS and stop him.

The air suddenly became too thick to breathe. Kat gasped and bent in half, wrapping her arms around her stomach as the weight of all she had lost pressed down on her. She so badly wanted to be the fun-loving, carefree girl again.

God, how could you have let this happen? Why would you let that monster destroy so many lives? She squeezed her eyes tightly together. *It's not fair. That Piece Of Shit should be in the ground, not all those innocent people.*

She rocked back and forth, thinking of her old life and how she was going to take it back until the sick feeling eased enough that she could sit up straight. She swiped her fingers over her cheeks, and looked out over the plaza.

Her doppelganger and group of friends were gone and the flow of students had dwindled down to one lone male, who was just emerging from the passageway. His shoulders were hunched over and his head was down so she couldn't see his face. He didn't look familiar, but she cocked her head, narrowed her eyes, and watched his back as he walked away.

As he neared the corner of the building, he looked over his shoulder as if he knew someone was watching him. Kat's heart stalled. It was the POS. He didn't have the cocky, crazed look he had in the photo that was burned into the backside of her eyelids, and his hair wasn't dyed black yet, but she had no doubt it was him. He turned back and proceeded around the corner, as normal as any other student.

Kat watched him go, but couldn't move as her legs had gone weak. She thought she had prepared herself for this encounter and expected her rage would get her through. But seeing him in the flesh was more frightening and devastating than she had imagined.

Don't do this. He has no power over you. He's just a man.

She rolled her shoulders, clenched her teeth, and forced herself to her feet. He was the reason she had come and she couldn't afford to let him get away and delay it any longer.

I'm coming for you, you evil son of a bitch! she thought and hurried after him.

The POS wove through the campus to the underpass and up to the street. As soon as Kat saw he was headed to the parking lot where she had left her car, she picked up her pace and turned right, past the Starbucks and row of shops, to the alley that ran behind the lot. She got to her car just as he was climbing into a white two-door Honda Civic with Kentucky license plates.

Kat gripped the steering wheel of her car as if it were a life line and followed him onto 14th Street and out onto Broadway. There was always heavy traffic around campus, but she managed to stay with him, and only once did more than a couple cars get between them.

The POS went through the drive-up of a sub shop, then drove to his apartment and turned into a small parking lot between two of the buildings that was designated for residents only. Kat pulled to the curb on the street and watched him walk up the stairs to the second level and enter the second door from the end.

As soon as he was inside, Kat inched the car up a few feet so she had a good view of the parking lot and the window of his apartment. She then settled in again for another wait, not the least bit sleepy this time.

FIFTEEN

As the afternoon wore on and the sun beat down on the car, the inside temperature rose and Kat peeled away a layer of clothing. She had a bottle of water with her, but only took an occasional sip, just enough to stay hydrated. She didn't want to have to leave her post to pee. But even without drinking a lot, by the time the sun settled on the top of the mountains,, it was a foregone conclusion she wouldn't be able to hold out much longer without finding some place to relieve her bulging bladder.

Kat turned her gaze in the direction of the campus and tried to visualize where the closest gas station or fast food restaurant was. She was still pondering that question when a movement in the corner of her eye drew her attention back to the windshield. She let out a gasp at the sight of the POS bounding down the stairs and almost peed her pants as she hurriedly scooted down in the seat.

The POS got behind the wheel of his car, backed out and turned onto the street, seemingly oblivious to the fact she was watching him. Squeezing her thighs together, she started her car and followed, praying he was going somewhere that had a bathroom she could use.

He drove past the campus to the Hill and turned into a parking lot on the back side of a strip mall that housed a small market, a diner, a laundromat, and Tony's, her favorite pizza joint. A knot of dread tightened in her stomach as she turned into the same lot and parked at the other end from his car.

“Where are you going?” she asked the air as he dropped coins into the parking meter and started walking up the sidewalk toward Broadway instead of taking the back stairs that provided a shortcut to the storefronts of the strip mall.

Kat didn’t take the time to pay the parking meter and hobbled after him as fast as she could go with a bladder that was near to bursting. “Please don’t go into Tony’s,” she whispered as he turn left at the street. She hurried to catch up, but he had already turned the corner of the building by the time she made it to the street. Cursing softly, she waddled to the end of the market just in time to see him pass the entrance of Tony’s and continue toward the corner of the L-shape mall. She halted and frowned. The only thing at that end was a diner, and it was only opened for breakfast and lunch.

The POS walked straight to a wooden door partially hidden behind the blue staircase to the second level, pulled it opened, and walked in without hesitation.

Kat had walked past that door dozens of times, but never once gave it a second look. It was just a plain wooden door. And as it had no business name on it or on the wall next to it, she assumed it led to a storage unit or a staff entrance. But that didn’t make sense. None of what she read about the POS mentioned him having a job. He had no reason to go into a staff entrance.

She hesitantly walked to the door and reached out for the handle. As she wrapped her hand around the metal, she spotted a small rectangle sign on the lower part of the door that she had never noticed before. It read: OPEN DAILY 4PM-1AM.

Her hand dropped to her side and a line creased her brow. What kind of business would not put their name up so customers could find them?

If her mind hadn’t been so waterlogged, she might have been able to come up with a rational explanation. But at the moment, all she could do was stare at the door in confusion. A sudden blast of music disrupted her thoughts and the delicious, spicy scent of pizza wafted toward her. She turned her head toward Tony’s just as the restaurant door shut. She hadn’t eaten since breakfast and her stomach growled with the thought of food.

She bit down on her lip and looked back at the wooden door. She didn't know where it led, and more importantly, if there was a restroom behind it. But she did know there was one in Tony's. With her bladder making the decision for her, she turned and wiggle-walked to the pizza place, praying she didn't pee her pants before she made it into the restroom.

It had been well over a year since Kat was last in Tony's. She and Michael used to come to the small pizzeria to meet up with friends at least once a week. It had been one of her happy spots, and stepping back into the familiar smells, the blaring music, the posters tacked up all over the wall of the bathroom stall released a flood of memories. She squeezed her eyes together to hold the tears back and forced up the image of the victorious smirk on the POS's face as he stood beside his car the night of the shooting. She was so close now and there was no time for sentimentalities to take over her mind and sidetrack her mission.

The small restaurant wasn't as packed as Kat knew it would be once the bars closed, but she still had to push her way through a group of people at the counter when she came out of the ladies' room. Ray, the owner, his graying hair pulled into a ponytail at the nape of his neck and a pair of glasses perched on the tip of his nose, was barking orders and snapping his fingers at the pizza makers as always. He looked directly at her as she stepped up, but instead of the wide grin and the, "Ciao cara," he always called out whenever he saw her, he frowned and turned away as if she was an abomination.

Kat swallowed back the sting of his rejection and lifted her chin a little higher.

"Excuse me," she said, when it became clear he was not going to acknowledge her.

Ray called out a name for an order pickup and purposely turned his back to her, pretending as if he hadn't heard her. Kat's spine went rigid and her eyes narrowed. He had always been so friendly and teasingly flirty with her before. But back then she was the perfect picture of a co-ed, not a goth dressed in a Punisher T-shirt.

A fire of injustice lit in her belly and she longed to give him a piece of her mind, but she couldn't afford to make a scene and draw attention. She swallowed her indignation.

"Excuse me, I have a quick question. Can you tell me what's behind the wooden door that's just down from here?" she said bitingly as she leaned over the counter and pointed in that direction. "I'm supposed to meet up with Dean Bradley, you know, the Dean of Students," she added to make sure he knew who she was talking about. "There's no sign on the door, though, and I don't want to barge into a private office."

Ray turned to her, his eyebrows raised as he looked her up and down over the tops of his glasses. "It doesn't have a name. People call it the No Name Bar."

The second he mentioned the name, Kat remembered hearing talk of a bar fashioned after a speakeasy, thus, the absence of a sign. No one ever said it was next door to Tony's, though.

Without saying anything more to Ray, she stomped out of the restaurant and down the sidewalk. She had never been treated like that before, and the rebel inside her had come to life and was steaming. She yanked the wooden door open and stepped in without thinking about what she was doing or that the POS was inside.

The bar was quite a bit smaller than what she expected it to be. Lights were turned low over the four oversized booths to her right and a couple high tables directly across the room from her. But strategically positioned track lighting and hanging pendant lights beautifully spotlighted the focal point of the room, the hand-crafted L-shaped bar and the rich wood wine rack and fully-stocked shelves of liquor behind it. The most notable aspect, however, was the absence of blaring music, the sports highlights on dozens of TV monitors, and the greasy smells of burgers and chicken wings that were standard fare in the bars that catered to the college scene.

Kat stood by the doorway blinking her eyes into focus. It was early and the bar hadn't been opened long, but still, the barstools lined up around the bar were full, except for two—one at the end by the waitress station, the other next to the POS, who sat huddled against the sidewall.

She swallowed back the lump in her throat and adjusted the strap on her shoulder. This was the moment she had been looking forward to and dreading at the same time.

"There's a table in the corner and a couple stools up at the bar, hon," the waitress said as she walked by with a tray of glasses filled with varying hues of amber.

Kat started and tried to smile, but even the muscles in her face had frozen at the sight of the POS. She could feel his evil vibe from where she stood even though he was across the room from her. And no matter how many times she told her feet to move, they remained stuck to the floor.

The waitress stopped again on her way back to the bar. "Are you looking for someone?"

Kat started. "Oh … no, I'm good. Thank you."

Before the waitress could say anything more, Kat awkwardly strode across the room to the empty stool next to the POS.

"Is this stool taken?" she asked the gentleman sitting on the left.

"No, it's all yours," he said with a wave of his hand.

Kat looked to the POS, who was staring intently into his tall glass of dark beer, and paused only a second before pulling out the stool. "Okay, good."

She shrugged off her coat and draped it over the back of the ladderback barstool, hoping to draw the POS's attention to her Punisher T-shirt. She hung the strap of her bag over the back of the stool too, and made sure the title of the comic book, The Punisher #1, was sticking up above the top before she sat down.

Her butt had no sooner hit the stool when the bartender stepped up and asked for an ID. She smiled sweetly at him as she pulled her bag onto her lap and tried not to look nervous. Even though she was legitimately twenty-one in 2017, the ID she had with her was fake, and she knew from experience bartenders were a lot more skilled at picking out a fake ID than car rental clerks. However, when she looked inside her bag for her wallet and saw the comic, she realized it was the perfect opportunity to hook the POS.

"I'm sorry, I've got so much stuff in here it's hard to find my wallet," Kat said sweetly to the bartender, placing the comic on the bar between her and the POS as she dug down deeper into her bag.

Out of the corner of her eye, Kat saw the POS do a double take and crane his neck for a better look at the comic. She handed her license to the bartender and tried not to squirm, but with pure evil sitting beside her and the bartender glancing back and forth from the photo on the license to her, it was hard not to.

When the bartender finally handed her ID back and asked what he could get her, she sagged against the back of the stool in relief without thinking how suspicious that might look. But when her eyes met the bartender's as she released the breath she had been holding, she realized her faux pas.

With a jerk, she straightened her back, grabbed up the table tent that listed the bar's offerings, and ordered the first thing she saw, the Happy Hour special—a beer and a slice of pizza. The bartender nodded without saying anything more and hurried off, as Kat made an extra effort to not outwardly show her relief this time.

Kat took her time rearranging the items in her bag before dropping the wallet back inside to give the POS a few extra minutes to study the comic. By the time she looked up and reached for it, the POS was stretched so far over the bar, he was almost completely off his stool. However, as soon as Kat reached out, he reared back and turned to his beer in one fluid motion, gripping his glass with such intensity it looked like he was fighting an invisible hand trying to take it away from him.

"Are you a Punisher fan?" Kat asked, her hand stalling above the comic.

The POS's cheeks turned a rosy red, but that was the only hint he gave that he heard her question.

Kat pulled the comic in front of her and flipped open the cover. "If you aren't a fan, you should be. Frank is fuckin' awesome!"

The POS shot her a sidelong glance, seemly startled she was addressing him.

"I do like the Punisher," he mumbled, looking back at his beer.

"I thought so!" Kat said with as much enthusiasm as she could muster. "I can always pick out a fan. It's like they have an extra special vibe about them."

The POS darted another sidelong look at Kat, then turned his head to her. Kat involuntarily shuddered as their eyes met, even though he didn't look anything like the psychotic killer she knew him to be. He did, in fact, looked to be more like a bewildered, shy nerd with his brown hair slicked back and his oversized lens glasses. One of those kinds of people who always stood on the outside and never fit in no matter where they went.

"I've been an off and on fan, myself. It was the Born series that really hooked me on Frank and turned me around. It was just so real when he came to terms with his fate and destiny, and finally accepted that was who he was," Kat said, using the writer of the series' own words to make it sound like she knew what she was talking about.

"Now, if only the writers could get to that same conclusion and quit fuckin' around with Frank and trying to change him into something other than what he is, I'd be a lot happier," she added. "I mean that whole Franken-Castle thing ..." She shook her head and scoffed in disgust. "What the hell were they thinking with that? I almost gave up on the whole fuckin' franchise right then and there, let me tell ya. I'm glad I stuck with it, though." Her voice was a pitch higher than normal and she knew she was rambling and talking way too fast, but the POS didn't seem to take notice.

His gaze lowered to the white skull on her T-shirt, which she guessed was because he was too shy to look at her and speak to her at the same time. "Actually, the Marvel Knights series ... do you know that one? Where they turned Frank into an angel?" He shot a glance up at Kat's face. She nodded, even though she had no idea what he was talking about.

He looked back at the skull. "In my opinion, that was the most ridiculous series. Frank is no angel and never will be. He's a broken man who was forced to accept the hatred of the masses by a system that is also broken." His last words came out with such passion they sent another cold shiver down Kat's spine.

"Yeah. Thank God, they ditched both of those series." Her voice sounded like an unintelligible squeak to her ears. She patted the comic and hurriedly added, "This new series is supposed to bring him back to his true self. Or so I've heard. I just got it from my uncle and haven't had a chance to read it yet, so I can't verify that's true. I have high hopes, though. I really like the old Frank best."

The POS's brow furrowed as he stared down at the comic. "I wasn't aware they had released a new one."

"Oh, they haven't. Not yet anyway. It'll be out in the stores in a couple months." Kat looked over her shoulder in the pretense she didn't want anyone to hear what she was about to say. She then leaned toward the POS and lowered her voice. "My uncle owns several comic book shops and has a friend inside Marvel who snuck him a pre-release copy of it. But don't tell anyone. No one is supposed to have access to this yet."

The POS's eyes widened and his face lit up like a young kid who had just been introduced to his hero. He timidly extended his hand, palm side up, and looked up at her with puppy dog eyes. "Would you … could I see it for a moment?"

"Oh, sure." Kat pushed the comic toward him. He picked it up reverently as if it were the Gutenberg Bible, his face shining with a hint of the insanity that would soon completely take over and turn him into a monster. Kat unconsciously scooted back on the barstool until she bumped into the man on her other side.

She ran her tongue around her mouth to bring some moisture back. "Have you heard the Punisher is going to be in the new Daredevil season?" she stammered.

"Yeah. From what I've read, it's going to portray Frank in his true light," the POS said without taking his eyes off the pages of the comic.

"I've heard that too. I'll know for sure tomorrow night after I watch it. I'll let you know how it is … if I see you around."

The POS visibly flinched and his gaze shot up to Kat. "Tomorrow night? It doesn't start streaming until the 18th. How do you get to watch it tomorrow night?"

"For everyone else it starts on the 18th. But for the privileged who have an uncle with friends at Marvel, we get to watch the whole season tomorrow night."

The POS gawked at her, his eyes shining with awe. "That's … Wow …" He laughed a nerdy, huh, huh, huh laugh and looked down at the cover of the comic in his hand. "I'm very anxious to see it." He glanced up through his lashes and right back down. "Do you think your uncle would mind, if … would he maybe let me come over and watch it with you guys tomorrow night?"

The room suddenly shifted and an uneasy, stranger-danger kind of knot twisted in Kat's stomach. Since everything she read about the POS said he was leery of strangers, she expected she would have to wave the bait in front of him several times before he took it. So his agreeing so readily on the first try caught her off guard.

"I don't know. I don't really know you."

The POS's face fell, and in an instant, he shrank back into himself and scooted backward on the stool until the wall stopped him. "Yes, of course, you're right. It was forward of me to ask. I'm sorry," he murmured, turning back to his beer.

Shit! What the hell am I doing? Why did I say that? This is exactly what I wanted. She looked down at her hands. From the second she started putting the plan together, she knew it wouldn't be easy, but she also knew it was the only way to get Michael back. *The sooner I get this over with, the better. So what's the issue? Stop being a coward. Just do it. This is a good thing,* she told herself.

Kat closed her eyes, took in a breath and steeled herself as she turned to him, her lips curled up in a fake smile. "Hi, I'm Olivia Flynn," she squeaked and extended her hand.

The POS slowly turned his head but didn't reach out. Kat left her hand hanging out there, praying she hadn't blown her chance, but fearing she had as he just stared at it. She was about to pull it back, sure she had missed her opportunity, when his clammy hand clasped around hers.

His touch sent a shock up Kat's arm and she felt like spiders were crawling under her skin. It was all she could do to keep from jerking her hand back.

"Patrick James," he replied, giving her hand one quick shake before releasing it.

She shoved her hand under the bar and wiped it up and down her coat.

"Well, hi, Patrick James. It's nice to meet a fellow Punisher fan." She lifted her glass in a mock toast and forced the corners of her mouth up into a smile before she took a big swig to expunge the bitter taste his name left on her tongue. As she wiped the foam from her lip with a napkin, the bartender, who had been hovering strangely close, asked if he could get her anything else. She shook her head and turned back to the POS.

"I guess what my uncle doesn't know won't hurt him? You're not going to run out and post it all over social media, right?"

"No, of course, not. I wouldn't do that." He laughed the same short, staccato laugh. "It's just … the Punisher is a hero to me in a way. I've been looking forward to the new Daredevil season ever since it was announced Frank would be in it. I'll be in your debt, and your uncle's, if you allow me to be in on your viewing."

"I'm looking forward to it too," she said, picking up the slice of pizza and taking a bite even though she was half sick to her stomach. But she needed the few extra seconds to calm her mind and decide how to work her next move. She chewed the bite twice as long as necessary and wiped her mouth with the napkin before she looked back at him.

"I should probably check with my parents and make sure they're okay with you coming over. I don't know what they have going on tomorrow night. I can give them a call right now and let you know in a sec if it's cool."

"Oh sure. I understand. I don't want to impose," the POS added, his face shining with hope.

Kat flashed him a fake smile as she picked up the comic book, tucked it into her bag, and slipped off the barstool. She walked stiffly toward the restroom, throwing a longing glance at the exit door as she passed. Halfway across the room, the bite of pizza moved dangerously into her throat and she ran the last few steps with her hand over her mouth, making into the stall just in the nick of time before it came up.

Once her stomach was empty, she slumped against the stall door. The cool metal felt good on her back, but her stomach continued to roil. She dropped her chin to her chest and tried to conjure up an image of Michael to give her strength, but all she could see was the POS's hopeful face. She shook her head to discard the disturbing image. He wasn't the innocent nerd he was pretending to be. He was a horrific monster. She needed to focus on that and be careful.

She walked to the sink, washed her hands, and rinsed out her mouth. "Get it together. He's evil and should be in hell," she whispered to the mirror. "And the sooner you get this over with, the sooner you'll have Michael back."

Kat stared hard at her reflection, daring herself to do what had to be done. Then with her lips pressed in a line, she gave a nod to confirm her acceptance of the challenge, fluffed up the bangs on her forehead, and walked back to her seat at the bar with her head held high.

The second the POS saw her coming, he jerked up and nearly fell off his barstool. If it had been anyone else, Kat would have laughed out loud at the look on his face, which was that of a little boy waiting to be picked for a team in gym class.

"Good news, my parents have nothing going, so it's fine," she said, slipping back onto the barstool.

His eyes grew round, then turned glassy and he looked down to hide his emotion. "You have no idea how much this means to me. Thank you."

"Oh, I think I know," Kat replied scathingly before she could stop herself.

He lifted his head, his eyebrows raised in question.

"I know because I'm as big a fan as you are," she hurriedly added to cover her mistake.

The question remained in his eyes as he gave a slight nod, then turned to his glass and took a long draw.

Kat internally winced. That was twice she had almost blown it.

"So here's my address," she said jotting it on a napkin and pushing it toward him. "It's the green house behind the one on the corner of 8th Street. You'll see a flagstone walkway leading back from the street. I've gotta work until 9:00, so would 9:30 be okay with you?"

"Sounds good," the POS said, sticking the napkin in his pocket without looking at it.

Feeling suddenly awkward, Kat reached out for the pizza. The mere thought of the greasy slice made her stomach pitch and she picked up the glass of beer instead. The beer didn't want to go down any better than the pizza, but she forced it down as the POS started talking about how Frank Castle was really just a victim of the system.

The more he talked, the more her stomach churned and the harder it was for her to feign interest and pretend to agree. It wasn't long before she knew she had to get out of there or she would throw up all over him. She pushed the beer back, wiped her mouth with the napkin, and gingerly stood.

"I should probably get going. I've got some things I gotta do before work," she said. "It was nice meeting you, Patrick. I guess I'll see you tomorrow night?" she added, forcing the words out.

He looked sincerely distressed she was leaving. However, before he could say anything more, she grabbed her coat and bag and hurried cross the room, praying she could make it out the door before she started gagging.

SIXTEEN

Daniel was no experienced sleuth, but somehow he managed to follow Kat around town without her noticing. Although, he was well aware he couldn't count the feat as a testament to his skill, or even contribute it to luck. She was so focused on the man she was trailing, he doubted she would have noticed if he put a neon sign and flashing lights on his car.

The man she was following looked vaguely familiar to Daniel and seemed to be just as clueless about being followed. But when Kat entered the No Name Bar, Daniel realized his invisibility factor would be coming to a screeching halt. The bar wasn't that big. He knew, because it was one of his favorite haunts. On any given week, he would stop in at least once, sometimes twice, to listen to the musical groups that performed there nightly. He couldn't imagine there being much of a crowd this early, and it wasn't that big of a place, so once he stepped inside, it would be near impossible for him to remain inconspicuous.

He stood in the shadows of the stairwell near the corner of the mall and stared at the door, debating whether he should risk going in or wait for them to come out. Waiting outside was the only sure way to keep Kat from seeing him. But if the event she had come to stop was going down in the bar, he needed to be there.

He balled his hands into fists. If only he knew why she was here. When she told him in the lab her journey was personal, his first thought was that she had come to get revenge on a boyfriend. But after ruminating on it all night long, he no longer believed that to be true. Mainly because he couldn't imagine a tech on the project, who would be well versed in the risks involved, would willing send a girl through the gravity field for something as trivial as a relationship spat. And the guy she had been stalking all day did not look like the boyfriend type. There was no doubt the guy was involved in Kat's mission, but whether he was a friend or foe, Daniel couldn't tell. And the fact the guy looked familiar added an extra layer of mystery.

Fuck this, Daniel thought. Tugging the bill of his baseball cap down low, he tucked his chin, and headed in.

Even in the dim light, he had no trouble picking Kat out. She stuck out like a pumpkin in a basket of lemons, even though she was sitting at the bar with her back to him. The guy she had been stalking was sitting in the last barstool next to her.

Daniel's eyes rounded in recognition. That was how he knew the guy. He had seen him sitting on the last barstool against the wall just like that many times. The guy was always alone and never once did Daniel see him talk to anyone.

With his curiosity aroused more than ever, Daniel strode across the room to the last empty stool on the short end of the bar next to the waitress station.

"Hey, Daniel, what's up?" the waitress said, stepping up to the bar to collect a round of drinks.

"The usual?" Brendan, the bartender, asked right behind her as he placed a napkin down on the highly polished surface in front of Daniel.

"Yeah, sure," Daniel replied robotically, straining to get a glimpse of Kat around Brendan and through the double rack of upside-down hanging wine glasses that inconveniently obstructed his view of Kat's entire head and most of the guy.

Brendan was back in less than thirty seconds and set a tall glass of pale ale in front of Daniel. Daniel bent lower over the glass and motioned for Brendan to come closer. Brendan hesitated, then leaned in, clearly confused by Daniel's actions.

"The girl with the black hair sitting at the bar next to the guy in the corner …" Brendan straightened and started to turn to look. "No! Don't look," Daniel hissed even though Kat was turned away from him and seemed to be totally engrossed with the guy she was talking to.

Brendan frowned. "What's going on? Are you in trouble?"

"No, it's not like that. I just need to find out what that girl and guy are talking about. Could you help me out? Stand over there and listen for a few minutes? Then come back and tell me."

Brendan took a step back. "Look, man, I don't wanna get involved in your domestic problems. That's not my thing."

"No, you've got it wrong. She's not my girl. It's a work issue. I think she … might be trying to sell some of our trade secrets. It would be bad if those secrets got into the wrong hands. Bad for the whole country," Daniel said, hoping the explanation he pulled out of the air didn't sound like a bad movie plot.

Brendan's eyes narrowed and Daniel thought for sure he was going to tell him to fuck off. However instead, Brendan put an elbow on the bar and leaned down, "What do you want me to do?"

"Just stand over there close enough to hear what they're talking about. But don't make it obvious you're listening."

Brendan nodded solemnly and strolled around the corner.

Daniel absentmindedly wiped the condensation off the glass with his thumb, his gaze locked on the distorted view of Kat he could see through the rows of wine glasses. The waitress came around again to see if he was ready for another drink, but after he distractedly brushed her off for the second time, she left him alone.

All of a sudden, Kat rose from her stool. Daniel dropped his chin and brought his right hand up to the side of his face, but she hurried past and went straight into the restroom. A second later, Brendan was back.

"I don't think you have anything to worry about, man. That guy she's talking to comes in here a lot. He's a strange duck, but I don't think he's any kind of spy. All they've been talking about is comic books. So unless your company secrets have something to do with the Punisher, I think you're mistaken."

"Do you know the guy's name?" Daniel asked.

"Sorry, I don't," Brendan replied. "He's always kept to himself and pays with cash. I've never even seen him talk to anyone before now. He doesn't even talk to Wendy," he gestured toward the waitress, "and you know how friendly she is."

Daniel gave a nod. "Okay, thanks. I owe you one. It's a relief to know I was worried about nothing."

"No problem, man," Brendan replied and moved down the bar to help another customer.

Daniel was still trying to figure out what Kat was up to when she came out of the restroom and walked back to her stool at the bar. A short time later, he watched her walk to the door alone. He got up and moved to an empty stool at the corner of the bar so he could get a better look at the guy she had been talking to. There was nothing special about him as far as Daniel could see, but it was obvious he was important to Kat.

Pulling his phone and pretending to check his messages, he snapped a photo and hurried out the door before Kat got too far away.

SEVENTEEN

After a restless night, Kat was up before dawn, sitting at the small desk and going over the final details of her plan. The one thing she hadn't thought to bring along, and was fretting over now, was a photo of the house. She had a decent memory of it as she had driven down the street multiple times before leaving 2017. But imagining it wasn't the same as having a photo. And her memory didn't include some of the minute details she now realized could make or break her mission. Like exactly where to stand for the best shot that would also keep her hidden from the POS.

When her stomach rumbled loudly, she looked down at her wrist and groaned. The front desk had granted her a late check out, but the morning had slipped away from her and now she had only thirty-five minutes to get ready. She hurriedly jammed the papers back into the notebook and jumped to her feet. The room tilted to the side and she grabbed the back of the chair to keep from falling over as she swayed with it.

She closed her eyes and inhaled deeply, waiting for the light-headedness to pass. But when she opened her eyes again, the ugly patterned drapes and orange loveseat were still swirling around her, and her stomach pitched.

Aghh, I don't have time for this! she thought, but the nausea was her own fault. The only real food she had yesterday was the fast food sausage burrito she picked up for breakfast. The couple bites of pizza she had at the bar couldn't be counted since she hadn't kept them down. She had briefly thought of running out to get something to eat right after she got up, but she made the mistake of taking the notebook out of her pack, and before she knew it, she was immersed in the plan for the day and every other thought fled.

Keeping one hand on the wall, Kat made her way into the bathroom. The hot shower helped to clear her head a little and also helped with the achiness in her muscles, but the dizziness stayed with her. The minute she dressed and checked out, she headed straight into the restaurant at the hotel and gorged herself on the biggest breakfast on the menu, knowing it might be her only meal of the day once again.

With real food in her stomach, she felt human again and for the first time since arriving in 2016, not lightheaded. She stood beside the car, her face tilted to the sky, capturing the warmth of the sun. One never knew what the weather would be like from one day to the next in Colorado, but more times than not, it was perfect. This was going to be one of those days.

Kat had nothing to do and all day to go before the POS arrived at the house. Michael had an early morning class on Fridays, and this was the weekend they had gone up to ski Vail. So once again she had missed her chance to get a glimpse of him.

She turned in the direction of the house to take her mind off of her heartache. She didn't really want to go to there in the daylight, but she still needed to figure out where to stand. Feeling a little numb, she climbed into the car and headed toward the cemetery.

Kat drove to a side street on the south side of the cemetery where she planned to park the car later that night. She pulled to the curb, got out, and jogged the short distance to the three-foot wrought-iron fence that boxed in the cemetery. There were several entry gates stationed around the perimeter of the fence for easy access, one just a few feet down from the house, which she planned to use for her quick escape.

She walked through the closest gate, but turned away from the paved paths the city had put in when it took ownership of the cemetery and trudged through the graves. She wasn't meaning to be disrespectful, and actually hated the thought of walking on top of dead people. Her grandmother once told her it was bad luck to do so. But there were a number of joggers out taking advantage of the beautiful day, and since she didn't exactly fit in, she didn't want to give any of them a good look at her.

She took her time meandering through the graves, reading the inscriptions on the headstones. The cemetery was a historical site for Boulder and the final resting place for many of the city's founding fathers, so the markers were old and interesting. She kept her gaze down and zigzagged across the uneven ground, doing her best to avoid walking directly over the tops of the graves.

Once she crossed an arched bridge over a drainage ditch that cut a line through the cemetery, she angled back into the grass and looked up. At that same moment, the toe of her clunky boot caught the raised edge of a flat grave marker.

She felt the jolt, but didn't have time to even flail her arms before she hit the ground hard and the air was knocked out of her lungs. More embarrassed than hurt, she hurriedly pushed herself up to her knees and sat back on her heels to examine her injuries.

The palms of her hands were scraped, but not badly, and her ribs and jaw ached where they had hit the solid ground. She could taste blood in her mouth from her teeth cutting into her lip, but her wrists and arms felt fine and nothing was broken. And that's all that really mattered.

Kat gingerly got to her feet with a groan and straightened her wig that had gone a skew. She silently berated her boots with a few choice words and looked to see if anyone was watching. When her gaze came around to the house, which was no more than ten yards in front of her, her breath whooshed out of her lungs again, this time in a gasp.

"Oh, no … no!" she mumbled, staring at a full view of the house.

Forgetting about her aches, she stumbled the last few yards to the fence and leaned against the metal to keep from falling down. *What the hell happened?*

That question had no sooner entered her mind when the

answer followed. It was September when she found the place and the shrubbery and trees were still filled out with summer leaves. It was early March now, and those same bushes and trees were in their dormant stage and nothing but sticks and twigs.

Kat gripped the metal bar of the fence harder and slowly moved her gaze from left to right, hoping against hope that she was in the wrong place. But no amount of wishing could change the fact that it was the house she had chosen and she was screwed. She had already given the address to the POS and had no way of contacting him to change it.

How could I have been so stupid? She had gone over her plan again and again until it was engraved into the back of her mind, and she was so sure she had covered every little detail that might cause her an issue. Yet she missed the simple fact that it would be a different season.

A car slowed as it passed and Kat realized how bad it looked for her to be staring directly at the house. She spun around and causally walked to a tree a few feet back from the fence. She eased to the ground and leaned her back against the trunk and pulled out her phone to make it appear as if she was just relaxing in a quiet spot. With her sunglasses on, no one could tell she was still forlornly staring at the house.

As her mind raced with thoughts of what to do now, Daniel's words came back to her, "*You can't undo an event that has already become history in your timeline.*"

She stared at the bushes that had been so full when she last saw them an elephant standing within the yard would have gone unnoticed. Now, not even a kitten had a chance of going undetected. She closed her eyes and dropped her head into her hands. Could Daniel be right? Was this the Universe telling her it wouldn't allow her to change things? She didn't want to believe it, but she was finding it harder not to. So many thing had gone wrong since she arrived. But why would the Universe go to all the trouble of sending her back in time if it wasn't to stop the POS?

Kat let her head fall back against the trunk and looked up at the small patches of blue visible through the clusters of green pine needles.

"What is it you want from me? Why am I here?" she whispered and waited for an answer or a sign even though she knew full well one would not be coming.

She stared glumly through the pine boughs, watching the varying hues of green change from moment to moment as clouds crossed in front of the sun. Several birds, who were also enjoying the brief reprieve from the cold weather, sang out to one another from somewhere high up in the tree. One in particular, whose trilling call was more annoying than pleasant, began to grate on Kat's already tense nerves. She tilted her head from side to side to find it, but the abundant clusters of pine needles sufficiently hid the bird from her sight until it hopped down to a lower branch and she caught the movement.

All at once, she sat up and looked back at the house. If the pine boughs could hide a bird so completely, wouldn't they also hide her? Especially at night with her dressed in black?

In one swift move, Kat sprang to her feet and rushed to the fence. She walked back and forth surveying the yard from every angle she could. Most of the trees in the yard had bare limbs, but there were two big Ponderosa Pines that were close together and had many of their long boughs intertwined. They looked like a good option, but she couldn't tell for sure from where she was standing.

She tucked her lower lip under her teeth as she debated whether or not to cross the street and check it out. She really needed to know before the POS showed up. But if someone were to notice her snooping around, they might think she was casing the place—which technically she was.

Kat looked around. The cemetery was deserted at the moment, and from the silence, it seemed the schoolyard that shared the block was as well. She stretched out her fingers, then drew them back into a fist and casually walked through the gate and crossed the street.

A wooden Forest Service sign, one that had been hidden in the brush and tree branches when she was there in 2017, looked out of place in the empty, winter-barren lot. She ambled over, feigning interest in what it had to say, all the while looking through her bangs at the pine trees she had set her sights on. She wasn't close enough to tell if they would sufficiently hide her, though.

Throwing another quick glance over shoulder to make sure there was still no one in the vicinity, she then dashed toward the pines, praying no one was at home in the house. She stopped behind the trees and looked out toward the street. She could see small patches of light through the twined boughs, but couldn't make out any distinctive shapes.

The corners of her mouth turned up in victory, but before the smile could reach her eyes she realized she wouldn't be able to see him through the needles any better than he could see her. That would make it extremely difficult to hit him, especially as her aim wasn't that good in the first place.

Kat rolled her eyes to the sky as the small bit of relief she had felt dissipated. *Come onnn. Can't you just let me have one win?*

She stepped around the tree, a few feet at a time. By the time the stone walk that led up to the house came into view, she was completely out in the open. She pressed her fingernails into her palms to keep from screaming out loud and hurried back to her original position behind the trees.

She studied the trees up and down. There had to be a way to make them work. They were the only real option. She took hold of one of the boughs. Though it looked stiff, it was actually quite flexible. That gave her an idea. She pushed another bough aside and stepped into the void.

Step by step, she wormed her way in until she was completely enclosed within the pine boughs. Several spots on her face burned where the sharp edge of a cone scraped her skin and she could barely move her arms with the tangle of branches pressing in on her on all sides, but she could see the walk.

The small victory was one Kat desperately needed, but she had no time to celebrate, for all at once, the scent of pine became suffocating and the boughs began to feel like restraints. She batted a branch away, but it sprang right back, the rigid needles coming close to poking her in the eye.

Her fingers began to tingle and the cage around her seemed to close in tighter, leaving her with no room to move. She gathered all her strength and struck out wildly, batting at the boughs to get them away from her. But for every branch she pushed away, it seemed two more took its place. Her heart was beating erratically as she shoved with all her might, and at long last she broke free and fell to her knees in the dirt. Gasping for air, she sat back on her heels and dropped her chin to her chest.

From the moment she first realized the POS must die, the only way she could imagine being able to go through with it was if there was an obstacle of some kind between them. Something to distort her view and make him appear as nothing more than an indistinguishable black shape. She had told herself he would suffer more if he didn't know who had done him in. But in truth, by her way of thinking, only killers could look someone in the eye and pull the trigger. And she wasn't a killer. She wasn't like him. That was why the location had been so important to her. But the fates or the Universe, whoever it was running the show, obviously didn't care about her feelings or about the mental anguish she would experience if forced to watch him die.

With a heavy heart, she got to her feet and staggered back across the cemetery. She slumped in behind the wheel of the car and looked in the direction of the house.

"Why are you making this so difficult? You led me to the time machine and planted the idea in my head to come back and stop him. I'm only here because you intervened and helped, and now you've abandoned me. Or have I been wrong about everything?" she mumbled.

Or have I gone completely insane?

As she stared unseeing into space, a memory from her youth floated into her head. It was an old adage her grandmother used to say to her: *"You always face the greatest opposition when you are closest to your biggest miracle."*

A small seed of hope sprouted. *Is that what's happening here, Grandma? Am I close? Cause I really,* really *need a miracle right about now.*

Holding onto that hope, Kat started the car and drove back to the hotel without thinking that she had checked out and had no room to go to. The minute she pulled into the parking lot and it hit her, she turned the car around without a second thought and headed toward Boulder Falls in Boulder Canyon.

The falls had always been her go-to spot whenever she needed to sort things out. She would climb up on the towering rocks and sit amongst the tall pines, letting the mist from the torrent of water cascading over the seventy-foot cliff cool her skin. Whatever was bothering her at the time would magically become insignificant. She knew there was no solution to her current situation, but she hoped a few hours of peace and serenity would help her get through it.

Ignoring the big 'Closed Until Further Notice' sign, Kat clambered over the split-rail fence and made the short hike to the falls. Her favorite spot was higher up in the boulders, but with her boots and the thin layer of ice still coating much of the rock that was shaded from the rays of the sun, her go-to spot was not an option. Fortunately, no one else was around, so there was no need for her to climb any farther to be alone.

She sat on a rock in a patch of sun and watched the water pour over the top and fall into a foaming rage at the bottom. It reminded her of her life that had once been so innocent, but was now such a mess. How had she let that happen? She used to be so strong and knew exactly what she wanted. And she wouldn't let anything get in her way of obtaining it.

The violence of the water pounding into the boulders at the base suddenly felt like it was inside her head. She bent over her knees and covered her ears to block out the roar, but then she could hear the small voice of her conscious, which was as bad, if not worse.

With a low growl rumbling in her throat, she rose and stomped back down the trail to her car, wishing the day was already over.

EIGHTEEN

Kat drove back into Boulder, through campus, past all the buildings she had spent so many class and lab hours in, by her old dorm, and Michael's and several other friend's apartments, hoping the reminder of all she had lost would boost her courage and resolution. But instead, all she came to realize was that the POS had not singlehandedly destroyed her life. He had taken Michael from her, yes, but all the rest she had given up on her own.

That revelation, on top of the guilt and everything else that was crowding her mind, was more than she could bear. She pulled into an abandoned strip mall and sat in her car, staring at the clock on the dashboard, her heart unconsciously jumping each time the hand bounced to the next minute. It had already been the longest day of her life and it wasn't over yet.

It was hard for her to believe that only two days ago she was in the lab with Jeff and excited about her impending journey. Then she arrived and things progressed so much faster than she expected them to. Which was good on the one hand. It meant the whole debacle was almost over and she would soon be going home to resume the life she was supposed to have. But on the other hand, she wished she had more time to get better prepared.

The conflicting thoughts and doubts festering in her mind were making her crazy. She wrapped her arms around her stomach and stared out the windshield, trying to make sense of it all. She didn't notice when the afternoon turned into twilight and then into dusk. The streetlights came on and the parking lot security lights kept the darkness at bay, but still, she sat staring into space until a sudden loud rap on the window next to her ear jolted her out of her daze.

"You okay, girlie?" a gravelly voice said through the glass.

Kat jerked her head around, her eyes wide as she looked through tear-fogged contacts at a bedraggled homeless man wearing a dirty quilted vest over a camouflage jacket. Straggly, gray hair stuck out in all directions from under a grungy, frayed baseball cap that had "Vietnam Vet" embroidered across the front. A long beard covered the lower half of his sun-browned face and was just as straggly and unkempt as the rest of him.

Kat brushed her hand across her eyes.

"Ever thing all right? You needin' some help?" the man reiterated, lines of worry adding to the numerous wrinkles that were permanently etched into the skin around his eyes.

Kat sniffed back the snot about to drip from her nose and returned her gaze to the dashboard. "I'm fine," she mumbled in a voice too low for the man to hear.

The man bent lower and peered through the window, making it clear he wasn't going to leave until he knew she was all right.

Kat internally groaned. *Just go away and leave me alone!*

The man rapped on the glass a little harder. Kat clenched her teeth and turned to face him.

"Just ..." Her words trailed off as she looked into his kind eyes and saw his concern for her. She snorted softly at the irony—a homeless man, who didn't know her from Adam, and who was the obvious one in need of help, was worried about her.

She lowered her head in shame and swiped her fingers across her cheeks, which unknowingly smeared the black streaks of mascara into smudges. Seeing her bag on the seat beside her, she pulled it onto her lap. She didn't have a lot of cash left, but she would be going home in a few hours and wouldn't be needing it anymore. She pulled out two twenty dollar bills and rolled down the window.

"Thank you for your concern, but I'm fine. Really." She held the twenties out for him to take and tried to smile, but it came across as more of a grimace. "It's just been a bad day. It's going to be better real soon, though."

The man straightened and took a step back as if the bills were a snake.

"I wasn't askin' for a handout, girlie. You've been sittin' here for some time, so I thought maybe you was needin' some help is all," he said. "Keep your money and keep them doors locked," he added. Then, with a tip of his head, he limped away, bent over from the weight of his pack.

Kat slumped back against the seat, feeling just as heavy of a weight pressing her down. Before stepping into the time machine, she knew exactly what she needed to do and was prepared to do it. Or so she thought. But she must have inhaled some of the cold gas Jeff pumped into the pod, because ever since she stepped out of the machine, her mind had been in a fog. And now the thought of killing the POS—a living, breathing person, albeit an evil, broken one—made her heart palpitate. That was a huge dilemma.

Oh Michael, I wish you were here to help me decide what to do.

She sniffed and looked down at the notebook she had filled with articles about the shooting that was sticking out of the pack. She picked it up, flipped it open to the first page and read:

> *A school year had ended. For many, a celebration of the final step toward fulfillment of a better future was in full swing.*
>
> *Then, just before midnight on Friday, the celebration turned into a nightmare, and a place of escape became a trap, when a man strode into a bar near the University of Colorado Boulder and opened fired. At least 17 people were killed and 38 wounded, with witnesses describing a scene of claustrophobia, panic, and blood. Minutes later, the police arrested Patrick James, 24, in the bar's parking lot.*
>
> *Witnesses told the police that Mr. James was wearing head-to-toe "tactical gear," including a ballistic vest and leggings,*

> *plus a gas mask and a long black coat. A few seconds before James walked in carrying several weapons, a gas canister was thrown into the bar through the front entrance. There was mass confusion, but as patrons were blinded by the smoke and gas, no one could find the exit. That's when the gunman walked in and said something to the effect of "I am the Punisher," according to one law enforcement official. He immediately began to shoot, pausing at least once, several witnesses said, perhaps to reload, and continued firing.*

The words began to jump around on the page as her hands started to shake and she couldn't read any farther. She closed her eyes. Patrick James had killed seventeen people and injured twice that many that night in April. Fifty-five lives and hundreds more extended family and friends had their lives changed by a single, horrid excuse for a human being. Those lives were now in her hands. She was the only one who knew what was going to happen and the only one with the means to stop it. If she didn't, they would die all over again.

She squeezed her eyes tighter. She had to do it even if it meant being condemn for all eternity. Her stomach twisted at the thought. Was there some kind of dispensation in the universe for a person who was forced into a hideous act in order to save others? Surely, those seventeen lives counted for something, right?

Her Fitbit buzzed on her wrist signaling there was one hour left before the POS arrived at the house. The time for speculation was gone. It had to be done. She had to get ready.

NINETEEN

With all that had gone wrong, Kat was feeling more than a little paranoid and circled the cemetery block twice before turning down the side street where she would leave the car. Lights glowed from the windows of small bungalows and craftsman style homes and dozens of SUVs and luxury cars lined the street, filling every available parking spot along the curb.

Of course there isn't any parking, she silently grumbled, tightening her grip on the steering wheel. She turned down the next block, then the next, and the next without luck. She clenched her jaw and chastised herself for not realizing people would be home from work and school at this time of night. It was another stupid oversight on her part, and this one might actually get her caught.

She slowly drove up and down the streets, going as far away as she felt comfortable, then back until she found a house with an empty space in front. The search took longer than what she had factored in and the pebble of panic in the pit of her stomach had grown into a boulder.

Kat patted the bulge of the gun in her bag, jumped out of the car, and hurried up the street. She had originally intended on cutting through the cemetery as she had done earlier in the day. But there was too much death on her mind as it was, and the thought of walking over graves froze the blood in her veins. She hesitated a second, staring into the darkness, then abruptly turned and moved at a fast clip down the sidewalk to go around the school.

Though the temperature had dropped nearly twenty degrees from the afternoon, all Kat noticed was her footsteps on the concrete, which to her self-conscious ears sounded like a battalion of soldiers marching. She tucked her chin to her chest, letting the hair of the wig fall down over her face, and hurried on, checking the time on her wrist every few minutes.

Once she turned onto the street the house was on, she breathed a little easier as there was no traffic and no sidewalks to amplify her footfalls. The one and only streetlight on this street was at the junction of the chain-link schoolyard fence and the cemetery wrought-iron fence. Her steps slowed and her paranoia escalated as she approached the circle of light. She scanned the area and didn't see anyone, but still, she couldn't shake the feeling she was being watched.

Kat hesitantly moved forward. The house was on the other side of the street no more than twenty yards away and the POS would be pulling up in fifteen minutes. There was no time to dawdle. She filled her lungs with air and held it, but as soon as she stepped into light, her legs nearly gave out. She grabbed for the fence and pulled herself into the shadows, breathing hard as her gaze darted wildly from side to side. The street was quiet, but again the hairs on the back of her neck stood on end with the feeling that someone was watching her.

You've gotta get to cover, so you gotta move, she told herself. She lifted the collar of her coat up around her ears with trembling hands and hurried along the fence of the cemetery, past the house to the corner at the other end of the street. There, she made a show of pulling her keys out of her bag and jingled them in her hand as she crossed to make it appear as if she was heading for one of the parked cars.

She casually strolled past the first car. Then she quickly ducked between the bumpers of it and the one ahead and darted into the trees on the empty lot. She pressed her back flat against a tree trunk and covered her mouth with her hand to muffle her wheezing breaths, but there was nothing she could do about the loud beating of her heart.

A cold, crisp breeze blew through the trees rustling up a few leaves that weren't glued to the still frozen ground. The air chilled her to the bone, but her forehead remained damp with nervous sweat. She twisted her neck and looked around at the two pines she had picked out earlier to judge the distance and the best path to get to them. She was well aware the POS could arrive at any moment, but she wasn't sure her legs would hold her up without the support of the tree behind her.

The lights of a car suddenly streaked through the trees. Kat made a small strangled sound and squatted. The car continued down the street. The next one could very well be the POS, though. With that thought in her head, she gathered her strength, pushed off the trunk, and dashed to the next tree.

She reached the two pines just as a car pulled up and stopped in front of the house. *Shit!* Without a second thought, she reached into her bag, retrieved the gun, and pulled the slide back, chambering a round like a pro. She flicked the safety off and turned her ear to the street, listening for the sound of the car door opening.

Seconds ticked off and Kat didn't move a muscle as she waited for the POS to get out of his car. As the seconds turned into minutes, her trepidation morphed into fear that he was having second thoughts and would leave before she could get off a shot.

"Come on. Get out of the car," she whispered, resisting the urge to step out and see what he was doing. As if their minds were connected, the creak of a car door pierced the silence. Then it slammed shut.

Kat jumped at the sound and almost dropped the gun. She wrapped both hands on the pistol grip and slowly inched around the tree to get a glimpse and make sure it was him. In the darkness, all she could see was the outline of a man standing next to a car staring at the front door as if trying to gather the nerve to go up and knock. He turned his head to the right and then left, and for that split second, his face was lit by the faint light of the streetlight and she could see it was him. But he didn't move. He just stared at the house.

What are you waiting for? she thought, not sure if she meant herself or him. She didn't actually need him to walk up to the house to shoot. But to hit him where he was standing she would have to step out from behind the tree. And if he was looking her in the eye, she didn't know if she would be able to pull the trigger.

She shifted her weight from foot to foot and adjusted her grip on the gun. *Come on. Just move already!*

Again, as if he could hear her thoughts, the POS rounded the car and hesitantly started up the flagstone walk, carrying a six-pack of beer.

Kat held her breath and stepped back into the boughs counting his steps. As soon as she was sure he was past the tree, she edged out until he was in her sights. The thought that only a coward would shoot someone in the back flitted through her head, but being a coward was the least of her worries.

She lifted the gun and aimed for the center of his back. The barrel wobbled in her trembling hands as she slid her finger through the trigger guard. The metal was cold, but her skin burned as it touched the trigger. She suppressed a shudder and adjusted her aim, picturing the bullet to hit in the exact spot as the one that had killed Michael.

This is what you've been waiting for. Pull the trigger.

TWENTY

Daniel followed Kat to the cemetery she had visited earlier in the day. When she circled the block and turned down the same street she had parked her car that afternoon, he drove back to Pleasant Street, parked alongside the wooded lot, and turned off the motor. He had no idea what her intentions were, but it was obvious she was interested in the house, and his gut told him something was about to go down.

He scooted down low in the seat and watched the cemetery, as that was the route she had previously taken. His head was full of possible scenarios, but nothing really made sense. The guy was too unassuming to be much of a threat, physically or romantically. A house in a nice, quiet neighborhood didn't add up either.

With all that was running through his head, he didn't see Kat walking down the street at first. It was a movement in the corner of his eye as she darted out into the streetlight's glow that caught his attention. He sat up and squinted, but the figure had already blended into the shadows and all he could make out was a slight movement along the fence. He relaxed a little as the person walked past the house, but when she came closer and he saw the long, black coat flapping, he realized it was Kat. Cussing his stupidity, he immediately collapsed over the console, though he was afraid he had already been made.

He heard the sound of keys jingling as she approached and

was sure she was coming to give him piece of her mind. The gear shift pressed uncomfortably into his chest and his mind raced to come up with an excuse as to why he was there.

Several agonizing seconds passed, then the sounds of footsteps and keys went suddenly quiet. He looked up at the same moment a shadow dashed past the passenger side window. He waited another second before he raised his head and peeked over the dashboard.

In the darkness, it took Daniel a moment to find Kat as her black attire melded in perfectly with the shadows. When she darted to the two trees she had been interested in earlier, he sat up with a jerk, realizing his suspicions were right. Something was going down. He reached for the door latch, but stopped as a car pulled up in front of the house. He tensed as the guy from the bar got out, but he didn' move until Kat stepped out from behind the trees and pointed a gun.

Kat's hands shook and her vision blurred as the image of Michael's body lying in the morgue swam behind her eyes. The blood had been cleaned off of him and his handsome face was perfect, except his coloring was wrong. His beautiful, olive-colored skin was as white as the sheet. She had never had to identify a dead body before. Never dreamed something like that would ever be asked of her. But his family was out of state and the police needed a quick identification of the victims. The pain and agony of the experience was devastating beyond belief and she wouldn't wish it on her worst enemy.

She swiped the back of her hand across her eyes and tried to refocus. But this time a different image appeared behind her eyes—the POS lying on a gurney with a man and a woman, who she knew to be his parents even though she had never seen them before, standing beside his body, pointing at her and calling out, "Murderer!"

Kat couldn't breathe. The lateral frontal pole, the small part of the brain that ponders the "what ifs" and thinks over what can be done differently, had been silent up to this point. But now, at this incredibly inopportune moment, it decided to kick in. Tears pooled behind her eyes and the gun barrel tilted toward the ground.

Ughh, she silently groaned, gritting her teeth. *This isn't murder. This is stopping one. There's no other way.*

The POS stopped a few feet back from the door of the house, and again just stood there, as if trying to decide whether or not to ring the bell.

Kat adjusted her stance and grip to keep the gun steady. Clenching her jaw, she raised the barrel and lined up the three white dots of the sight to hit the center of the POS's back. Her finger touched the trigger.

Pull it, she commanded. Her finger didn't obey.

The POS reached up and pushed the doorbell.

Kat's heart was beating so hard, she was sure it would break out of her chest any minute. *It's now or never.*

Her finger tightened on the trigger, but came short of pulling it back. She squeezed the grip tighter. The barrel started to wobble again. She clenched her jaw and stared at his back. A second later, she hissed through her teeth and dropped her hand just as the POS was lit by the beam of a porch light and a large man wearing a scowl appeared in the doorway.

Kat instinctively ducked back into the shadows of the tree and came up against a rock-hard, muscled chest. A hand clamped over her mouth as she opened it to scream. Another hand jerked the gun from her hand and snaked around her waist, pulling her close.

"Unless you want to be caught with a gun, you'll stay still and stay quiet. Do you understand?" a man hissed softly in her ear.

She didn't recognize the voice and wasn't sure who had captured her. She gave a slight nod to acknowledge she understood.

"… wrong house. There is no one by that name here," the man at the door said.

"Are you sure?" the POS asked, sounding confused.

The man huffed. "I think I know who lives here and I've never heard of Olivia Flynn. You have the wrong house." With that he slammed the door shut, leaving the POS standing on the doorstep.

The POS stood there for several long seconds before turning and slogging back to his car, his shoulders and head slumped in disappointment.

As soon as he drove off, the hands released Kat. She whirled around and rammed hard into her captor, hoping to knock him down so she could run. He stumbled back a few feet, but caught her by the arm before she could get away. She looked up at him, then her eyes went wide and her mouth dropped open.

"What the hell are you doing here?" she spat after the shock passed.

He lifted the gun and made a show of flipping the safety back in place. "What are you doing here?"

Kat's brow creased in confusion for a second as she stared at the gun. Then her failure rushed back to her and she felt as if an elephant was sitting on her chest. *I let him get away.*

"Oh God, what have I done?" she mournfully whispered.

The world tipped upside down and her knees buckled. Daniel reached out with his free arm and caught her just as she was going down. However, all Kat was aware of was the sea of guilt and pain that had risen up and engulfed her and the faces of the seventeen she had let down that zipped through her mind one by one.

Daniel hastily stuck the gun in the back of his waistband, picked Kat up in his arms and carried her to his car. She remained limp and unresponsive even after he buckled her in. If she had been anyone else, he would have taken her straight to the emergency room to have her checked out. But knowing they would ask questions he couldn't answer, he decided it would be too big a risk.

The scent of apples tickling her nose brought Kat back to reality. She lifted her gaze and blinked until Daniel's piercing eyes came into focus.

"Take a sip of the tea. It will help," Daniel coaxed as he pressed a steaming cup of chamomile tea into her hands.

"Where am I?" She looked around at the unfamiliar sofa she was sitting on and the fluffy, faux Sherpa blanket draped around her shoulders.

"You're in my apartment. I didn't know where else to take you."

"Your apartment?" Kat whispered. All at once her foggy brain cleared. She sat up and twisted side to side like a caged animal looking for an escape. Daniel's hand shot out and grabbed the cup of tea from her as she pushed up from the sofa, but her legs were numb and tingly and she crumbled right back down.

"No." Kat shook her head, scooting away from him until the back cushion stopped her. "Why did you stop me? I needed to shoot him," she stammered.

"I didn't stop you. Although, I fully intended to once I saw the gun in your hand. But you lowered it all on your own before I got to you."

"Why did you want to shoot that guy? Who is he?" Daniel added.

Kat heard only half of Daniel's words, as the anguish of her failure hammered loudly in her head. She covered her face with her hands. "I couldn't do it," she mumbled. "I didn't want to be a murderer like him."

Daniel moved next to her on the sofa and put his hand on her leg. "That guy's a murderer? Did he kill someone in your family?"

A long sorrowful moan came from deep within Kat and her shoulders began to shake. Without hesitating, Daniel gently pulled her to him. She melted into his chest as his strong arms folded around her and she clung to him as tears racked her body.

By the time Kat's torrent of tears ceased, Daniel's hoodie was soaked through, but he continued to hold her as she trembled and sniffed.

Eventually, Kat's exhaustion and the warmth of Daniel's arms reduced the raging storm in her head to a low hum. She felt safe, and that was something she hadn't felt in a long time. But she knew it was only temporary.

She also knew she needed to figure out what to do, but her energy was gone and her eyes were so heavy she could barely keep them open. She tried to stay strong against the temptation of sleep's sweet abyss, but it soon won out and she drifted off.

TWENTY-ONE

Kat shifted and snuggled deeper into the warm body next to her. The arm across her chest was heavy, but it felt good to be held. She hugged the arm and a smile lifted the corners of her mouth as she breathed out, "Michael," with a sigh of contentment.

She buried her nose in the soft fabric of his shirt and inhaled deeply. In the next heartbeat, her eyes shot open and she went stiff. Something was wrong. She moved her eyes side-to-side, but everything was a gray blur. Her contacts were coated with a film from her tears, and on top of that, she had slept in them, so it was like looking through a piece of wax paper. Her other senses were working just fine, though, and she didn't need her eyes to know the man she was snuggled up against was not Michael. This man smelled of Old Spice deodorant and had a faint background scent of Irish Spring soap. Michael only used Axe body products.

All at once, being cradled wasn't as comforting and the arm on her chest felt more like a restraint holding her down. To make matters worse, her brain was also in a fog and she couldn't remember where she was or how she had gotten there.

She tilted her head back and blinked at the man's face. Her eyelids scraped against what felt like sandpaper and his features blurred into one distorted blob. She gritted her teeth and gingerly moved his arm down to her waist, going slowly so she wouldn't wake him.

As soon as she got her arms free, she removed her contacts without thinking she had no case to put them in. Her only thought was to get away, and to do that she had to be able to see. She held her contacts in one hand, rubbed her fingers into each eye, and blinked several times. Once her vision cleared, she looked around. Nothing about the room looked familiar, except for her bag and coat that were thrown over a chair by the door.

Kat closed her eyes and weighed her chances of squeezing out of the man's embrace and getting out the door without waking him. At that moment, the man let out a soft hum right next to her ear and shifted in his sleep, tightening his arm around her. She held her breath, afraid to move.

She remained stiff for what seemed like forever before she twisted her neck and tilted her head back to brave a look at her captor, whose aqua eyes were staring back at her.

Butterflies took to flight in Kat's stomach as they always did when she looked into Daniel's eyes, and for a moment she was lost. But then the events of the previous night returned. She pushed away and broke out of his embrace.

Heat raced up her neck to her cheeks. "You were following me?" she asked, glaring at him.

His eyebrows rose and he shifted to sit up a little straighter. "Yes, I followed you. From the time you left the lab."

Kat's mouth dropped open, then closed as he nonchalantly sat there acting as if he had done nothing wrong. "What the hell? Who do you think you are?" she spat, her nostrils flaring with rage.

Daniel bristled at her tone. "I'm a physicist who knows a hell of a lot more about how time and the universe works than you do. *That's* who I am."

Kat jerked back as if he had slapped her in the face. "Yeah, well ... you have no business interfering in my affairs!"

Daniel's face instantly turned hard. He placed his elbows on his thighs and leaned over them. "It became my business the second you stepped into the time machine I had a hand in building. I told you when we first met, altering an incident that had already taken place can lead to an unpredictable chain of events, which could have dramatic consequences in the universe. I wasn't going to sit back and let you cause irreparable damage without at least trying to stop you."

"You don't need to worry about stopping anything because I—" The rest of the words stuck in Kat's throat and she couldn't finish the sentence. She fell back against the sofa and covered her face with her hands. "Oh God, I've ruined everything," she muttered between her fingers.

"Look, I'm sorry for your loss." Daniel struggled to find the words to ease her anguish, but he had no experience with grief stricken females. "I've never personally known anyone who's been murdered, so I don't know what you're going through. But I think you're being too hard on yourself. Killing another person is not as easy as you might think. If you had succeeded, you would have just traded one torment for another."

"It was the only way to save Michael," Kat whispered.

"That wouldn't have kept it from haunting you any less. My dad was in Nam. He never talked about it to anyone until a couple years ago. It's still hard for him, even now after forty-five years. He had to kill a lot of the VC to keep them from killing him and his friends back then and he still has nightmares about it to this day. The guys who have come back from Iraq say the same thing. It's traumatizing to take another's life, even if they are an enemy. They say the remorse stays with you the rest of your life." He scooted a little closer and reached out a hand, then thought better of it and pulled it back.

"I don't really know you, but you don't seem like the type that's capable of murder and can then just forget about it. And just imagine, if someone who's been trained to kill has difficulty coping with the aftermath, how do you think you would fare?"

A part of Kat's brain knew he was right, but it didn't make it any easier to accept. She thought her love for Michael was strong enough to give her the ability to do anything. Mothers have been known to lift cars to save their child, so she should have been able to shoot the POS to save Michael. But again, she was wrong. And knowing that was almost as upsetting as knowing he would die all over again.

"You don't understand," Kat said after a lengthy pause. "Patrick James isn't just a guy, and he didn't go into a war zone. He's going to walk into the Bison Bar with an M&P15 assault rifle on April 29th and kill seventeen people. Thirty-eight others will be seriously injured."

Daniel's eyes widened and his lips parted in shock.

"My boyfriend, Michael, was one of the seventeen. He had just finished his senior year at CU and was going to walk the next weekend. He had his whole life ahead of him, and then it was gone. I came here to get it back for him. I was going to kill James so he couldn't kill the others. But I … I couldn't do it." The last words were filled with tears. Kat swallowed hard and lifted her gaze to Daniel's face. "I was too chicken to pull the trigger and now they're all going to die because of me."

"Oh, come on. You can't possibly believe that nonsense. You aren't responsible for their deaths," Daniel broke in.

"But I am. I know what's going to happen. And I had the opportunity to stop it, but I couldn't do it simply because I didn't want to be thought of as a murderer. I ruined my one and only chance, 'cause even if I did manage to get James to talk to me again, he'd never trust me enough to follow me out to another secluded spot."

Daniel didn't know what to say or what to think. He had gone through a range of moods over the past two days, from shock that the machine had actually worked and brought someone back through time, to indignation that Kat was using the machine for her own petty vendetta, to fear of how her actions would affect the future and the universe. But now his only thought was to comfort her.

"Killing James isn't the only way to save your boyfriend, you know. Why not just stop Michael from going to the bar that night?"

Kat gave a slight shake of her head. "I won't be here at the end of April. The machine blows up on March 20th, remember? If I'm not back before then, I'll be stuck here with no life at all, because the other me will be living my life."

A muscle in Daniel's jaw twitched. "Okay, so you need to think of another way. You still have what … nine days to figure it out? We should be able to come up with something else in that timeframe if we put our heads together." He was grasping at straws and he knew it, but she had touched something within him and he didn't want her to leave.

Kat snorted and looked to the ceiling to keep from crying. "I don't have enough money to stay here another nine days. The hotel room is almost double what I planned for. I also have the cost of the rental car, so there's only enough cash left for two more days at best."

A heavy silence settled between them. Daniel knew he could solve her money problem in an instant by offering her his place. He could also drive her around to wherever she needed to go, so she could return the rental car. But he already felt a strong need to protect her after just one day and he wasn't sure he could afford the emotional cost of having her near twenty-four hours a day for another week or more.

Kat rose from the couch. "It was wrong of me to dump my problems on you. I think I should probably just go. Thanks for the use of your sofa. I hope … I hope you aren't going to lose your job because of me."

She had no idea where she would go and she was in no rush to get back to 2017, but it was bad enough she had messed up her own life. She didn't want to be responsible for messing up Daniel's life too, although she feared it may be too late for that. She had already given him more information about the future than he should know.

She wearily picked up her coat and bag and turned to the door. Just as she reached for the knob, she remembered her car was still parked on the street by the cemetery. Her hand paused on the knob as her muscles involuntarily spasmed with the thought of walking back to get it.

"If you were to stay here, you wouldn't have to worry about money."

Daniel's words broke through Kat's thoughts, but she didn't turn around.

"You could save even more if you return the car and used mine. That'll give you the days you need to figure out how to save your boyfriend," he added.

Kat turned to face him, a sliver of hope shining on her face. But seeing him standing by the sofa made her think of the sacrifice he would be making for her.

"Aren't you the physicist who doesn't believe the past can be changed?" she asked softly.

Daniel flushed, but the left side of his mouth turned up in a sly smile at the same time. "Yes, I am. But what scientist wouldn't take an opportunity to prove his theory is right when it's presented?"

Kat had to force herself to look away. She needed to be able to think clearly and she couldn't do that if she was looking into his eyes. "Your theory could also be wrong, you know."

"That's true. There's always that possibility." He gestured to the bookshelves against the wall. "Half of those books over there are proof of that. They're filled with theories that have since been proven wrong. That's part of being a scientist, encountering a setback or two … or ten."

Kat knew he was trying to lessen the tension in the room with a little humor, but she was in no mood to joke around. There were too many important decisions needing to be made and she kept going back and forth between whether or not to accept Daniel's offer. She desperately wanted the extra days to finish the job she had come to do. At the same time, she was afraid she wouldn't be able to pull the trigger, even if by some miracle she could get the POS to agree to meet up with her again. And her guilt would be ten times worse knowing she had messed up Daniel's future for nothing.

A hand suddenly took hold of hers. She tensed at his warm touch, but didn't pull away as his fingers curled around hers. She stopped herself from looking up, though. If she did, she would just be drawn into his spell again.

"I've never believed Michael was supposed to die that night.

He shouldn't have been there. We were going to have dinner with my parents, but we got in a fight. I think a higher force in the universe knows his death was a mistake too, and it sent me here to correct that mistake. That probably sounds ridiculous to you, but so many things have happened to support my belief. Unexplainable things, like following you into Mallory's lecture where I learned about the time machine."

"Me?" Daniel interrupted.

"Yes, you." Kat nodded her head. "I didn't know who you were, or I didn't think I did, but something compelled me to follow you. Then I learned that Jeff, a friend of Michael's who I didn't even like, worked at the lab. He's the one who ended up helping me, and if you knew him, you'd know that was totally out of character." She shrugged. "It seemed the Universe had mapped out every step for me. It just all fell into place so easily back there and I thought it would be the same here—I come, shoot James, and get back home without anyone being the wiser. But you were in the lab when I arrived."

She paused to swallow the tears that had suddenly congregated in her throat.

"Now, because of me, your future will be changed. I think … I actually might be the reason you left this job. It kills me to think I ruined things for you, but then if you hadn't left, Jeff wouldn't have taken your place and I wouldn't have had someone on the inside to get me here. So that makes me wonder if you're part of the Universe's plan. Or was it just an unfortunate coincidence you being in the lab?"

She sighed. "It was so simple in 2017. Now it's all convoluted and confusing, and it's making me crazy. And I hate that the Universe dragged you into this without your consent. It's not fair and not right that you're now going to have to pay the price too."

"So you're saying you think God is in the murder business and He's designated me as the hit man?" Daniel butted in.

Kat started and lifted her head to deny Daniel's statement, but then she saw the glint in his eye and the smirk on his lips and knew he was just messing with her. She glowered at him in return.

"I'm kidding!" he said, tightening his hold on her hands as she tried to pull away. "Look, I don't like to stomp on anyone's religious beliefs. If you want to believe there is a higher being up there in Heaven acting as a puppet master, controlling everyone on this earth and every event that takes place, that's your prerogative. But then you also have to believe there was a reason why I was in the lab on Wednesday and that I am part of the plan. And you have to accept my help. That's all there is to it."

Kat was too exhausted to even try to think through what he was saying. She shifted from one foot to the other to get some feeling back in her legs, but her whole body seemed to be on the verge of shutting down.

"You don't know me very well, but I can assure you I'm no one's pawn," Daniel stated matter-of-factly. "No one controls my future or forces me down a path I don't want to take. When and *if* I leave this project, it will be because I no longer believe in it, or I no longer feel I have anything to contribute. Neither of those reasons have anything to do with you."

"You don't know that," Kat whispered.

"I do," Daniel replied vehemently, giving Kat's hands a small shake. "I was at the lab late on Wednesday because I was concerned about some minor fluctuations in the gravity chamber that had recently shown up on the graphs. No higher being had anything to do with that. I was there on my own accord, doing my job as I'm paid to do. And I'm glad I was. I wouldn't have met you if I hadn't been there."

Kat looked up into his eyes that radiated intelligence, but also vulnerability, love, and fear, and her heart lurched with a sudden longing that scared her.

"Look, let's go pick up your car, then come back here and get a few more hours of sleep," Daniel added, seeing her hesitation. "It's only 1:30. And if you're like me, you can't think straight when you've had so little sleep. You can take my bed and I'll take my roommates'. He's at his girlfriend's and won't be back until Sunday. Then, in the morning we can discuss this rationally. Between the two of us, I'm sure we'll be able to come up with something. How does that sound?"

In Kat's current state she didn't have the wherewithal to argue or object. She was barely able to direct him to her car, and thank God he drove slow on the way back to his apartment so she didn't lose him.

Once inside, she dumped her two bags beside the door and stumbled into the bedroom after him. Her boots and her coat were the only things she removed before she fell onto the bed.

Daniel went to get a blanket from a closet. When he came back a minute later, she was already asleep. He stood beside the bed for a minute as a mixture of emotion splayed across his face. He then walked into the second bedroom, flopped down on the bed, and fell into a deep sleep almost as fast as she had.

TWENTY-TWO

Kat's eyes were red and swollen as she stood rigid between her two lawyers and stared at the round seal of the State of Colorado hanging on the wall behind the judge as he shuffled papers around on the bench and prepared to read her sentence. Her mom, dad, Cathie, and Michael sat in the first row directly behind her. Her mom was sniffling, her dad was silent and stoic, but Kat could feel his disappointment and pain burning into her back.

"The court is satisfied beyond a reasonable doubt that the defendant, Katelyn Michelle Chambers, is guilty of first-degree murder." The judge looked over the rim of his glasses that were perched low on his nose. "Ms. Chambers, I have never seen a more impenitent defendant come into my courtroom. You cruelly and callously took the life of a man who had caused you no harm, and from all indication, who you didn't even know. Yet throughout the trial you have shown no empathy. I find that reprehensible, and so, in compliance to the laws of the 20th Judicial District Court in Boulder, Colorado, I hereby order ... for the offense of the murder of Patrick James ... that the defendant, Katelyn Michelle Chambers, spend the rest her life in prison with no eligibility of parole," the judge stated and struck his gavel on the sound block.

Kat jumped and her eyes shot wide open, then fixed on the thin strips of sun leaking through the slats of the closed blinds. Her heart raced with fear and shame from the dream. She rolled to her back with a loud groan and cupped her face with her hands, her fingers steepled over her forehead.

"Oh God, whatever made me think I could kill someone?" She asked herself, and then, "What am I going to do now?"

There was a light rap on the door. She raised her head just as the door cracked open.

"Oh good, you're awake. I thought I heard you in here," Daniel said from the doorway.

Kat instinctively pulled the blanket up to her chin to hide herself even though she was fully clothed.

"I've made coffee if you'd like some," he added, lifting his cup as if she needed proof. "And I thought you might like your backpack." He raised it in the air as well before setting it on the floor against a chest of drawers next to the door. "The bathroom is right through that door. Come out whenever you're ready," he added, pulling the door closed as he turned away.

Kat didn't know why Daniel was being so nice, especially since she hadn't been. She didn't deserve his charity, or anyone's for that matter. She was an awful person and an even worse friend. She should just go home before she completely destroyed his future too.

She forced herself to get out of bed, wash her face and brush her teeth, but she didn't bother to change her clothes. Then with her pack slung over her shoulder, she walked into the living room with the full intention of leaving.

Daniel had on the same shirt he had been wearing the night before too, and tufts of his hair were standing on end. At the sound of the bedroom door opening, he jerked up, and in one swift move slammed shut the notebook he'd been perusing and set it on a TV tray that substituted as an end table.

Kat immediately recognized the notebook as her POS album and frowned. She hadn't noticed it was gone from her pack. "You went through my backpack?" she accused incredulously, her gaze going from the album to Daniel.

He hastily rose. "No! I wouldn't do that."

Kat marched to the table, picked up the album, and held it out. "So you're saying this jumped out of my pack, walked over, and threw itself in your hands?"

Daniel flushed and shoved his hands into his jean pockets. "I didn't go through your backpack. It fell out on the floor when I picked up the pack to take into you. I know I should have put it back, but it opened to an article on James and … " He shrugged his shoulders.

Kat glared at him for a long moment, trying to foster a sense of indignation, but she was too drained to care. And it didn't matter anymore anyway. She stuffed the album into her backpack and walked to the door.

"Where are you going?" Daniel asked as she reached for the door knob.

"Home," Kat answered simply and pulled the door open.

"What about James?"

Her knuckles turned white on the door knob and she closed her eyes. She didn't want to discuss her failure anymore. "It's over. I blew my chance," she said through the tears that clogged her throat.

"You're giving up?" His tone sounded almost accusatory.

Hearing someone else say it out loud made it sound even worse than it did in her head. She stepped over the threshold.

"Where is James now in your time. In 2017?" Daniel called out.

Kat paused. What possible difference did it make where the POS was? "Where do you think he is?" she snapped. "He's in jail, where he'll be for the rest of his life," she added without turning around.

"Exactly!" Daniel hastily crossed the room. "James didn't kill himself like so many shooters do. And he wasn't killed by the police. That's why you couldn't kill him."

Kat gave Daniel a quizzical look over her shoulder.

"Come back in, please. Let me explain," he added.

Kat didn't move or say anything, but her hesitation spoke volumes. Daniel took hold of her elbow and gently pulled her back into the room. When she didn't resist, he guided her to the sofa and gently sat her down on the edge of the cushion. He sat next to her, facing her, their knees almost touching.

"Unless you've studied physics it's not easy to understand, so you're going to have to trust that I know what I'm talking about. Stephen Hawking … you know who he is, right?" She gave a slight nod and he continued. "Hawking came up with a hypothesis called the Chronology Protection Conjecture. It states the laws of physics will prevent time travel on all but submicroscopic scales. In other words, the universe will not allow anyone to change the past."

The blank look on Kat's face and the skepticism in her eyes made it clear she wasn't grasping what he was saying.

"Look … let me put it this way. You couldn't kill James because if you had, it would violate the laws of physics and blow apart the basis of our existence. So the universe went into self-protection mode, so to speak, preventing you from pulling the trigger and changing the future."

Kat shook her head and turned her eyes to the ceiling to keep from crying. "So what you're saying is, there's no point in me staying because the universe is against me?"

"Yes, I mean, no. There is a reason for you to stay." He picked up Kat's backpack lying on the floor next to her feet, pulled out the album, and opened it to the first article on the bar shooting.

"According to these articles, James had planned his attack for months." He flipped a couple pages and pointed to a photo showing multiple homemade bombs in James' apartment. "He went to great lengths and intended to kill a whole lot more people than he did. The guy had over six-thousand rounds of ammunition, a hundred round magazine, body armor and other tactical gear, and all of it ordered online."

Kat gazed down at the photo and back up at Daniel. She was not following him, but from the satisfied look on his face, he obviously thought he was on to something.

"Don't you see? There are a lot of bombs in these photos. To create that many in the next six weeks, he would have to have the equipment on hand or ordered by now. He might even be in the process of assembling the bombs as we speak. Also, the stuff he ordered online, and possibly even the guns we know he purchased, could be in his apartment right now. Or some of it probably is. And the authorities would be interested in knowing that, don't you think?"

A small fissure of understanding cracked the thick wall Kat had erected in her mind, but it wasn't enough to make her fully grasp his line of logic.

"I thought you just said the laws would prevent us from doing anything to him."

"That's not what I said. I said the laws won't allow you to change James' future. In the future, he goes to prison. So we just need to see that he still gets there, which should be no problem if we show the police what he is planning. This way the future remains the same and the universe will be happy."

Kat looked back at the photo as she mulled over what he said. "The sentence for planning a murder isn't the same as carrying one out, is it?" she asked.

"Probably not. I don't know the law, so I can't say what his sentence might be. The bombs will elevate the charge to a higher offense than a straight shooting, though. As far as they know, he could be planning to use the bombs in a terrorist attack. They take the threat of terrorism very seriously, and a charge like that would come with a decent amount of time, I'm sure.

"But it doesn't matter how long his sentence is. He just needs to be in jail in April so this doesn't happen." Daniel pointed to the album. "And with the evidence I've seen in this book, I think it's safe to say we've got enough to put him there."

"Not we," Kat corrected. "Just me."

"But I—"

"No!" Kat held her hand up, palm out. "I appreciate you wanting to help, but I can't let you jeopardize your future any more than you already have. I don't want you on my conscience too."

Daniel's eyes darkened to the color of a stormy sea. "Like I told you before, no one but me has any say in my future. And what makes you so sure my future will be affected if I help you anyway?

I already know what happens. I've read through the list of victims' names and I don't know any of them. I've never been in that bar either, so my life is not directly affected whether James does or does not shoot up the place."

As soon as those words came out of his mouth, he realized how bad they sounded. "Look, you just can't call up the police and say, "Hey, I know this guy who is going to shoot up a bar.""

Kat shrunk back. That was exactly what she had planned to do.

"Come on … you can't possibly think it's going to be that simple?" Daniel asked incredulously after seeing her reaction. "They don't know who your are. As far as they know, you could be a crazy person or a jilted girlfriend looking for revenge. If you want them to take you seriously, you're going to have to give them proof the threat is real."

"You have the facts to substantiate your claim, but you'll need to go through all these articles and pull out just what James has done up to this point in time." He patted the album. "If you include something he buys or does in a week or two from now, they won't find it and that could lead them to believe the tip isn't legit. And with your strict timeline, it's going to take both of us to pull it all together."

Kat blinked, stunned to hear how much thought he had put into this, and for a moment, she couldn't speak. She had always thought his eyes were beautiful, but it seems his character was too.

Why couldn't I have met him earlier?

Immediately following that thought, a rush of cold seized her to her core. She hurriedly looked away so he couldn't read her face and know what she was thinking.

What's the matter with me? I'm about to get Michael back. I can't be daydreaming about Daniel. Michael is the only man I want.

"Not true," a small voice said in the back of her mind, but she purposely ignored it.

"What if the police don't act on the tip?" Kat asked.

He shrugged. "There's always that chance. But with the increase in mass murders that have taken place over the last decade, they'll likely look into it. I think what it will come down to is how much of this information we can pass along and how much evidence they can collect right now."

Kat's brows drew together. She hadn't thought about that. *Shit, I would have blown another chance!*

She looked down at the album Daniel was still holding. This was her problem and she hated the thought of bringing him into it, but he was right. She did need help. And he already knew what was going to happen so his future had already been affected. She reached for the album.

"What do you think we should we start with?" she asked, looking up at Daniel. His face lit up with the cutest little smile and she couldn't help but smile back, even though she wasn't happy with the idea of involving him in her mess.

TWENTY-THREE

Daniel's apartment was a typical single man's abode in that it had minimal furniture, all of which had seen better days. He had no kitchen table, so they had to spread the articles out on the coffee table after he cleared it of his own papers and books. It didn't take them long to fill the coffee table and soon the floor was cluttered with papers as well.

They worked side-by-side late into Saturday, pouring over the information in the articles and piecing together a timeline of his activities, taking only a quick break to return the rental car. Every one of the articles documented the results of the attack. Many mentioned the POS had prepared for months and listed some of his preparations. But as it turned out, only one article had the actual dates of purchases and only for three of the items.

Kat had been sitting cross-legged on the floor for over two hours when she let out a groan of frustration and threw her pen, which landed in an empty pizza box laying on top of a pile of papers.

The POS had purchased the gas mask kit on February 28th and the ballistic chaps and groin protector a week later. But he didn't order the ballistic vest and throat protector until April 2nd, so that took the confirmed items they could use down to two.

More importantly, they found no dates of purchase for the most damaging items in his arsenal—the 100-round magazine, the guns, the massive amount of ammunition, and the bomb making materials. Though they were both certain some of it was already in his apartment, they had no way of knowing what was and what wasn't.

"The police aren't going to do anything just because he bought a gas mask and some ballistic gear. We need to know about the big stuff, like the guns. I'll bet anything he has some of it stashed in his apartment right now, but how are we going to know? And all the stuff he's ordered online … we need to find out when he did that." She looked around at Daniel, who was lying on the sofa. "You don't happen to know how to hack into a credit card company so we can look into his account, do you?"

"Yeah, no … sorry. That's not my forte," Daniel said, rolling his head from side to side to stretch his neck. "I do know how to pick locks, though," he added in jest.

Kat perked up and twisted around to face him. "You can break into his apartment?" Her voice came out as a squeak.

Daniel paused in mid-stretch. "I was joking. I don't break into people's homes."

Kat rose up on her knees and sat back on her heels. "But do you really know how to pick a lock?"

He slowly turned his head and looked at her. "Yeah … in my first two years of undergrad I worked in the lock shop at Northern Arizona. But that—"

"So you could actually break into his place and see what he has?"

He abruptly sat up. "Look, just because I *know* how to pick a lock doesn't mean I go around doing it. Talk about changing my future! If I get arrested for breaking and entering, my future will definitely get changed."

"But you won't get caught. We'll wait in the parking lot for him to leave. Then I'll stay in the car and be the lookout while you go in and check out his room."

As Daniel slowly shook his head side-to-side, Kat jumped up, hurried to the sofa, and plopped down beside him.

"It's not like you'll be stealing anything. You're just going in there to see what he has as far as weapons and equipment and such.

Ooo, you might even be able to find a copy of his credit card bill, to show what he's ordered. You'd be in and out in five, maybe ten minutes max, and we'd have everything we need to put him away."

Daniel opened his mouth to respond, but Kat went on before he could say anything.

"I know this is asking a lot," she stated as if having read his mind. "But please don't say yes or no yet. We've had a long day and this stuff is totally draining. And we shouldn't make a major decision like this when we're not one hundred percent. So let's both sleep on it and discuss it again tomorrow. We can't do anything tonight anyway, and things might look different in the morning. Or maybe one of us will have an epiphany overnight that will solve the problem. "

Daniel drew his hand down over his face. "You're right. There's a lot to think over and we could both use some sleep," he said.

Kat hadn't realized how much tension she was holding in until it flowed out with his words. But as the silence grew between them, an uncomfortable feeling settled in.

"If it's okay, I think I'll head to bed now. I'm really tired," she said rising. She stood beside the sofa to see if he would say anything more, but he remained silent. "Okay … I'll see you in the morning," she added awkwardly.

Once inside the safety of the bedroom with the door closed, she pulled off her wig and wig cap, threw them on the dresser, and collapsed on the bed. She had kept up with the disguise, thinking Daniel already knew too much about the future. Plus, she was afraid it would be awkward if they met in the future. And she wouldn't know how to explain Daniel to Michael.

She stared up at the ceiling and raked her fingers through her long, tangled hair. She had been so certain of what she was doing when she left 2017. But not much had gone the way it was supposed to ever since she arrived in 2016, and she was no longer sure of anything.

"So is this what you had planned? Did you put Daniel here to help me?" she whispered. "Cause I gotta tell ya, keeping me in the dark is not working so well. How about a sign or something since you obviously have a specific plan in mind. It's just wasting everyone's time and energy to let me bungle things and then go back and try to fix em."

She dropped her forearm across her eyes. She wanted so badly to believe her being here was proof the Universe was on her side and it would help her succeed. But it was getting harder to hold onto that belief.

Please don't let the POS destroy all those lives. Help me find a way to get him arrested.

She didn't think she would be able to fall asleep with all that was on her mind, but the stress and tension was as good as a sleeping pill. Her thoughts began to blur together and it wasn't long before she was lost in the world of dreams, sleeping in her clothes for the second night in a row.

TWENTY-FOUR

Kat woke with a start and clutched a handful of sheet. She blinked up at the ceiling and tried to calm her beating heart from the terror of another nightmare. In this one, she had lost Michael and was running from place to place trying to find him, stopping only to ask their friends and his professors if they had seen him or knew where he was. No one, not even Cathie, knew who she was talking about. No one had ever heard of a Michael Bellwood. He didn't exist to anyone but her.

She took in a shaky breath and blew it out slowly, fixing her gaze on a large art print of a guitar on the wall. She stared at it for several minutes before realizing it wasn't a guitar at all. It was the sun setting behind a grove of trees growing on the banks of a body of water. The contour shape of the trees, the sun setting on the horizon, and the reflection of both in the water formed the illusion. As she studied the trees that shaped the body of the guitar and the skyscrapers that formed the tuning pegs on the head, the last of the dream faded into the abyss, but the tightness in her chest remained.

Beyond the door she could hear the sound of water running in the kitchen. Daniel was up, and from the sound of it, was making coffee. She closed her eyes and rolled to her side as a fresh wave of guilt gripped her.

She knew she should leave and let him get on with his life, but the odd connection she felt with him stopped her every time.

She had never felt such a bond with anyone before, not even Michael. Daniel had found a way in and now held a permanent place in her heart, and it happened so quick it sort of scared her. But at the same time she liked having him there. He made her feel safe and loved, although she couldn't explain why.

But it wasn't up to her anymore anyway. Asking him to commit a crime was probably the final straw to push him over the edge. It wouldn't surprise her a bit if he was waiting for her to get up, so he could tell her to leave.

Kat heaved a sigh as she gingerly swung her legs off the bed and staggered into the bathroom like a drunk. She stood in front of the sink and looked forlornly at her reflection in the mirror. The girl staring back with the pale skin, dark circles under her eyes, and hair that was partly matted to her head and partly sticking out in all directions looked like a thirsty vampire without the fangs. The only thing left of her old self, her blue eyes, showed her disgust.

She turned away, stepped out of her clothes and into the shower. She took her time, standing in the hot spray twice as long as usual. She then dressed in her last clean outfit, a black T-shirt and black skinny jeans. With extra care, she applied her makeup and shoved her hair up under the wig cap. She wished she didn't have to wear the wig, but a little voice in her head insisted she not let Daniel know what she truly looked like.

After making the bed, she looked around the room for something else to straighten up. She was stalling and she knew it, but she didn't know where she would go when he told her to get out. She looked at the door, then squared her shoulders, and walked into the living room.

Daniel was sprawled out on the sofa, talking on his phone.

"... I'll let you know." He looked over his shoulder at the sound of the bedroom door opening. When he saw her, he sat up and hurriedly added in a lower voice, "It shouldn't be more than a few days, but it all depends on how it goes." He paused to listen.

Kat's stomach dropped. Was he talking about her? Who was he talking to? She walked into the kitchen as casually as she could, pretending she hadn't heard what he said.

"That's great. I appreciate it. I'll keep you posted." Another pause. "Yeah, thanks. Bye."

Kat's mind was in such a whirl she missed the cup as she poured the coffee.

"Damnit!" she spat as she set the pot down, grabbed a sponge from the sink, and quickly mopped up the coffee. She turned back to the sink just as Daniel stepped up and they nearly collided.

She looked up into his bloodshot eyes that had dark bags under them and a wave of guilt sent a rush of heat to her cheeks. She forced the corners of her mouth up in a smile, doing her best to act normal.

"Good morning," she chirped sweetly and looked down as she stepped around him so he wouldn't see the anxiety on her face.

Daniel crossed his long legs, leaned his butt against the other half of the sink, and watched her, saying nothing. Kat became even more nervous under his penetrating stare and clumsily dropped the sponge twice as she rinsed it out. He didn't seem to care and didn't move, forcing her to step around him again to get her coffee. She wrapped both hands firmly around the cup before she turned back to face him.

His jawline was outlined with dark stubble and his hair was tousled from sleep, but he looked sexier than he ever had. Her cheeks and ears began to burn. She dropped her eyes as she lifted her cup to blow on the hot coffee, praying he couldn't tell how flustered he was making her.

"How did you sleep?" Daniel asked breaking the silence.

"Um …" She looked up through her bangs. "… good."

"I'm glad someone did. I slept lousy."

Kat's hands started to shake. She rapidly set the cup on the counter. "I'm sorry. I told you I would take the sofa—"

"No, it wasn't that," Daniel said cutting her off. "I woke up at three-thirty thinking about things and couldn't get back to sleep."

Kat felt weak and sagged against the counter.

"Did you know your physical presence here violates the second law of thermodynamics, which states entropy, which is basically the degree of disorder, can't be decreased in a closed system such as the universe? So according to what I've held to be true, you shouldn't have been able come. But here you are. And there is no research, data, or test results for me to fall back on to give me an inkling of what to expect now."

Kat suddenly couldn't breathe.

He uncrossed his legs and pushed off the counter. "You say I led you to the time machine in 2017, and then I was in the lab when you came through. Since I don't believe in coincidences, I can only assume this joint path we are on was predestined. The scientist in me wants to believe the laws placed me in your way to protect the past. My heart is telling me we were brought together so I could help stop the atrocity James has planned. That's the dilemma that kept me up most of the night. How do I make an analytical decision without facts or data to support either side?"

Kat stared at him wondering if she was supposed to answer. But he went on.

"I can't, so I have to throw them both out, which leaves me with only my conscience. It tells me if I do nothing, I will be just as guilty for the deaths of those people as James is. I couldn't live with myself carrying that kind of guilt."

The lump in Kat's throat grew bigger. She wasn't able to follow all of what he was talking about, but it kind of sounded like he was going to agree to pick the POS's lock.

"I've never broken into someone's home before, but I'm willing to give it a shot … no pun intended. I just called in and lied to my boss, telling him I was sick and wouldn't be in for the next few days. But I suggest we do this as soon as possible before reason returns or I chicken out."

The feeling of dread that had turned Kat to stone evaporated in the blink of an eye. But it took another heartbeat for the elation to register in her brain, as it had been a long time since she had experienced that feeling. Her somber face changed to glowing, and with a squeal, she threw her arms around Daniel's neck and whispered, "Thank you," in his ear.

Daniel lifted his hands to hug her back, but she moved too quickly, gave him a peck on the cheek and turned away.

"I'll be right back," she said as she ran into the bedroom.

He stood there, his hands still raised, and stared at the open door. She hadn't given him a chance to tell her what else had kept him awake. That was the thought that sending James to prison wouldn't save Michael. He tried to find fault with that notion, but since the laws of physics wouldn't allow her to kill James, he found it hard to believe they would allow Michael and the other sixteen people to live. However, he had no proof to substantiate Michael would still die, and he had been wrong before, which was why he had hesitated to bring it up.

"So I'm ready. Let's go," Kat said excitedly, as she came out of the bedroom.

Daniel gaped at her and spread his arms wide. "When I said as soon as possible, I didn't mean this second. I slept in these clothes last night and I need a shower." He lifted his wrist and looked at his watch. "And it's only 7:30. James is probably still in bed … like I wish I was," he added under his breath.

Kat looked down at her wrist and two pink splotches lit up her cheeks. "Of course, I'm sorry. I'm just a little anxious to get this over with."

While Daniel went in to shower and change, Kat sat on the sofa, making a list of the materials and equipment the POS had used in the attack. It was quite a long list, but there weren't that many specific items that would raise an eyebrow or give the police reason to think this was someone planning a mass murder.

She fell back against the sofa cushion and closed her eyes. If only the time machine hadn't blown up on March 20th, she could just wait around until she had all the evidence she needed. But wishing couldn't make it so.

So I guess it's all on you, she thought, addressing the unseen body she was convinced was orchestrating the whole thing. *I know you didn't send me here to fail, so there better be some good stuff in that apartment, 'cause I'm running out of time.*

TWENTY-FIVE

Daniel talked Kat into stopping for breakfast before they headed over to the POS's apartment. They also stopped at a big box store to pick up a cheap burner phone so they would have a way to communicate while he was inside. It was after 9:30 a.m. before they got to the complex.

The resident parking lot was full and the POS's car was in the same spot as when Kat was last there. The street was lined with cars as well, but they were able to find a spot a few yards down from the POS's building, which gave them a view of the second-floor balcony and the top of the stairs leading down to the parking lot.

Kat drummed her fingers on her thigh and fidgeted with the flap of her bag, which was a lot lighter now that the gun was no longer in it. Her nerves didn't seem to understand she wasn't the one breaking into the apartment and were as tight as the wig cap on her head.

"You know it may be awhile before he comes out," Daniel said after she shifted her position in the seat for the tenth time in fifteen minutes.

"I know, but I can't help it. I'm nervous … and not only about breaking in. What if we don't find what we need?"

He shrugged. "I can't imagine that will be a problem. James was well prepared. It takes time to assemble that much stuff and put together the bombs. And we already know he's a planner, so I'm betting he has started to work on the assembly."

Kat automatically nodded her head, but she wasn't convinced and went back to biting her lip and fidgeting with the strap of her bag.

"So how did you and Michael meet?" Daniel asked.

Kat stared through the windshield, recalling the first time she saw Michael play soccer. Cathie's brother played on their high school varsity team and she had gone with Cathie to cheer him on against their school's biggest rival. It was a hard fought game, but Michael, who was the varsity goalie, even though he was only a sophomore, made a spectacular diving save in the final seconds, stopping the opponents from tying the score. At that moment, she knew she would marry him one day and she had loved him ever since.

It took Kat so long to respond, Daniel opened his mouth to repeat the question, but she started talking before he could get the words out.

"I've had a crush on Michael since the eighth grade. He was two years ahead of me and didn't know I was alive until my best friend introduced us at a party when I was a sophomore and he was a senior. We dated off and on that year, but I was way more serious about our relationship than he was. He didn't get serious until he came home on winter break his first year here at CU. I don't know what changed, but those two weeks were magical and we were a couple from that point on."

It had been a long time since Kat talked with anyone about Michael. Her friends and family all seemed to think mentioning him would be bad and would take her farther down her destructive path. But in reality, talking about Michael was exactly what she needed. Her memories and her dreams for their future poured out of her until it suddenly hit her in midsentence how boring her rambling must be to Daniel.

Kat flushed and turned in her seat. "I'm sorry. That was … weird. I don't know what came over me. I don't usually talk about him to strangers." Her cheeks heated up more. Daniel could hardly be considered a stranger. "What about you? Do you have a girlfriend?" she hurriedly added to hide her embarrassment.

Daniel looked over with a jerk. "Me? Um … no, no one at the moment. I've been concentrating on my classes, research, and the lab. They take up most of my time. What little extra I do have I spend getting in a few runs on the slopes."

Kat perked up at the mention of skiing, one of her favorite pastimes. Talk of skiing led into talk of hiking, and it didn't take long for them to fall into a comfortable banter just like they were old friends.

They had a lot in common even though Daniel was four years older than Kat and had grown up in a family of seven, whereas she was an only child. Not only were they both avid skiers and hikers, they both loved Harry Potter, country music, and Broadway musicals, which Michael never wanted anything to do with. Daniel had also taken a year off after getting his bachelor's degree to backpack through Europe, something she had wanted to do for as long as she could remember. She had gone so far as to plan out the entire trip, but Michael decided he wanted to get started on his career right away, so she had put her dream on hold. She didn't realize the disappointment of that decision still lurked in the back of her mind until Daniel started talking about his adventure.

Daniel was easy to talk to, and Kat found herself sharing secrets she had never divulged to anyone else, even her thoughts of suicide. And Daniel listened without judgement or a lecture, which not too many people in Kat's life seemed to be capable of doing, especially since the shooting. Soon she began to wonder what her life would have been like if she had met Daniel earlier. As the day wore on and that fantasy took on more substance, she realized what she was doing.

Stop this! she silently chastised herself. *Daniel's a great guy, but I'm getting Michael back soon and I'll probably never see Daniel again once I leave here.*

She seized on that belief with her whole heart. But there was no denying the attraction she had to Daniel and how easy it was to slip into his world. And after suffocating in the world of depression for more than sixteen months, it was nice to feel normal again and laugh and talk about the silly stuff of everyday life.

As they commiserated over the deaths of Dumbledore, Hedwig, and Fred and talked about all their favorite Broadway shows amongst numerous other topics, she made an extra effort to keep her mind from drifting. When the glare of the sun hit her in the eye, she looked down at her Fitbit in surprise. Other than one quick bathroom break, they had been sitting in the cramped seats for almost eight hours straight and she was suddenly aware of every one of those seconds.

She shifted uncomfortably and groaned as her lower back seized. As bad as she ached, she knew Daniel had to be feeling worse. His seat was pushed all the way back, but even with that, there was no room for him to stretch out his long legs. But he wasn't complaining, so she clamped her lips together and kept her misery to herself.

Once the sun dipped below the mountains, the gray clouds turned pink, then a vibrant Bronco orange, and the temperature inside the car immediately cooled along with their moods. Daniel had moved the car earlier in the day when a spot opened up closer to the building, so they had a view of both the POS's car and the stairs. Kat fixed her gaze on the top of the stairs, willing him to show, but she was beginning to have doubts he would.

Daylight faded fast, and as her hopes faded along with it, her thoughts turned to what she would tell the police if they couldn't get the evidence they needed. She stared unseeing through the windshield lost in thought and didn't see the POS walk out of his apartment and start down the stairs. It was Daniel's poke on her arm that jerked her back to the present.

She looked up just as the interior light on the POS's car went on, spotlighting him as he climbed behind the wheel. With a soft squeal, she scooted forward on the seat and knocked over the giant-size bag of gummies Daniel had picked up at the gas station, sending little colored bears flying all over Daniel's lap and onto the floor.

She paid no attention to the mess and watched the POS as he backed out and drove away. When his tail lights disappeared around the corner, she turned to Daniel, her eyes wide and questioning. His face looked pale in the beam of a small flashlight he had turned on, and all at once it hit her that he was putting a lot on the line for no reward or glory.

"Are you sure you're okay with this?" she asked haltingly.

He glanced up from collecting the bears and right back down. "Nah, I thought I would just sit here in this cramped box all day for my health."

Kat's spine went rigid. He could joke at a time like this?

Paying her no attention, Daniel dumped the last few bears into the bag and proceeded to put on the rubber gloves they had purchased along with the burner phone. He then reached into the duffle bag on the floor behind Kat's seat to retrieve a navy hoodie and a flat leather case that looked like the business card holder her father used. He donned the hoodie before he looked back at her. His face was grim and all business.

"Okay then, are we ready to do this?"

There were so many words bouncing around inside Kat's head she couldn't pick out the right ones to say. He was risking everything to help her and if he was caught… She involuntarily shudder and pushed that thought from her mind.

"You've got the phone and my number's been plugged in. If James comes back, give me a call," he said, pulling on the door latch.

A strange, out-of-body sensation came over Kat as he got out of the car and she felt like a bystander watching him from a distance. The slam of the door broke the spell and with a jerk, she opened her door and scrambled out.

"Daniel, wait," she called out.

He stopped in the middle of the street and turned his head toward her as she ran to his side.

She put her hand on his arm wanting to tell him he didn't need to do this, but again the words wouldn't come. She gazed into his eyes, hoping he could read her face and know how much this meant to her.

At that moment, two young men emerged from a ground floor apartment and walked toward the parking lot. Kat and Daniel both turned their heads and watched the pair get into a car and back out. When the car's headlights illuminated them standing in the street, Daniel drew Kat into his arms and pressed his lips against hers. His action took her by surprise, but more startling was the pleasure she felt in his soft lips and the electricity that set every cell in her body on fire.

"Get a room!" one of the young men yelled as the car drove past.

To Kat's disappointment, Daniel pulled away.

"Sorry. I thought a couple would look less suspicious than two people lurking about," he said seemingly unaffected by the kiss. He patted his pocket where he had put the lock picks. "Right. I'll see you in a few." He walked across the street and headed for the stairs as casual as if he was going to visit a friend.

He had reached the top of the stairs before Kat recovered and whispered, "Be careful," but he was too far away to hear. She resisted the urge to touch her lips that were tingling from the kiss and folded her arms across her chest instead. She didn't know what had just happened, and she wasn't sure she wanted to know. She told herself her racing heart and the warm tingly feeling was just the anxiety of breaking into the apartment mixed in with the fear of getting caught. But a small part of her brain didn't buy into that explanation.

Lights of a car suddenly glared in her eyes making her realize she was still standing in the middle of the street. She jumped back, more shaken then before. This wasn't the time or the place to sort out feelings. She needed to stay focused and keep a lookout for the POS. But she knew she would never forget the feel of Daniel's lips on hers, for it was now burned into the back of her brain.

TWENTY-SIX

Daniel casually walked to James' door and knocked. James reportedly lived alone and it was said he didn't have any friends, but the media had been known to be wrong and Daniel wasn't willing to take the chance this was one of those times. He waited a few seconds after knocking, then tried the doorknob, hoping he would get a break and it wouldn't be locked. He didn't actually believe he would be that lucky, and it turned out he was right. There was also a deadbolt, but no way to tell if it was locked too. He briefly glanced over both shoulders, then pulled out the leather lock pick case.

He had opened hundreds of locks just like the one on the door and it typically took him three minutes or less. But he had never picked a lock to break into an apartment, and this lock appeared to be old, which in most cases translated into more time. He wiped his hand on the leg of his jeans out of habit and started to work.

Five minutes later, sweat was dripping into his eyes as if he was running a marathon, and he was beginning to worry James would return before he got in, or a neighbor would notice how long he had been standing there and come to check on what he was doing. The time was inching toward seven minutes when he finally felt the last pin fall into place and the keyhole turned.

Don't let the deadbolt be engaged, Daniel thought as he leaned into the door. To his relief, it swung open. Without hesitating, he stepped inside and closed it behind him. There was a strong odor of gasoline in the air and it was cold, as cold as the outside. A cross-breeze swept through the room rattling the vertical blinds covering the double windows. James had left all the windows open to air the place out, which explained the cold.

The thin strips of light shining through the slats of the blinds from a lamppost outside were enough to let Daniel get an idea of the layout of the room. Much like most college apartments, James had a minimal amount of furniture, but the ominous feel of the place was not like any other Daniel had ever experienced.

He pulled out his flashlight and slowly scanned the room. A white skull with dripping teeth, the symbol of the Marvel character, the Punisher, shined back at him from every wall. In a corner next to a computer desk was a stack of shipping boxes. On the kitchen counter was a heap of Styrofoam next to a gas can and a paint bucket.

He reckoned the paint bucket held the homemade napalm, but he needed to be sure. Cautiously, he walked into the kitchen, making sure he kept his steps light so the neighbors below wouldn't hear him. As he got closer, he noticed a gas mask lying on the counter on the other side of the stove.

He used the screwdriver sitting next to the bucket to pry off the lid and a concentrated cloud of gas fumes billowed out. His eyes watered and the inside of his nose burned as he fanned the air with his hand to disperse the fumes. Then, holding his breath, he peeked inside. As he hoped, the bucket was half full of a creamy white substance he knew to be napalm. He replaced the lid, pounded it down in place, and blew out his breath, mentally ticking off one of the items he had hoped to find.

Daniel knew coming in what the POS was planning, but to see actual evidence of it in person was unnerving. He inhaled deeply, blew it out through his mouth, and moved to the boxes in the corner by the desk. There were six boxes in all. The top two held softball size firework shells, the ones James used to make into bombs. The next box had three tear gas cannisters, then there were two boxes of ammunition, one filled with thousands of rounds of .22 caliber for the assault rifle, the other holding .40 caliber for a handgun. The last box had chemicals, some of which Daniel was familiar with, some he was not. It also contained a roll of yellow wire, several rolls of aquamarine duct tape, and a roll of orange cord that was labeled Detonating Fuse.

None of the items in the boxes, other than possibly the amount of ammunition, pointed to the atrocity James was planning. Daniel looked around. He needed to find the assault rifle. Clenching his jaw, he walked back to the kitchen and pulled opened the first of three doors. It was a small coat closet. The second door was a sparsely stocked pantry that held nothing of interest, and the last door led into James' bedroom.

Daniel paused in the doorway and shuddered as he stared at the crumpled red, satin sheets on the unmade bed. He was wearing rubber gloves so he wouldn't have to touch anything, but his stomach didn't have that protection and rumbled with an uncomfortable feeling. He forced his feet to move into the room and pulled open the closet door. There were a couple dozen collared shirts hanging on hangers as well as three sports coats and a heavy winter jacket. On the floor were a couple pairs of shoes and boots and a stick Dirt Devil vacuum.

He turned back to the room. Similar to the living area, there was little furniture: a bed, a nightstand, and a small chest of drawers. A door at the foot of the bed led into a bathroom. A quick examination of it provided nothing of consequence, except several bottles of anti-depression medication.

Daniel returned to the bedroom, his gaze again drawn to the red sheets. Everything in the apartment was drab and neutral color, except for the sheets and the splash of red on the posters, which was there to imply the Punisher and blood went hand in hand. An unwanted vision of James lying in bed fantasizing about the bloodbath that would be coming sent an icy shiver down Daniel's spine.

He started to turn away, then stopped and looked back at the bed. If he had a rifle in an apartment like this, he would most likely keep it under the bed. He dropped to his knees, peered under, and hissed, "Yes," as he spied something wrapped in a towel. He reached for it, but his arm wasn't quite long enough. He lowered his head and scooted part way under the frame. At the same moment his fingers touched the towel, the phone in his pocket buzzed.

The vibration startled him. He reared up, hitting his head hard against the rail of the bed.

"Son-of-a-bitch!" he growled and swiftly wiggled out. He yanked his phone out of his pocket as he got to his feet and hit the answer button. "Is he back?" he asked before Kat could say a word.

"What? No, not yet. I was just wondering what was taking you so long? Have you not found anything?"

Daniel dropped his hand that was holding the phone and let his head fall back as he sucked air in through his teeth and tried to slow his hammering heart.

"Daniel? Are you there?"

He lifted the phone back to his ear. "Yeah, I'm here … barely."

"Did you find anything?" Kat repeated.

"I was in the process of pulling out from under the bed what I think might be the rifle when you called. I'll tell you what I find when I come out," he said and lowered the phone, thinking the call was ended.

"Wait! Don't hang up!" she yelled loudly, guessing that was what he was about to do.

He put the phone back to his ear and snapped, "What?"

"Don't hang up. I want to know if it's the rifle."

Daniel rolled his eyes, but didn't waste the time to argue. "Fine," he said and hit the speaker button. He placed the phone on the floor beside him and wiggled back under the bed.

As soon as he got hold of a handful of towel, he started pulling. He guessed that he had hit the jackpot by the weight. As soon as he unwrapped the red and white Budweiser beach towel, he saw he was right.

"It's here," he said staring down at the weapons lying on the towel.

"The rifle?" Kat asked, her voice quivering.

Daniel shook his head in response, before realizing she couldn't see him. "Yeah, the rifle and two hand guns."

Kat's relief came out as a small, Ohh. "Have you found any of the other stuff that will incriminate him?"

"Some ammunition and napalm. I don't know if that will be enough."

"Damn," she said softly, then louder into the phone, "Well, we know he's ordered stuff online. Did you find any confirmation of that?"

"I haven't checked the desk yet." He rewrapped the guns and pushed them back under the bed. He then picked up his phone and made sure nothing was out of place before he walked back into the living room.

He had already been in the apartment twice as long as he expected and wanted to be, and his stomach was painfully tight knowing James could be back at any minute. He laid the phone down beside the computer and shuffled through the papers cluttering the desk. They were mostly research articles and part of a paper on microRNA biomarkers that James was preparing for a class.

"I'm not seeing any kind of orders," he said out loud so Kat could hear him.

"Is his computer there? Can you get into it?"

Daniel touched the mouse. The monitor immediately lit up with a password request box. "It's password protected."

"Damnit!"

He pulled open the top drawer of the two-drawer cabinet beside the desk and sat down in the chair. "He has a filing cabinet too. I'm looking through it now." He thumbed through the files that were neatly labeled and alphabetized. They all pertained to school—research, schedules, separate folders for each class, and lab work and notes. The second drawer was a continuation of the first with a few personal folders for rent, grant applications, scholarships, and one labeled bank, but it had no statements in it. There were no online order confirmations to be found either.

Daniel closed the drawer and looked over the desk again. The desktop calendar had a red circle around the date April 29, but that wasn't any help. As he pushed the chair back to rise, he noticed a black computer bag propped against the wall behind the tire of James' bicycle. He pulled the bag out and unzipped it, not expecting to find anything useful in it either.

At first glance, he thought he was right as it only held one black, spiral-bound Composition Book, the kind used to take notes in class. He pulled it out anyway and opened it.

Scribbled on the first page was an underlined header that read: *The questions*. Under that was: *The meaning of life*, and then *The meaning of death*. The next few pages held a series of calculations for the value of a life, the value of death, and the value of a murderer.

"Holy shit!" he breathed softly, realizing he might have found something after all.

"What is it?" Kat asked, perking up.

He ignored her and flipped through the next few pages that had more ramblings on life and death and the value of each. His stomach clenched tighter with each page he turned and the bag of chips and gummy bears he had eaten earlier moved up into his throat.

Halfway into the book, James had outlined a self-diagnosis, documenting his broken mind with several pages of bullet-points. Toward the back, James had moved onto his plan, first listing the pros and cons of different methods of killing, then sketching out the layout of different sites, the majority of which were the Bison Bar, its exits, its table setup, even the best parking spot to park in. And finally, a detailed timeline of his attack. His entire methodical plan to kill as many people as possible in a single act of violence was written out in the notebook.

Daniel slumped back in the chair and closed his eyes. He had already read multiple articles about what James had done and knew a lot of the details, but reading the workings of a demented mind was far more disturbing. He felt dirty, sick, and more shaken than he ever remembered being.

"Daniel, are you there?" Kat asked when he hadn't said anything for several minutes.

Daniel jumped. He had forgotten she was still on the phone.

"Yeah," he croaked. "I'm almost done. I'll be out in a sec."

He sat up and hurriedly clicked photos of the pages before he shoved the notebook into the bag and tucked it back in place behind the bicycle tire. He pushed the chair back in exactly the way it had been and glanced around the room to make sure everything was how it was when he entered.

"I'm coming out. Is it clear?" he asked Kat as he put his hand on the doorknob.

"Yes," she replied.

A second later, the door open and Daniel hurried across the balcony and down the stairs. Kat ran to him as he crossed the parking lot, excited and anxious to hear what he found. His lips were pressed into a grim line and without saying a word he took her arm and guided her to his car.

Once they were both inside the car, he put the key in the ignition. However, instead of turning it, he sat back and stared at the steering wheel. Adrenalin had kept him going and his hand steady while he was in the apartment, but now that he was out, the tension he had been holding in and the revulsion of what he found hit him hard. He knew Kat was dying to know the particulars, but he also knew he couldn't talk about it at the moment without breaking down. He didn't want to do that. Not in front of her.

Kat turned in the seat to face Daniel. His face was extremely pale and not from the light of the flashlight this time. She laid her hand softly on his arm. "Are you okay?"

Her touch brought him back to the present. With a jerk, he reached out and turned the key in the ignition.

"I'm fine. I just need some time to process what I found," he said and shifted the car into drive.

It was nearly impossible for Kat to stay quiet and hold in all the questions sitting on the tip of her tongue, but she could see Daniel was definitely *not* fine. His silence and white-knuckle grip on the steering wheel confirmed that. Whatever he had found in the apartment had really shaken him up, and though a part of her was afraid to hear what it was, a larger part really wanted to know.

She silently followed him into his apartment and stood by the door wringing her hands as he went straight into the kitchen, grabbed a beer out of the fridge, and guzzled it down.

"Daniel—" she started.

"I'm going to take a shower. I smell like gasoline," he said cutting her off.

Then, without saying anything more, he walked into his bedroom and slammed the door behind him, leaving Kat standing by the front door not sure what to think.

TWENTY-SEVEN

Kat grappled with her emotions and tried to keep the fear at bay, but it wasn't easy after seeing Daniel's reaction to whatever he had found in the POS's apartment. She curled up on the sofa with the blanket from the back wrapped around her shoulders and stared at the bedroom door, her imagination racing with different scenarios, each more horrific than the one before it.

At the sound of a door opening, she sat up straighter, but the bedroom door was still closed.

"Well, hello there," a male voice said behind her.

Kat whirled around as a tall stranger wearing an amused smirk dropped his keys on a small table beside the door. She scrambled to her feet, clutching the blanket tightly around her as if it were a shield and would protect her.

The stranger waved his hand through the air. "No need to get up on my account," he said and walked into the kitchen.

He pulled a beer from the fridge and foraged around in one of the cabinets, coming out with a bag of cookies, which he proceeded to devour between gulps of beer.

"Who are you?" Kat demanded once she had regained her voice.

"Me? I'm Nick. I live here. Who are you?"

Kat had forgotten all about Daniel having a roommate.

"I'm Kat," she automatically replied and immediately realized what she had done. Heat rushed up her neck. “I prefer to be called Olivia,” she added.

Nick walked into the living room with his beer and cookies in hand and dropped into a chair. “So where’s Dan?”

Kat’s cheeks burned hotter. “He’s … in the bedroom.”

“Yeah?” A sly grin spread across Nick’s mouth as he lifted the bottle to take another swig.

“No, it’s not like that,” she blurted out. “We’re just friends.”

Nick’s eyebrows raised and his smile grew wider. “Okay … whatever.”

At that moment, Daniel emerged from the bedroom, his hair still damp from the shower.

“Oh, hey,” he said seeing Nick. “I didn’t think you’d be back this early.” Before Nick could reply, Daniel added, “Can I talk to you for a second?” He swung his arm toward Nick’s room.

Nick gave Kat a wink as he got up and walked into his room with Daniel.

“What’s up?” Kat heard Nick say as the door closed.

She stood beside the sofa until Daniel came out a few minutes later and joined her in the living room. He sat down in the chair Nick had vacated. “He’s going to stay with his girlfriend a few more nights.”

Kat sank onto the sofa. The silence that ensued was as thick as a wall between them, but neither wanted to talk about what happened while Nick was in the apartment. She stared unseeing at her lap, listening to the patter of water in the shower as Daniel rested his forearms on his knees, clasped his hands together, and stared at his feet.

When Nick finally reemerged, he had a bulging backpack in hand. “Okay, bro, I guess I’ll see ya later. Don’t do anything I wouldn’t do.” He gave Kat another wink and walked out the door.

Daniel looked over his shoulder and mumbled, “Thanks, Nick. I owe you one.”

As soon as the door clicked shut, he turned to Kat and they both started talking at once.

“I’m sorry, you go ahead,” Daniel said.

"I …" she started, but as she lifted her gaze and saw the sadness and pain in his eyes, the words stuck to her tongue. She licked her lips. "I shouldn't have asked you to break into his apartment. It was selfish of me and …" Her words trailed off and her gaze fell to her lap.

The sofa cushion shifted as Daniel sat down beside her. His hand closed over hers. It was warm, but she still shivered at his touch.

"You have nothing to be sorry about. It was my choice to go in, and I'm glad I did. I'll admit it was horrifying and the most repulsive thing I have ever done. But I made it out and no harm came of it. And I got what we needed. So it's all good."

Kat's head jerked up. Her eyes were glassy, but her curiosity shone through as well.

"He has a bucket of homemade napalm sitting on the kitchen counter in plain sight. The rifle and two handguns are under his bed. But what's going to cinch it for us is his journal that's got his whole, sick plan written out in black and white. I didn't take the time to read it word for word, but I read enough to know it should put him away for a very long time."

Kat's hand flew to her mouth and she didn't know whether to laugh or cry.

"Now, all you have to do is get the information into the hands of someone who will investigate it before James carries through." He pointed to the articles spread out on the coffee table. "That may be the hardest part. Several of those right there mentioned people who knew about James' obsession with killing for years, and did nothing about it."

"I know. I was furious when I read how he could have been stopped. No one took him seriously just because he's smart. But they'll have to now that you found the notebook. Too bad you didn't just snatch it so I could hand solid proof over to the police."

"I thought about it, but he would have noticed it was gone and might have run or sped up the timeline for the attack. But I snapped pictures of most of the pages. We can print a couple out to send to the police."

"Wait … you took pictures? You never mentioned you took pictures!" Kat scooted to the edge of the cushion.

"I—" Daniel started.

"I want to see them," she cut in, pulling her hand out from under his and turning it palm side up.

"Nooo … I don't think that's a good idea. The guy is a psychopath. It made me sick to read what I did. I can't imagine what it would do to you."

"I can handle it," Kat replied, giving her hand a bounce to reiterate she wanted his phone.

"No."

Kat's eyebrows rose, and if looks could stab, he would have had a dozen cuts. "No? What do you mean no? You can't keep those pictures from me! They aren't yours. I demand you let me see them … *now*."

Daniel's eyes went hard and a tic appeared in his jaw, but he kept his tone even. "You already know his plan. You know what he does. You don't need to read the sick workings of his mind. And I don't need you closing up on me and reverting back to the girl who couldn't get out of bed."

Kat lifted her chin. "That's not fair. I had just lost the love of my life. I've come a long way since then and I want to see the pages."

Daniel held her glare for a few seconds, but he knew from experience with his four sisters that he had no chance of winning. He dropped his eyes with a shake of his head. "This is a mistake."

"Maybe. But it's my mistake to make." She lifted her palm higher.

Daniel shook his head again and hesitantly reached into his pocket and retrieved his phone. He unlocked it with his thumb, handed it to Kat, and walked into his room without saying anything more.

Kat knew she should probably apologize, but instead, she looked down at the phone and opened the gallery of pictures. The first image was the page of calculations showing different variables as to the value of men, good and evil, and life and death. Her stomach clenched painfully, but she flipped to the next photo and read on, and then the next photo. Tears started to freely flow down her cheeks when she got to James' self-diagnosis and she couldn't go on.

With a shuddering breath, she set the phone down, dropped her chin to her chest, and closed her eyes. A deluge of sobs pushed against the back of her throat, but she knew if she let even one escape, there would be no stopping the rest. And she was afraid to sink into that world of depression again. If she did, she may not survive it this time.

How could she not have known reading the POS's actual notes would be far worse than reading the articles published about him? Once again, her stubbornness had led to trouble as it so often did.

She didn't hear the bedroom door open, but sensed Daniel's presence. Through a crack in her eyes she saw his feet standing in front of her. She opened her eyes more and slowly moved her gaze up his body. Her lip quivered with her effort to keep from breaking down. When she reached his face, she sprang to her feet and threw herself into his arms.

"It's all right. I've got you," Daniel said tenderly, wrapping her in his embrace.

She clutched him as if he was the only thing keeping her from falling into the abyss, but he didn't mind. From the moment she collapsed in his arms in front of the house on Pleasant Street, he had felt an overwhelming need to protect her. It started in his gut, then moved into his brain, muddling it completely, before it settled in his heart.

Enfolded in the warmth of Daniel's arm, Kat listened to the sound of his strong, steady heartbeat drumming in her ear, and her own heart's rhythm began to match his. Her anxiety level began to ebb, taking the threat of a breakdown with it, and her deathlike grip relaxed, but she didn't let go. It had been a long time since she felt anything other than sadness and anger, and she missed the yearning to be loved and the achy heat that was building between her legs.

Kat tilted her head back to tell Daniel he was right. That she should have listened to him. But the passion burning in his eyes stopped her. Warning bells went off in her head and she knew she should step away, but her body took on a will of its own. She reached up and lightly ran her fingertips along his jawline to his chin.

Daniel tensed under her touch and his hand that had been stroking her back stilled.

Their eyes locked. His pupils were dilated, almost completely covering his irises, and just like a black hole, they sucked her in. Her head began to spin and she felt lost, but found at the same time. The warning bells continued to ring, but she could no longer hear them through the rush of air going in and out of her lungs.

She lowered her gaze to his lips and timidly lifted a finger to test and see if they were as soft as she remembered.

Daniel trembled and gooseflesh pimpled his arms, but he showed no other signs of the ripples of shock coursing through him.

Kat unconsciously wet her lips with the tip of her tongue as she slid her hand around to the nape of his neck and gently pulled his mouth down to meet hers. Their lips barely touched, but the shock wave could have flattened Denver.

Kat didn't close her eyes and neither did Daniel, so she not only felt the intensity of the kiss, but saw the explosion in his eyes. He pulled back, just slightly, and moved his hands up under her hair below her ears, lightly caressing her cheek with his thumb as he searched her face. She watched a gamut of emotions splay across his face. He then closed his eyes, and in slow motion, leaned in and gently pressed his lips to hers.

Gentleness was the last thing Kat wanted, though. A desperate need to be touched and to be loved had taken over and she could no longer think rationally. She wove her fingers through Daniel's hair as his one hand moved to her waist and the other to her butt pressing her into him until they were one instead of two.

His tongue slipped between her parted lips and she tasted the sweetness of the gummy bears.

Kat moaned low in her throat and opened her mouth a little

more to welcome him in. She had never felt such a hunger, such desire before, and she didn't want to ever let him go. But when his hand moved under her shirt to her bare skin, his searing touch was an awakening jolt to her brain. She pulled back with a start.

Daniel looked at her through half-closed eyes that held a mixture of confusion and lust—the same emotions swirling inside Kat.

She stepped out of his embrace. "I'm sorry," she mumbled in a voice just above a whisper, though she wasn't sure if she was talking to Daniel or to Michael. "I …" Her brain was muddled from the strong desires still pulsing through her and she struggled to find the right words. "I shouldn't have done that. I don't know what I was thinking."

She turned away and hurried into the kitchen to put some distance between them. Her body ached to be back in his arms and she felt flushed. But most of all, she was confused. She took a glass from the cabinet, filled it with ice from the automatic dispenser on the refrigerator door and held it to her face.

What was I thinking? How could I do that to him? Again, she wasn't sure if she was referring to Daniel or Michael, as the question could be applied to both.

Daniel stood in the spot where she left him, his arms hanging limply at his side.

"I was thinking I would go to the library and use their computers to submit a tip to the *Safe 2 Tell* site. They guarantee anonymity and supposedly don't trace where the tip comes from," Kat stated, trying to find an excuse to get away so she could sort through her emotions.

He gave a slight nod, but Kat was standing at the sink with her back to him, waiting for a verbal reply. When none came, the tightness in her chest intensified. She turned and stiffly walked to the sofa to retrieve her bag.

"I don't know how long it will take, so I don't know when I'll be back," she said and turned toward the door.

"It's too late," Daniel said before Kat could take a step.

It's too late? she repeated in her mind, thinking he meant it was too late to stop the POS. She whirled around.

"It's Sunday. The library closes early on Sundays."

It took Kat a moment to process what Daniel said. She looked down at her wrist and saw that he was right. Her gaze darted around the room and stopped on the bedroom door.

"I'm going to bed," she stated without thinking. Her eyes grew wide as soon as the words came out of her mouth. "I haven't had a good night's sleep since this whole thing started," she hurriedly added to make sure he hadn't mistaken her statement for an invitation. "And I want to get up early and get this done so you can have your room and your life back."

There were only a few seconds of silence before Daniel spoke, but it seemed like an hour. And all he said was, "Sure."

Kat clutched her bag to her chest feeling empty inside. She slowly turned, then stopped, wanting to say something else, but not knowing what.

"Please don't be mad at me," she finally whispered.

Daniel closed his eyes and a tic appeared in his jaw. "I'm not mad at you," he said without emotion and without looking at her.

A lump rose in Kat's throat. She stood there another second fighting the urge to throw herself back into his arms. Instead, she mumbled, "Good night," in a strangled voice, hurried into Daniel's bedroom, and closed the door before she did something no "I'm sorry" could take away.

TWENTY-EIGHT

Kat tossed and turned all night, her emotions ping-ponging from one extreme to another. One moment she was horrified and ashamed of what she had done. The next, she tried to justify it as a normal reaction for having been deprived of the basic human need to be loved for so long. Then her betrayal and guilt would sweep in. And in between those bouts of emotions, questions as to why Daniel's kiss and touch seemed so familiar would flit through her brain. The culmination of all resulted in another night of little sleep and bigger bags under her eyes.

As dawn broke, she was tired of wrestling with the blankets and got up to shower. She was sitting on the sofa in the living room on her third cup of coffee when Daniel ambled out of Nick's room. She thought she could just pretend the previous night hadn't happened, but her heart remembered and flipped at the sight of him.

She forced the corners of her mouth up in a smile and tried hard to sound nonchalant as she called out, "Good morning."

Daniel plodded straight to the coffee machine without so much as a grunt. Kat's smile slipped and her shoulders sagged, but as soon as he turned with a cup of coffee in hand, she straightened her spine and fixed the smile back on her face.

"So I was just making a list of everything you found in the apartment to give to the police. What I have listed is the M&P15,

two handguns, napalm, bullets, and the journal. Did I get everything?"

Daniel brought his coffee with him into the living room and sat down at the opposite end of the sofa. He looked grumpy, but Kat pretended not to notice.

"He had two full cases of ammunition and a couple boxes of those round plastic shells he used for the bombs. The ones in the photo in the album. There was other bomb making stuff, too … chemicals and rolls of wires and fuses."

"Oh, good." Kat's voice came out an octave higher than normal. She winced, but added the items he mentioned to the list and leaned back. "Wow, this should definitely be enough for the police to take action."

She picked up her bag and rummaged around inside rearranging the items before placing the notepad in. She could feel Daniel's eyes on her, but she didn't look up. She didn't know what to say and she didn't trust herself after last night.

"Look, I'm sorry about last night," Daniel said, breaking the silence first.

"No, don't say that." Kat's heart lurched as she looked into his eyes for the first time since the kiss. "You have nothing to be sorry about. I'm the one who should be sorry … am sorry. I … it's just been so overwhelming, so emotional, you know, losing Michael and all. I got carried away for a moment at the thought of seeing him again." She looked down at her hands, then glanced up through her eyelashes. "Can we just forget about last night? Say it didn't happen? You've been so sweet and good to me. And it feels like we've been friends for a lot longer than we have. I don't want my stupidity to ruin it all."

She held her breath, not sure what he'd say.

"I think the emotions of the day took us both by surprise. And I agree with your suggestion. We should forget about it. And you don't have to worry, it won't happen again. I swear," he said, lying through his teeth, but he didn't know what else to say. He wasn't the instant love kind of guy. Had never, in fact, come close to being in love before. And though he didn't know if what he felt for her was love, it was more than he had felt for any other girl he had ever known and he didn't want her to leave.

Kat felt her tension flow away, and in the moment of relief, she almost threw her arms around him to say thank you. She caught herself just in time, smiled, and gave him a nod instead.

"I'm so glad you see it that way. There aren't a lot of people who would have done what you've done for me and I'd like to stay friends." She watched a pink tinge color Daniel's cheeks and hurried on to keep it from getting uncomfortable again, "The main library doesn't open until nine, so let me take you out for breakfast. It's the least I can do since you've let me crash here."

Daniel smiled. "You're on. I've got to grab a quick shower first. I'm not going in to work, but I can't ditch out on my classes. It would put me too far behind. They're stacked on Mondays, Wednesdays, and Fridays from one to four, so I'll be able to go with you to the library this morning."

While Daniel was getting ready, Kat went in to apply her makeup and try to hide the circles under her eyes, which took the same amount of time as he did to shower and dress. They had breakfast at a popular local diner near campus and arrived at the library fifteen minutes after it opened.

Kat's library card was back in Cathie's apartment in 2017, but she wasn't worried. She got a guest pass at the front desk to access the computers, which was better anyway. If the police did decide they wanted to speak to the person who submitted the tip, they would find Olivia Flynn's name on the log-in, not hers.

The tip form wasn't long and didn't take much time to fill out. Daniel had downloaded the pictures he took of the POS's murder book to a thumb drive, so Kat was able to attach a couple of the most damning photos to the form. She hit the submit button, then sat back and stared at the confirmation screen in a daze.

Daniel gave her a second before he placed his hand on her shoulder and said, "Come on, let's get out of here."

When she didn't move, he took her hand, pulled her up, and led her out to his car. When he slammed the door shut, she flinched.

"Are you okay," Daniel asked, climbing into the driver's seat.

"Yeah, I'm fine," she said and shook her head. "I was just wondering … what do you think it will be like when I go back to 2017?"

Daniel blew air out through his teeth. "That's the million dollar question, isn't it? I wish I could tell you everything will be wonderful and your life will turn out just as you always dreamed it would. But this is a whole new frontier and you're the first pioneer to explore it. So no one can tell you for sure what you're going to find."

"That's not what I meant. Do you think I will remember all this? Remember the way it originally happened? Remember you?"

"I don't know," Daniel answered, his voice suddenly husky.

"Do you think you'll remember me?"

He looked hard into her eyes as if trying to memorize the placement of every small dot of gold swimming in the pool of blue. "I don't think anything could ever make me forget you."

Kat looked down at her hands. She wanted to remember him too. It seemed wrong for it to be any other way. But she also knew it would probably be better if she did forget.

Daniel cleared his throat. "We have a couple hours before I have to be in class. How about a short hike?" he suggested to take both their minds off her leaving.

TWENTY-NINE

The next few days were a waiting game with Kat anxiously watching every news cast on TV, going to the library to read the newspapers, prowling the apartment, or lurking around campus trying to get a glimpse of the POS. He did show up for class on Tuesday, which didn't surprise Kat. It had only been one day since she put in the tip and she had no expectations the police would move that fast.

Her hopes raised when he didn't show up for class on Thursday and she had Daniel drive her over to the his apartment to see if there was any sign of police activity. The complex was quiet and there was no yellow tape on his door, and no mention of the POS on the news that night either.

Thursday evening it started to snow and didn't stop until mid-day on Saturday. With almost ten inches on the ground, Friday classes were cancelled and all news channels were suggesting people stay indoors and off the roads unless it was an emergency. And there was still no mention of the POS's arrest.

Early Saturday morning, Kat was sitting cross-legged on the sofa with a cup of cold coffee in her hand staring blankly at the TV screen when Daniel walked out of the bedroom. They had each decided to push aside the memory of the kiss, but the evidence that it still lurked in the recesses of their minds was obvious by the distance they maintained from each other.

Daniel padded to the coffee machine. There was a quarter pot left, but it was cold. He looked over his shoulder. "How long you been sitting there? Did you get any sleep at all?"

Kat jumped and looked over her shoulder. She hadn't heard him walk out of Nick's room. "I got in a few hours," she replied and turned back to the TV.

Daniel took the mug out of Kat's hand, made a fresh pot of coffee, and refilled hers and one for him. With two mugs in hand, he sat down next to her, just far enough away so no part of him touched her. He handed her back her mug, took a sip of his coffee, and looked up at the screen.

"No news?" he asked even though he already knew the answer. He could see it on her face.

Kat shook her head. "I don't understand. How could they not do something with all the evidence we supplied?" She shifted her position and turned slightly to look at him. "I have to go back tomorrow. What am I going to do if they haven't arrested him?"

"You don't know that they haven't. He could be sitting in a cell right now. Being from Colorado you know how it is when a snow storm like this comes through. It's takes precedence over everything else. All other news has to wait."

Kat looked to the ceiling as tears pooled behind her eyes. "I can't go back until I know I've stopped him."

He took her hand in his. "You can. And you *will*. You have to go back. This is not your time."

Kat looked down at his hand on hers. She knew he was right, as he always seemed to be, but that didn't take away the numbness that had settled over her.

"Look, you've done everything you possibly can to stop James. I mean, for God's sake, you risked your life and came back in time. I'm sure the police are looking into him, but they have to make sure they have everything in order to make a charge stick. That may take some time." He gave her hand a little shake. "Tell ya what, let's leave the police to do their work while you and I take the day off and hit the slopes. It's still plenty early so we shouldn't have any trouble getting up to Loveland. The conditions should be pristine with all this new snow."

"I don't have my equipment or ski gear," Kat muttered despondently.

"You can rent equipment. As for ski gear, all you need is a coat and I'm sure Nick's girlfriend has one you can borrow. You two are about the same size."

Kat scoffed. "I doubt Nick's girlfriend is going to want to loan her stuff to a total stranger."

"Oh, I think she will. If Nick vouches for you. I'll go call," Daniel exclaimed, jumping up and racing into the bedroom for his phone before Kat could come up with any other objections.

Much to Kat's surprise, Nick's girlfriend was just fine lending her a coat and even a pair of snow pants. In less than an hour, they were on their way up the mountain.

They took the chairlifts all the way to the top where the trails hadn't been completely tracked out and still offered some decent powder. The day was overcast and a few flakes floated in the air as Kat stood on the ridge and stared apprehensively down the black diamond run littered with moguls. She hadn't been on skis for over eighteen months. On top of that, she was totally out of shape. But as soon as Daniel let out a hoot and pushed off the edge, she clenched her teeth and followed. To her amazement, her muscle memory came back almost immediately and she made it to the bottom with only one fall. After that invigorating first run, she felt more confident and skied the rest of the day with only the snow and the mountain on her mind.

At the end of the day after their final run, they stopped in the basin lodge for a beer and stayed until it closed. Kat could hardly keep her eyes open on the way back to Boulder, and her legs were stiff and wobbly as she climbed the stairs to Daniel's apartment. She went straight into the bedroom without turning on the TV to check the news, shed her clothes into a pile at the foot of the bed, and for the first time since arriving in 2016, she slept through the night without a single nightmare.

The next morning, when she opened her eyes and rolled to her back, her body was quick to remind her how out of shape she was. With careful movements, she stretched her arm and leg muscles one by one to the drone of the TV coming from the other room. Daniel had the sound turned low so she couldn't make out actual words, but the steady, monotone voices told her he was watching the news.

She let out a moan, not only because of the ache that ran from her ankle to knee as she grabbed hold of her toes and stretched her calf, but because it just hit her that it was her last day in 2016. She stared up at the ceiling and waited for the weight of failure to fall on her again and the tears to follow, but neither happened.

She cocked her head and wondered why. Had her brain finally accepted Daniel's beliefs that the laws of physics wouldn't allow the past to be changed? She cocked her head the other way. That couldn't be it because she *had* changed the past just by being here. A dull ache started behind her eyes.

I'm not a physicist so what do I know. I did everything I could. If the Universe doesn't want me to succeed, I can't fight it. But why send me back here if I couldn't do anything?

She had a feeling that question would never be answered, but that wasn't anything new. From the moment she learned about the time machine, it seemed she had been running head first into a hurricane force wind for answers and she was worn out. She hated the saying, "It is what it is," but in this circumstance it fit.

All right then, I guess it's time to go home and just accept whatever future you have picked out for me.

THIRTY

Daniel didn't know what mood Kat would be in when she came out of the bedroom, but he prepared himself for the worst, knowing it was her last day. But it wasn't a sullen Kat who called out, "Good morning," as she shuffled into the kitchen and poured herself a cup of coffee.

She turned around as she lifted the mug to her mouth and saw him watching her over his shoulder, a look of surprise on his face. "What?" she questioned, lowering the mug.

Daniel shook himself out of his shock. "Nothing," he said way too fast.

Kat gave him the same look his mother used to when she knew he was lying and the heat of a blush move up his neck.

"I'm just surprised you're up so early," he said. The heat spread to the tip of his ears as he realized it was after ten. "Did you sleep well?" he added to change the subject.

Kat padded over and eased down on the sofa beside Daniel. "I did actually. Skiing yesterday really wiped me out. It's been awhile since I was last up. I missed it. So thank—"

Her words cut short and her head whipped around to the TV. Big as life on the screen was the POS's mugshot. Daniel looked over a second after Kat and sloshed coffee down his pant leg as he scrambled for the remote to turn up the sound.

"... was arrested after bomb making supplies and several guns, including a M&P15 assault rifle, and ammunition were found in the suspects apartment," the announcer stated. "The anonymous tip came in through *Safe 2 Tell Colorado*, a tip line that was set up after Columbine—"

"Oh my gawd," Kat whispered, then louder, "Oh my gawd!" She turned to Daniel, her face beaming. "We did it!" she squealed and threw her arms around his neck.

The hug lasted several seconds too long, but only because of their elation and nothing more. She pulled away and turned back to the TV.

"I can't believe it. He's in jail. He won't be able to kill all those people." She sobered and her eyebrows raised. "Michael isn't going to die." She flipped her head around to Daniel. "Michael isn't going to die now, is he?"

Daniel hesitated to search for the right words. Truthfully, he didn't know what she would find when she went back, but his gut told him it wasn't going to be what she expected. But the thought of extinguishing the light in her eyes with his scientific hypothesis made his heart ache.

"With James locked up, it will be virtually impossible for him to shoot Michael."

Kat looked thoughtful for a moment, then her face radiated with expectation. "I've got to get back. I've got to see him." She jumped up and started toward the bedroom.

"Wait!" Daniel called out after her. "There are people working in the lab right now. You can't go in there until they leave."

Kat looked over her shoulder. "That's fine. It'll take me a little while to get ready." Her nose wrinkled as her smile grew bigger. "Michael is so going to *freak* when he sees me in this getup."

"No, you don't understand … there will be people there all day. You won't be able to go back until tonight after everyone leaves."

"Oh." Her face went blank for a moment, then her brow raised in comprehension. "That's right. I don't go back until after ten." She shrugged. "So I guess I have one more day to enjoy 2016." Her eyes twinkled and her mouth turned up in an impish grin. "Let's go down to Pearl Street!"

Daniel stared at her for a long moment trying to catch up to her mood swing. "Sure. We can do that."

The sky was luminescent, the air had a scent of freshness, and the ground looked like someone had sprinkled diamonds over it. An overall great day to be alive. Kat opened her arms wide and lifted her face to the heavens with a silent thank you to whoever had made it possible.

She twirled in a circle feeling as light as air and saw Daniel walking to his car. Just as he was about to open the door, a snowball hit him in the back. He yelled out, but reached down and scooped up a handful himself. Within minutes they were both laughing and covered in snow from head to toe.

At the mall, she threaded her arm through his and practically skipped along, pulling him from one shop to another where she ogled and awed over the merchandise. They ate a late dinner at a way too expensive restaurant that Kat had always wanted to go to, which depleted the rest of her cash, along with extra that Daniel had to throw in. Then they drove up the highway to the lab.

It had been one of the best days Daniel had spent in years. He wasn't a talkative kind of guy, but Kat wasn't a typical girl and he talked more in this one day than he had all others in the last month combined. But the chatter and light mood of the day waned as they headed out of town.

Daniel parked in front of the lab, but neither attempted to get out of the car.

"I want you to know I have decided to destroy the machine," he said at last, staring straight ahead.

Kat's heart froze. She jerked around in the seat. "You aren't going to send me back?"

"No, I'll send you back. That's where you belong. But no other person will ever be able to travel through time. At least not with this machine."

She opened her mouth to ask "Why?" then shut it.

Daniel went on as if she had asked. "Every time a traveler goes through time, it puts a ripple in the universe. You're the first, so the ripple is small and shouldn't have much effect. But the propensity for the rich and powerful to abuse the machine and change the past for their own gain is great. As more people come through, more ripples will get added. Soon they'll form a wave and eventually a tsunami. Everything we know and love in this world could vanish with one man making one change. I can't let that happen."

"But they'll just fix the machine like they did before, won't they?" Kat asked.

"Not if I do it right. Though I know it'll just be a temporary fix. It's inevitable another physicist will someday build another machine. But I hope that once the failure of this machine gets out, or the believed failure, I should say, others will be deterred from moving forward with any time travel plans that are in the works."

He glared at the building as if it was an enemy. "That may just be wishful thinking on my part, but at least the next time machine won't have my name associated with it, and I won't be responsible for the downfall of humankind."

They sat in silence a few more minutes before Daniel looked down at his watch. "It's getting late. We should get going."

Daniel opened the door to the lab with his keycard and followed Kat in. One florescent bulb illuminating the hallway behind the reception desk was enough light for them to move through the lobby without turning on any other. He proceeded down the dark hall toward the lab, using memory and the faint light of the exit sign shining at the end to guide his way. When he stepped through the door of the lab, he could have easily passed for the Hulk as his face was grim and green from the glow of the machine's lights.

Kat stopped in the doorway, her gaze going to the little red flashing lights near the ceiling. Jeff hadn't mentioned anything about missing minutes on the security video for March 20th, but she could see the cameras were working so they should record her when she got into the machine.

She puzzled over that for a second before it dawned on her. The whole time she had been wondering if running into Daniel when she first arrived was an unfortunate turn of events or the Universe placing him there to help her stop the POS. Now it was obvious it was the latter. He was also here to take care of any evidence left behind. She shook her head in disbelief. The whole thing had been a set up and the Universe played them like pawns.

"Wow," she whispered. *Was everything scripted then? The kiss?* Her heart lurched at the thought of Daniel's lips. *Why would the Universe do that to me … to us?*

"Olivia, I need a look at the instructions your friend wrote out for you," Daniel called out. When she didn't respond, he turned sideways in the chair. "Olivia!" he called out louder.

Kat jerked and looked over at him questioningly, forgetting for a moment he only knew her as Olivia.

"Could I see the instructions your friend wrote out for you?" he reiterated.

"Oh … sure," she replied, digging into her bag as she hurried into the control room.

It took him longer than it had taken Jeff to get the machine ready, but watching him, Kat knew she would never have been able to do it without him. Finally, he turned in his chair and rose.

"It's all set," he said, but didn't move.

Kat didn't move either. She stared into his eyes until tears began to build. She was excited about seeing Michael again, but afraid she wouldn't remember Daniel. That upset her more than she wanted to admit.

"You know how to get into the pod better than I, so after you," Daniel said, swinging his arm around to the doorway.

She nodded and he followed her to the machine. She paused beside the metal casket, then at the same time, they both turned and fell into each other's arms.

"I don't want to forget you," Kat whispered into his ear.

Daniel squeezed her tighter. "You'll have Michael, so it won't matter. Just love him and have a great life."

A tear slipped out of the corner of her eye. She quickly brushed it away and stepped back. "I will," she said with a forced smile. "Thank you for all you did … for me and for the victims. I couldn't have done it without you. I'm not just saying that. I mean it."

He smiled, took her arm and helped her up into the pod. She pulled out the gas mask that was right where she had stashed it. His eye widened in surprise, then he nodded his approval.

"You know, I don't think anyone has thought about a gas mask, but it's a great idea. I'm glad your boys on the other end have their shit together."

Kat squeezed in and laid back, her arms at her side. Daniel reached up for the lid, then paused and stared into her eyes, which was all he could see of her face through the gas mask. They were brown when he first met her, then a sapphire blue, which he knew to be her true color, and now they reflected a greenish tint from the machine's lights. As he stared into them, it suddenly hit him that her eyes were the only real part of her he knew.

"What's your real name?" he blurted out without thinking.

Her eyes widened and a little crinkle appeared between her brows. He couldn't see her mouth to read her lips and couldn't make out the garbled murmur that came through the gas mask to know if she told him or not, but logic told him it was for the best. Knowing would be too much of a temptation to look her up.

"Take care of yourself," he said with a sad smile and closed the lid.

RETURN

"No man ever steps in the same river twice, for it's not the same river and he's not the same man."
Heraclitus (circa 535-475 BCE)

THIRTY-ONE

September 2017

As soon as the pod lid sprang open, I sat up, yanked the gas mask off and crossed my arms over my chest, rubbing both of my biceps at the same time to bring back some warmth. I was expecting the cold this time, but that didn't make it any better. If anything, it seemed even colder than before. My teeth chattered and my fingers felt like icicles, but I pushed myself up, thinking only of getting to Michael.

It was all I could do to lift my stiff legs over the edge of the pod and slip down the side to the floor. I could barely feel my toes and it took all my concentration to slide one foot in front of the other. It didn't help that the room was exceptionally dark, even the control room. The thought that was strange flashed through my head, but I didn't have time or the mental capacity at the moment to dwell on it. I was too concerned about tripping over the cables that I remembered littering the floor and getting out of there fast to be concerned with anything else.

I shuffled my feet along to keep from tripping and pushed aside several obstacles with the toe of my boot. I didn't feel as many cables as I thought there should be, though. Again a small nagging tickled the back of my mind telling me something wasn't quite right. I pushed it aside. The only thing that mattered was throwing myself into Michael's arms as quickly as possible. All other issues could wait until later.

The hallway leading to the front door was just as dark as the machine room, but I somehow made it through the boxes stacked against the walls without breaking anything. The front lobby area was packed with more boxes. I staggered through and out to my car. My fingers were stiff with cold and it took me several tries to get the key in the lock and then in the ignition. When I finally got the car started, I turned the heater up to high, and shifted into reverse.

My car was equipped with a backup camera, but my dad had taught me to always look in the rearview mirror to make sure it was clear before backing up. I lifted my gaze to the mirror and there was a crystal teardrop hanging on the chain that used to hold Michael's pocket watch. My hand flew to my mouth. I had really done it. I stopped the POS from killing Michael.

I blinked rapidly to suppress the tears of joy. The last thing I wanted to do was show up at Michael's with black mascara streaks running down my cheeks. I breathed in and out through my mouth for another minute, my heart near to bursting, then checked in the rearview mirror again, this time to make sure my makeup was still good.

I felt giddy as I backed out, and turned onto the highway. Thank God I had been to Michael's apartment enough times I could drive it blindfolded, because my head was still swimming and fuzzy from the effect of the machine and I found myself zoning in and out. At one stoplight, I sat lost in the thought of seeing Michael again long after the light had turned green. A honk from the car behind startled me out of the fantasy. I jerked up and clutched the steering wheel as I pressed down on the accelerator. The only driver's license I had with me was Olivia Flynn's, and being she wasn't a real person, it would not be good to get pulled over by the police.

I kept my spine rigid and my mind on the road the best I could the rest of the way to Michael's. When I turned down his street, I noticed his car wasn't parked where it usually was, but I didn't dwell on it. Knowing he was only a few feet away was the only fact I could focus on at moment.

My heart was racing a lot faster than what my feet could go as I sprinted up the stairs to the second floor. I was panting by the time I made it to Michael's door. I put my hands on my knees and dropped my head to slow my breathing and heart rate. But only for a second, as I couldn't wait to see Michael's expression when he opened the door and saw me dressed as a goth. It was going to be priceless.

I filled my lungs and slowly blew the air out one more time, then straightened. My hand was shaking as I lifted it to knock, but an odd feeling came over me before I could. Something wasn't right. I couldn't put my finger on it, but I knew it was so.

I stared at the number 208 on the door, my hand still frozen in the air. It blurred in and out of focus, then pulled away as if I was looking at it through the wrong end of a telescope. At the same moment, a rush of heat swept over me. My forehead grew damp and my palms were suddenly clammy. I placed my hand on the wall to steady myself.

I had been dizzy and lightheaded the first time I went through the machine, so my reaction wasn't really a surprise. I gnashed my teeth and silently berated myself for not staying at the lab until my head cleared and the effects of the time travel wore off. When Michael sees me like this, he's going to be worried, and I can't tell him what's going on.

For two seconds I thought about going back to my car and taking the time to recoup, but Michael was just on the other side of the door and I was so anxious to see him.

I forced myself to rap on the door twice. My heart filled my chest, leaving no room for my lungs to expand, but I was holding my breath anyway so it didn't matter. I put my hand on the wall again to keep from swaying and fixed a smile on my face. As the door knob rattled, my smile stretched wider, then quickly drooped as a thirty-something woman appeared. My gaze darted from her to the 208 on the door and back.

"May I help you?" the woman asked when I said nothing.

"I …" I looked over my shoulder and down the familiar hallway, wondering if I had come to the wrong building. As I turned back to the woman, another wave of lightheadedness washed over me and my words slurred. "Is … is Michael here?"

"Michael?"

"Michael Bellwood." My mouth was so dry I had trouble spitting out the words.

"I'm sorry, there is no one here by that name. You must have the wrong apartment."

All at once, every ounce of blood in my body pooled to my feet and a rush of memories flooded my mind: a chapel filled with flowers and rows and rows of people and more standing along the walls; a shiny black coffin hovering over an empty grave; a granite angel weeping and holding drooping flowers in its hands draped over the top of a headstone; the name Michael Bellwood etched into the stone.

"No!" My hand went to my mouth and I staggered back a step as the world started to spin. Then the gray fog that had been hovering at the edge of my mind closed in. Again, everything around me pulled back as if I was looking down a long tunnel. In the next instant, it all went black.

THIRTY-TWO

I blinked and turned my head away from the bright light shining in my eyes.

"Well, there she is. My name is Ethan. Can you tell me your name?" a male voice asked.

I blinked again and tried to focus. A band just above my elbow tightened as a man with black, curly hair and a mustache, who was holding a flashlight in the air, came into focus.

"Do you know your name, Miss?" Ethan asked again.

Of course I knew my name. "Katelyn Chambers." I croaked, my voice sounding like a two pack a day smoker.

Ethan smiled. "Well, Katelyn, you are in an ambulance on your way to Boulder Community Hospital. Do you remember what happened?"

My confusion doubled as the words *Boulder Community Hospital* silently repeated in my head. Before I had the chance to tell him I didn't remember, the back doors of the vehicle were yanked open and the gurney I was laying on was swiftly pulled out and wheeled through large, automatic, sliding-glass doors.

Two nurses immediately took over for Ethan. As everyone started talking and asking questions at once, my head began to throb. I closed my eyes.

The next thing I knew, a strong, stringent smell of alcohol wafted into my nose. I opened my eyes and found a woman in navy scrubs leaning over me, sticking a needle in my arm. Beside her was an IV bag hooked on a metal pole and the soft beeping of a heart monitor was coming from somewhere behind my head.

I lifted my shoulders off the bed and a stab of pain shot through my head behind my eyes. At the same moment, the heart monitor erupted with a loud, annoying beep. I winced and eased back down as the nurse looked up from her task.

"Well, hello," she said cheerfully. "How are you feeling? Any pain?" she added as she applied a piece of medical tape over the needle to hold it in place and then went about attaching the IV tube.

"I have a headache," I replied through dry, cracked lips.

"I'm not surprised," the nurse responded, her attention still focused on the IV bag.

"Where am I."

"In the emergency room at Boulder Community Hospital. You collapsed and hit your head pretty hard on the concrete. You've got a concussion and a nice little goose-egg as a result."

I tried to picture what had happened, but the effort, along with the loud beeping, made the throbbing in my head worse. The nurse must have seen me cringe because she added, "I'll ask the doctor and see if we can get you something for the pain." She finally pushed the button to stop the beep and asked, "Would you like me to turn the lights down?"

I started to nod, then froze as another stab of pain rewarded my effort. "Yes, please," I squeaked.

She turned off the bright lights shining directly on me, which was an instant improvement. But she no sooner walked out when another woman walked in, wheeling a stand holding a laptop. As it turned out, I had come in with no purse or identification on me, and since no one was with me, the hospital had none of my personal information. I thought it was odd I didn't have my purse, but it was just as odd I couldn't remember what happened.

I had no trouble recalling my medial history, my address, my phone number, even my health insurance company, though. And when she asked who my emergency contact was, I was cognizant enough to give Cathie's name and not my parent's. My mom would go into hysterics if she got a call from the hospital in the middle of the night.

After the nice lady left, I lightly touched the sore spot on my head and tried again to recall how I had gotten it. A memory—or was it a dream?—lingered at the edge of my mind. I tried to bring it into the light, but it made the throbbing in my head worse.

It was pure bliss when the nurse returned a short time later and added some pain medication to my IV drip, but I still wasn't able to tell the doctor, who came in a minute after that, why I had collapsed. He explained to me that on top of my head injury, my blood pressure and pulse had been high, and I showed signs of hypothermia when I first arrived. My body temperature had been rising nicely and was almost back to normal, and my last blood pressure and pulse readings were also back in the normal range, which was all good.

He asked me a lot of the same basic medical history questions the lady did, which I answered with no problem. He also threw in the standard mental status questions such as: who was president, what year it was, and what day it was. I fumbled a bit on what day it was, but he had to stop and think a moment himself, so he didn't count it against me. He was still waiting on the blood workup to come back, and because I had passed out twice, he wanted me to have a CT scan to make sure there was no hemorrhaging going on in my head and to rule out every other area of concern.

As soon as the doctor left, I was taken down to radiology. Once I got back to the room, I'm not sure if it was the pain medication, or if it was just my body's defense against my head trauma, but I couldn't keep my eyes open. I drifted in and out of a light sleep cycle where I was half asleep, but still somewhat aware of what was going on around me. So it seemed the nurse was gone only a minute when she returned to tell me all the test results had come back negative. The clock on the wall, however, said it had been well over an hour.

I still felt lightheaded and my brain was still a bit foggy, but I was starting to feel more like myself. I called Cathie to come pick me up and told her bring my wallet from my purse too. She had been calling me all night and was already in a panic since I hadn't answered. Hearing I was in the hospital further freaked her out and she fired off questions I couldn't answer, as I still hadn't pieced together what had happened. I didn't want her to know that, though, and put her off with an excuse of, "I'll explain when you get here." After I hung up, I prayed I would be able to do so.

The doctor wasn't happy about me going home. He wanted me to stay the night for observation since I had passed out twice. I told him I wouldn't be alone and also made it clear I knew he couldn't hold me against my will. So like it or not, he had to release me. With that, he flipped my chart closed and huffed out. The nurse returned a few minutes later with a stack of papers for me to sign, releasing the hospital from liability since I was leaving "against medical advice."

While I signed, she pulled the plastic bag filled with my clothes out of a little closet in the corner of the room and set them on the foot of the bed. She gave me another stern lecture about how concussions were not to be taken lightly and tried to talk me into staying the night before she left. But I was adamant. It seemed like it had been years since I'd slept in my own bed and I just wanted to go home.

As soon as the nurse closed the door behind her, I scooted to the edge of the bed and reached for the bag of clothes. I understood the purpose in the design of hospital gowns, but it was so drafty and I was anxious to get out of it. I stretched the drawstring opening of the bag and pulled out the black wig, the black coat, T-shirt and leggings.

Just like that, as if someone had pulled a cord and raised the curtain, the last bit of fog in my head vanished. Fortunately, I wasn't still hooked up to the heart monitor or else I'm sure it would have signaled a "code blue" as memories began to take form and my heart started pounding like a sledge hammer.

I sat on the edge of the bed with the wig in my lap staring blankly into space as memories of the massacre in the bar and everything that followed paraded into my head. It was dizzying, and even more so because I also had a perfect memory of the ceiling of the bar collapsing after a semi-truck ran into the building, killing Michael and the others on that same April 2016 night. It had been the worse night of my life, or so I thought. But compared to the recollection of the mass murder, it was nothing.

I shuddered at the horror that memory instilled in me and closed my eyes as I twisted a piece of the wig's hair around my finger. I couldn't believe I had actually gone back in time, faced a mass murderer, and stopped him. But the memories were too vivid to be a dream. And I had the wig and the clothes as added proof, so …

The door suddenly burst open and nearly slammed into the wall as Cathie rushed into the room, came straight to the bed, and sat down on the mattress beside me.

"How are you doing?" she asked softly, putting her arm around my shoulder and giving me a squeeze.

"I'm fine. It's just a bump on the head."

I could practically see her mind churning with questions about what happened, but I didn't know what to tell her as I was still struggling to sort out the truth myself.

"Did you bring my wallet?" I asked before she could start drilling me.

"Oh, yeah." She dug in her bag and handed me my rainbow colored credit card wallet. When I took it from her, she noticed the wig in my lap. "What's that?"

"Oh, just a wig." I didn't look up because I knew she was an expert at reading me.

Cathie put her hand over mine. "Kat, what were you thinking going over to Michael's old apartment? Why would you want to dredge up all that pain?"

My back went stiff and my head swiveled around to look at her. I didn't remember going to his apartment until she mentioned it. "H … how did you know I went to his apartment?" I stammered.

"I asked the nurse what happened. She told me you had collapsed at Crestview Apartments."

I looked at a space over her shoulder as I recalled how sure I had been that Michael would be there.

"You've been so brave. So much stronger than I could have ever been. And it's okay, normal even, for you to have a relapse. But trying to deal with it on your own is not a good idea. Why didn't you come to me about it? You know I'm always here for you. So is your mom."

Cathie's voice was husky, the way it got when she was holding back tears. I knew if she started crying, I would too, and I was tired of crying. I had spent sixteen months doing so. I was tempted to just tell her about all the bizarre thoughts tumbling inside my head and see if she could help me make sense of them. But most likely she would think my head injury was a lot worse than the nurse said, or else I had lost my mind. To be honest, I was beginning to wonder that myself. But if I was going insane, I wanted to find out now before I did something even more stupid.

I scooted my butt around and put my bent knee up on the bed so we were face to face. As I tucked my hair behind my ear, her eyes went wide and her brow rose.

"Oh my God, what is that on your neck?" she exclaimed before I could say anything.

My hand immediately went to the spot where I had put the tattoo and my heart stalled. I wasn't going insane. It was all real. Going back in time. Getting the POS arrested. Daniel. But what good had it done? I stopped the POS from killing Michael, but still lost him.

I could see my shocked look in the reflection of her eyes, and she had the same expression on her face. But a sense of relief that I wasn't hallucinating and hadn't incurred brain damage when I fell trickled in to replace the shock.

"It's a tattoo of the Chinese symbol for courage," I said, just as awed as she was. I pulled down the neck of the gown so she could see my clavicle and the tattoo there. "And this one is the Chinese symbol for love."

Cathie looked from the tattoo to my face and back to the tattoo. "You don't even like tattoos. When did you go get those done?" She couldn't take her eyes off of it.

"They're temporary. I put them on ..." I glanced up at the wall clock and saw it was after midnight, "... yesterday."

Cathie shook her head. "Why?" She looked up at me with a frown. "What the hell is going on?" She was so flustered, it was hard not to laugh.

"I'll tell you, but only if you promise not to repeat any of it. But I don't want to do it here. I think you're going to need a drink when you hear it, so let's go back to the apartment where there's wine."

Worry mingled with the shock on Cathie's face as I changed into the black Punisher T-shirt and leggings and laced up the clunky black boots. This, on top of everything else, must have put her at a loss for words because she didn't say a thing.

She remained silent as she drove me to where I had left my car. The doctor said I couldn't drive for the next couple of days, but I wanted to pick up my bags. There was stuff in them that would support my story. We then drove to the apartment and I sat quietly on the sofa while she poured herself a glass of wine and me a glass of water.

She looked edgy and I felt bad that I was the cause of her stress, but I knew her stress level was going to get a lot worse before it got better. She sat on the sofa facing me and I eyed her over the rim of the glass as I took a sip, unsure where to begin.

"You're killing me here, Kat. What the hell is going on? The tattoos, those clothes ..." Her words trailed off.

"I know. It's crazy, and believe me, it gets crazier. But please try and keep an open mind. And hear me out before you jump to conclusions or say anything. Okay?"

Cathie nodded. "Just tell me already. The suspense is freakin' me out."

"Yeah, well, I'm kind of freaked out too." I took in a deep breath and started in.

"Michael didn't originally die when the ceiling collapsed in the bar. He died in a mass shooting along with the sixteen others."

Cathie shrank back and her brow creased, but she held her tongue as she promised.

"A man by the name of Patrick James was the shooter." I paused. The name slipped off my tongue so easily and I didn't feel the need to throw up. I suppressed a smile, knowing it would only make me look crazier.

"I was a basket case after the murder and couldn't function at all. I lost my scholarship and my apartment. I was even thinking of killing myself. But then I learned about a former professor right here in Boulder who had built a time machine."

At the mention of a time machine, Cathie's expression went from "Oh my God, you poor thing," to, "Okay, you're just messing with me now."

"This is the part where I don't want you to jump to conclusions," I hurriedly added to let her know I understood how ridiculous it all sounded.

"But seriously? A time machine?" Cathie replied.

"I know. I said it was crazy, but you gotta hear me out before you judge me or call for a straightjacket. Okay?"

She nodded and didn't say another word as I went through the rest of the story. The only thing I left out was the kiss and my feelings for Daniel. For some reason I couldn't tell her that.

When I finally stopped talking, Cathie didn't move for a nano-second. Then all at once, the blank face she had held throughout my tale crumbled and she leaned in and threw her arms around me.

"Oh honey, I've been expecting this. You've put on such a great show for everyone since you lost Michael, but I could see the sadness was still there in your eyes."

I went stiff in her arms. She didn't believe me. I pulled back.

"I'm not making this up. I went back in time to save Michael, but there are laws in the universe that protect the past and I couldn't stop him from dying."

She put a hand on each of my shoulders and looked me in the eye. "Of course you couldn't. No one could have. It was a freak accident. The truck driver had a heart attack and lost control of the truck. No one could have foreseen that."

I pressed my lips together. My disguise and collapse at Michael's apartment wasn't enough to convince her. I stood and moved to the desk where I had set my backpack and pulled out the gun. I turned back to Cathie with a smug smile and watched her mouth drop open. She jumped up off the sofa.

"Is that real?" she whispered, clearly shaken.

"Yes. It's the gun I bought to shoot Patrick James." I set it on the desk, pulled out the paperwork from the rental car company and the thumb drive with the picture from James' murder book, and sat down in front of my laptop. "Come over here. I want to show you this."

Cathie stayed put, but I knew her curiosity would eventually win out. I inserted the thumb drive and pulled up the file with the photos. As I opened the first one, I could feel her standing over my shoulder. I slowly clicked through the rest of the pictures. She gasped out loud on the page where James had diagramed the layout of the bar. Once I clicked off the last one, I looked around and saw tears running down her cheek.

"Cathie—" I started and reached out to take her hand, but she reached around me and picked up the rental car contract.

She perused it for a moment and looked up at me. "This is dated March 10, 2016," she whispered.

"Yeah. It's like I told you. I went back in time."

She shook her head. "I'm going to need more wine." She started to turn away.

"Wait," I said and swiveled back to the laptop. I brought up Google and typed Patrick James in the search box. A page of results instantly appeared. On the righthand side of the page was a box that had his mug shot and short synopsis of his life and downfall.

I stared at the photo, but instead of feeling rage, I felt sorry for him. I opened the first article from the Denver Post and let Cathie read through the details, which were exactly as I had described.

"This is you? This anonymous person? You did this?"

"Yeah, I stopped him." I craned my neck to look at her and saw her face was as white as snow. "You need to sit down." I got up, took her arm, and led her back to the sofa.

We were both shaken by all that had happened and sat in silence lost in our own thoughts.

My brain was working overtime trying to come to terms with the memories of both timelines. It was surreal thinking that just yesterday my life was completely different than what it was now. Although … it wasn't. But like a bad dream, the lingering emotions of that other time were still there. They were already fading into the background, though, taking the horror and darkness with it.

It didn't make it any easier to believe or accept I still lost Michael after all I went through. And I didn't understand why the Universe would lead me to the time machine and send me back in time when it knew I wouldn't be able to save him and the others?

I mulled that question over, but I couldn't make sense of it no matter how hard I tried. The only thing I could see I gained from it all was that in this timeline his death, though traumatic, didn't destroy me like his murder had. But the hole in my heart was still there and I still miss him and think about him every day. I probably always will.

The anger I had held on to so tightly after his murder was gone, though. My friends and my parents saw to that. They helped me move past it and all the other levels of grief because I didn't push them away after the accident. And never once did the thought of killing myself enter my head either. That was all new in this timeline.

I laid my head back against the sofa cushion and closed my eyes. A vision of Daniel stared back at me from behind my eyelids and I felt a flutter in my stomach. Was he the reason the Universe sent me back? Was his future the one I was supposed to change? The memory of the deserted lab when I returned floated into my head and my eyes shot open.

"Oh my God! Is that what this is all about? You wanted him to destroy the time machine?" I silently asked the unknown force I still felt was responsible for the whole mess. *"You used me to protect yourself?"*

For a fleeting moment, a sense of indignation burned in my chest, but it didn't last. If I hadn't gone back, I wouldn't have met Daniel and would have never known the touch of his lips on mine. And I would still be distraught over Michael's murder and be contemplating suicide.

The Universe *had* given me back my life, and, in an odd sort of way, a better future. Not the one I dreamed of having, but better than the world of darkness I had before. That was something to be thankful for, I guess.

I let my mind wander through everything that had happened since Michael's accident. How I had thrown myself into my studies and was now a senior at CU. But even in this better timeline, the one thing I hadn't been able to do was entertain the thought of dating again. It seemed pointless because I knew no one would ever be able to take Michael's place in my heart. But I can now see that I was wrong about that too. I don't have to push Michael out to let another person into my life. My heart is plenty big and there is room enough for both Michael and someone else … someone like Daniel.

The thought of Daniel tugged at my heart. Could he be the one I was supposed to be with all along? Or was the connection we had just in my imagination?

It has been eighteen months for him since I stepped into the machine, and I have no idea what's happened in the time since I left. He was the physicist who knew the laws and how time travel worked, not me. I don't even know if he will remember me or what happened. Or maybe he will remember and not want anything to do with me, because I completely ruined his future. I shifted uncomfortably and blinked up at the ceiling to hold back the tears as that possibility ran through my head.

"I don't know why you chose me, but you put me through hell. Do you know that?" I silently said to the Universe. *"So you owe me. And the least you can do in return is don't let Daniel hate me. Please."*

THIRTY-THREE

Six months later

Madison gathered up her books and stuffed them into her book bag. “So are you coming tonight?” she asked. “Jeff is going to be there,” she added teasingly as she scooted her chair back.

She had met me at Starbucks to swap notes on a class we had together. I had made a rash decision to change majors from neuroscience to psychology this semester and she was helping me catch up.

“What’s that supposed to mean?” I said looking up from my laptop.

“Oh come on, you know. He’s got a huge crush on you. And I think you two would make a cute couple.”

I sat back in the chair as the memory of the other timeline and his confusion of his crush streamed through my head. He hasn’t ever expressed those feelings to me in our current timeline, but now that I know, I can see it in his eyes. And I’ve gone out of my way—nicely—to make sure he understands that I value our friendship, but that’s all it can ever be.

“Jeff and I are just good friends,” I replied.

“Right now maybe. But I think he would like to be something more.”

I could feel my cheeks heating up. “You aren’t going to be

happy until you hook me up with someone, are you?"

She lifted her left shoulder as she tilted her head to the side and gave me a sly smile.

"Jeff knows we'll never move past the friendship stage. He's accepted that, so you should too," I added.

"If you say so. See you at 6:30. Bring a bottle of wine," she said and walked away.

I shook my head as I watched her go. She had been playing matchmaker ever since I lost Michael. I looked over the top of the trees to the snowcapped mountains. They were exceptionally beautiful with the sun reflecting off the white tips and the sapphire blue sky behind them. It was almost too perfect a scene to be real.

I never used to like March. I thought of it as a transitional month and just plain blah. But lately it had come to hold a special place in my heart. My thoughts drifted to a faint memory of another March. Those memories weren't as prominent as they once were, except for two—eyes the color of the Caribbean Sea and lips as soft as rose petals.

I smiled at the memory, let out a sigh, and turned back to my laptop as a tall man in sunglasses stopped beside the table.

"Is this chair taken?" he asked.

"No, it's all yours," I replied with a wave of my hand and returned my focus to the screen without paying any more attention to him.

"Is it all right if I share the table with you then?"

I glanced up. The sun was behind him and all I could see through the glare was a halo around his short, sandy-colored hair and his black-rimmed sunglasses. "Oh sure, help yourself," I said, stacking my books on top of each other to give him a little more space.

He sat down, pulled out a book, and we both delved into our work.

"Daniel, wait up!" someone up the street yelled.

My heart stalled and my head pivoted to the side as a young man ran up to another with dark brown hair. They then proceeded down the stairs to the pedestrian underpass that led onto campus.

An unexpected wave of disappointment hit me and a sharp ache pricked my heart.

I had tried to find Daniel after I came back, but he was as good as a ghost and I couldn't dig up a single digital footprint on him. I even asked Jeff's friends who were physics majors if they knew him. One did, but he said Daniel moved out of state right after the project he had been working on was cancelled. He had no idea where Daniel was now. The thought of never seeing Daniel again was as painful as losing Michael, and though I had resigned myself to that reality, it still hurt.

I bit down on my lip and turned back at the same moment the guy sharing my table turned around from looking the same way. He had removed his sunglasses and as our eyes met, I forgot how to breathe. I never expected to see that particular shade of blue again, somewhere between aqua and teal, except when I closed my eyes or in my dreams.

A line appeared between Daniel's brow and he quickly looked down, as if he was embarrassed for staring. I, on the other hand, couldn't drag my eyes away. I thought I had lost him and it was all I could do to stay in my chair and not throw my arms around him.

He cleared his throat and glanced up at me sheepishly. "Please don't take this as a cheap pick-up line, but have we met before?"

I opened my mouth, but my reply caught in my throat. In the time we were together I never let him see me without the wig on, so there was no way he could know I was the girl who traveled back in time. And I wasn't sure what his reaction would be if I told him.

My tongue felt thick, but I tried to sound casual as I replied, "You look familiar too. Are you enrolled here at CU?" My voice came out a pitch higher than normal. I cringed on the inside.

"Yeah, just came back this semester to finish up my masters."

"Oh," I said with a nod.

"It's just … your eyes remind me of someone I once knew," he said.

I suddenly felt hot and queasy and my heart grew too big for my chest. I wanted so badly to tell him it was me, but all I could do was sit there and stare.

He tilted his head to the right. "She had a tattoo, though."

My hand immediately flew to the spot where I had placed the tattoo. Daniel's brow drew together as he squinted and studied my face.

"Hey Kat," a guy from one of my classes called out as he passed the table.

I looked over and the spell was broken. Daniel lowered his gaze as I gave my classmate a tweak of a smile and responded, "Hey," back.

"Your name is Kat? My old roommate, Nick, once met a girl named Kat," Daniel said, looking me in the eyes.

"Um … actually, it's Katelyn. Katelyn Chambers. My friends call me Kat."

"I thought your friends called you O?"

My heart stalled and my mouth formed an O.

"It is you, isn't it?" Daniel asked.

"I didn't know if you'd remember me," I said softly, my voice filled with tears.

Daniel reached out and took my hand. The second our skin touched a fire ignited within me.

"I told you nothing could ever make me forget you," he said tenderly.

Our eyes locked and the connection we had was as strong as it had been in 2016, but neither of us seemed to know what to do.

"Look, I hate to leave, but I have a class in ten minutes and I can't miss it," he said breaking the spell. "We need to talk, though, so would you meet me for a drink tonight? I know this great little bar. It doesn't have a name." He smiled his crooked smile and I almost lost it.

"I know that bar too. I would love to have a drink with you tonight." I stopped myself from adding, "And every night from now to eternity."

He gave my hand a squeeze and rose. "Does 5:30 work?"

I didn't trust my voice to say anything more than, "Perfect."

"Great." He turned and my heart ached that he was going to walk away so soon after I had just found him. But to my surprise, he walked around the table, leaned down, and planted a passionate kiss on my lips that spoke of a promise of tomorrow.

"I'll see ya later then," he whispered into my mouth before he pulled back and walked away.

I may have answered him, I may not have. I don't know, because my heart was beating so hard all I could do was sit there and watch him go. But thank God, I didn't tear up until he was out of sight.

I looked to the sky to keep the tears from falling and burst out with a half laugh, half sob at the sight of a fluffy white heart-shaped cloud sitting directly over my head. I thought the Universe had deserted me, but I guess it was just giving me a little time to make sure I had completely healed and to figure out what I really wanted.

Just like that, the dormant princess inside me awoke and the old belief that my prince would save me and we would live happily ever after emerged from the darkness. But my prince's name wasn't Charming. It was Daniel.

I hurriedly collected my books and laptop and pulled out my phone as I jogged across the street and down the steps to the underpass, surprised that my feet were able to stay on the ground.

"Cathie, you're *never* going to guess who I just ran into!"

A Note from the Author

Thank you for reading **NEXT TIME I SEE YOU**. I hope you enjoyed it. It would mean a lot to me if you could take just a moment of your time to leave a quick review and let me know your thoughts. And please tell your friends, for in case you didn't know, word of mouth is an author's best friend.

Other novels by M.J. Bell:

Chronicles of the Secret Prince:
Book I, Before the Full Moon Rises
Book II, Once Upon a Darker Time
Book III, How Dark the light Shines
(All available now in print and eBook)

To keep informed on more projects from M.J. Bell, please 'like' my Facebook page, **MJ Bell Author**, or check out my website at **http:www.mj-bell.com.**

Happy reading!

About the Author

M.J. Bell is an award-winning author (Gold from Mom's Choice Awards) of the Teen/YA Fantasy trilogy, *Chronicles of the Secret Prince*, and the science/fantasy, *Next Time I See You.*

Having escaped the mosquito-infested land of Iowa where she grew up, and the scorpion-infested land of Arizona where she was transplanted for way too long, she now lives happily ever after in Colorado, spreading magic wherever she can as a full-time writer, full-time babysitter, full-time cheerleader, full-time cook/ housekeeper, and full-time taxi cab driver.

She loves to hear from readers through her FB page at

MJ Bell Author

Or her website at

http:www.mj-bell.com

78269697R00151

Made in the USA
San Bernardino, CA
04 June 2018